This book is dedicated to my mother, Doris.
Thanks for believing.

ALAN McDERMOTT

GRAY REDEMPTION

THOMAS & MERCER

Text copyright © 2014 Alan McDermott
All rights reserved.

Published by Thomas & Mercer, Seattle

www.apub.com

Amazon, the Amazon logo, and Thomas & Mercer are trademarks of Amazon.com, Inc., or its affiliates.

ISBN-13: 9781477818510
ISBN-10: 1477818510

Cover design by The Book Designers

Library of Congress Control Number: 2013920516

Printed in the United States of America

Prologue

Saturday, 21 April 2012

Ben Palmer placed the bloodied knife on the table and removed the tape covering Kan Tek Kwok's mouth.

'I know that you've been passing sensitive material to Alphaco,' he said, his voice calm. 'Just tell me what you shared with them.'

It was, in fact, a lie. He neither knew that Kwok was selling trade secrets to his client's rival technology firm, nor did he care. His remit for the current assignment was simply to extract information, and in this particular field he had no equal.

'I swear...'

It wasn't the answer Palmer was looking for. He placed the tape back over Kwok's mouth and picked up the knife, which he'd found in his subject's kitchen drawer. It was probably fine for slicing vegetables, but it had taken a lot of effort to cut through the man's fingers. *Still*, he thought, *it all adds to the effect.*

Palmer ran the knife down Kwok's bare stomach and over the two marks created by the Taser. The file he'd been given showed the man lived alone, and fortunately he hadn't been entertaining that evening. After getting him to answer the door, Palmer had stunned him with the electroshock device. While he was still reeling from the shock, Palmer had flipped him over and administered an injection between his shoulder blades. He had then closed the curtains while the neuromuscular-blocking drug—derived from curare, a relaxant which left the recipient unable to move any of his voluntary muscles—took effect. Unlike other varieties—such as suxamethonium chloride, which also affected the involuntary muscles such as the diaphragm—this derivative allowed the patient to breathe unaided. The result was that Kwok was unable to put up any resistance whatsoever, but could still feel every ounce of the pain being inflicted.

'I can make this last all night, Kan,' he said, moving the knife down to Kwok's bare genitals. 'It would be better to tell me now, while you can still father children.'

Palmer placed the blade on the man's penis and applied a little pressure while making a sawing motion—not enough to break the skin, but sufficient to bring a look of horror to Kwok's face.

'I'll count to five,' Palmer said. He got to four when his phone rang and he knew it was work related—less than a dozen organisations and governments had this number, and his circle of friends could be counted on one hand.

'Think about it,' he said to Kwok and hit the 'Accept' button. 'Palmer.'

James Farrar had been through Tom Gray's file twice, but as he'd already suspected, there were just two associates known to be in Asia. In order to prioritise them, he had been in touch with the Government Communications Headquarters to get a breakdown of recent calls made to their known numbers, specifically anything from the island of Jolo. Within twenty minutes GCHQ had come up with the information he wanted.

Farrar closed down Gray's electronic file and opened the one for Timothy Hughes. Once it had passed through security protocols and loaded, he looked for the current address. Minimising the file, he opened another screen and searched for resources in the area. The results showed that the nearest was in Japan and currently working a case, and Farrar didn't have the authority to pull him off it for his own needs.

What he could do, though, was bring in some outside help. Given the sensitivity of the mission, it would have to be someone he could trust, and that narrowed it down to just one man. Despite this, he was reluctant to mention Tom Gray's name. After careful consideration, he decided to limit the mission to locating and, if possible, eliminating the quarry: Len Smart, Simon Baines and one other, as yet unidentified.

Farrar looked up the number in the database and dialled.

'Palmer,' he heard when the call was connected.

'Ben, it's James Farrar. I have an urgent job for you.'

'Sorry, gonna be a bit busy for the next few days.'

Farrar cursed silently. Palmer was the only man he could turn to, the only one he could trust. He had performed other jobs for the organisation, and Farrar knew that operational secrecy was a given.

'How much are they paying you?' he asked the freelancer.

'Three hundred ...' Palmer replied, and Farrar knew from previous negotiations that he had to add 'thousand' to the end. He also suspected that Palmer had doubled the fee he was currently earning, but that wasn't his concern. All that mattered was getting him on board.

'I'll give you five hundred if you can start now.'

The offer brought a pause in the conversation. 'Sterling,' Palmer said eventually.

'Dollars,' Farrar insisted.

Another pause, then: 'Write this down.' He gave Farrar an Internet URL consisting of letters and numbers, one that couldn't be guessed or stumbled upon accidentally. Palmer also gave him a twelve-digit code to enter when he got to the website.

'Once you're in, enter the job details and hit "Send". You can also upload files and images. Don't worry, it's secure.'

'How secure?'

Palmer explained that it used 2,048-bit encryption and a one-time 28-digit key, which meant even a supercomputer would spend a lifetime trying to unscramble the garbled message.

'I'll have access to the message in an hour. Please make sure the money is transferred to the usual account before then.'

The phone went dead in Farrar's hand. Now that he had secured Palmer's services, all that remained was to get his hands on half a million dollars. As an idea came to him, it brought a smile along for company. He still had control of Tom Gray's Manila bank account, which had a balance a shade over the sum he needed. The smile grew as he considered the irony of using Gray's money to pay the man sent to kill him, and he thumbed through the list of contacts in his phone in search of the account manager for the Philippine National Bank.

———

Palmer put his phone away and looked down at Kwok. The man had tears streaming down his face and a pool of urine had formed between his legs.

'You got lucky,' he said, extracting another hypodermic needle. Kwok had overheard his conversation, but that was the least of Palmer's worries: he had seen his face, and that sealed the man's fate. Palmer stuck the needle into his subject's carotid artery and delivered double the normal dose. As he waited for the drug to take effect, Palmer straightened his wig and considered an explanation for his current employers. He settled on reporting that Kwok had been innocent and collecting the fee, which he had tripled for Farrar's benefit.

Kwok's breathing was becoming laboured, and Palmer prepared to leave, replacing the hypodermics in their case and stowing it in the inside pocket of his jacket. He sat there for another minute until Kwok took his last breath, then he left the house, quietly closing the door behind him. As he walked to his car, he removed the bloodied surgical gloves and screwed them into a ball before wrapping an elastic band around it to stop them from unravelling. The ball was discarded down a storm drain, along with the hairpiece.

He drove the car to a secluded wooded area and removed the false licence plates which he had stuck over the originals. He wiped them down before digging a shallow hole in the undergrowth and burying them.

No loose ends.

Palmer drove back to his rented apartment, curious to see what the urgent mission entailed.

Chapter One

Sunday, 22 April 2012

The radar indicated a small vessel a mile ahead, apparently stationary in the water. According to his GPS it was within fifty metres of the rendezvous point, and the captain made a small course correction to intercept it.

'Just where you said they'd be, sir,' he said to Timmy Hughes, who had just entered the cabin.

'Anyone else around?' Hughes asked.

'Nothing larger than a canoe for twenty miles.'

Hughes stepped onto the deck and switched on the Carlisle & Finch searchlight, playing its beam out over the bow of the twenty-metre yacht. It was a couple of minutes before he located the small craft and its four occupants. Using hand signals, he indicated for the captain to slow their approach, and a few minutes later they pulled alongside the craft. Hughes threw out a rope, and it was caught by one of the males, who tied it to a ring on the wall of the inflatable. Hughes walked the rope to the stern and tied it off, allowing his visitors the chance to climb onto the swim-deck attached to the transom.

First aboard was the familiar figure of Len Smart, and Hughes gave his old friend a hug.

'Good to see you, man.'

'You too, Timmy. You haven't changed a bit.'

Hughes grabbed an inch from his own midriff. 'Maybe a couple of pounds heavier.'

He looked over the transom at the others. 'Who are your friends?'

Len leaned over and gave Sonny a hand up. 'This is Simon Baines. He joined the regiment shortly after you left.'

The men shook hands.

'Looks like you're doing okay for yourself,' Len observed. 'Nice boat.'

'Business has been great for the last couple of years,' Hughes said. 'I struggled at first because everyone was going to Viking Securities, but once Tom Gray sold up, the company lost its reputation. They raised their prices and cut the wages for the people in the field, so a lot of the contractors came to me instead. I approached all of Viking's clients and offered to do the same work for a twenty per cent discount, and the rest is history.'

The final two passengers had clambered aboard, and the male came over to shake his hand.

'Hello, Timmy.'

The voice was familiar, but not the face. It was a few moments before realisation hit him.

'Tom?'

'I hear you've been stealing my clients,' Gray said with a grin, his amusement increased by the look on Hughes's face.

'But you're dead. It was all over the news.'

'It's a long story. I'll tell you over some food.'

Once Hughes got over the shock of seeing a ghost from the past, Gray introduced his female companion. 'This is Vick.'

Hughes held out a hand while simultaneously straightening his short-cropped brown hair. For a man approaching his mid-forties, he still had the looks and physique the ladies found appealing.

'Welcome aboard,' he said in his most charming voice.

Hughes led the party down to the main cabin and offered them seats while he went to the galley. He was back moments later with a champagne bucket full of beers on ice.

'Something for the lady?' he asked Vick, but she was already reaching for a beer. He disappeared again and was back five minutes later, this time carrying a plate of bread, butter and cold meats.

'So, tell me how you happen to be in the middle of the Sulu Sea a day after a terrorist attack on Jolo.'

'You hear about that?' Gray asked, making himself a sandwich.

'It was all over the local news.'

Gray gave him a rundown of events over the last year, starting with his injuries in Abdul Mansour's attack and the government's subsequent subterfuge in declaring him dead while spiriting him out of the country. He glossed over the following year and took up the story at his kidnapping in Basilan.

Vick was nursing her third bottle of beer and the alcohol—combined with her first full stomach in months—was taking its toll. Her head was on Gray's shoulder, and her eyes told the others in the cabin that sleep wasn't far away.

Hughes sat back in his chair and took a swig of his beer. 'I've alerted Carl Levine and Jeff Campbell to the danger, and they are taking their families into hiding. There's nothing to stop you calling the media in London and letting them know that you're still alive.' he said.

Vick looked at Tom through tired eyes. 'Tim's right. You could just call the newspapers and this would all be over.'

'It's Timmy,' Hughes corrected her with a smile.

Gray sighed. 'You have to think like James Farrar. He's sitting at home listing the options open to us, and going to the press is right at the top of the page. If I was him, I would have a blanket DA-Notice on anything mentioning my name'

DA-Notices—called D-Notices until 1993—come in five varieties, with DA-Notice 05 dealing with British security and intelligence. Although they are advisory requests and not enforceable by law, it would be a very brave editor who chose to ignore one.

'What about social media?' Sonny suggested. 'Get yourself all over Twitter and Facebook. They can't censor that, can they?'

'Trust me, they'd find a way. Besides, I don't have accounts, and if I create one and claim to be alive, who's going to believe me? There must be a few million crackpots on the Web, and I'd just be the new nutter on the block.'

'So what have you got in mind?' Hughes asked.

'I haven't got a plan as such, but the first step is to get back to England, and that isn't going to be easy without a passport. Even with one, you can bet every port will be keeping an eye out for us.'

'Sounds like you're going to have to sneak in,' Hughes said. 'I may know just the man.'

He disappeared up the carpeted stairs, and Gray made himself another sandwich. He took in the sumptuous surroundings and for a fleeting moment considered cruising around the South China Seas for a few weeks, but the urge to get his life back soon put a stop to such thoughts.

Hughes returned with a handful of towels and put them on an empty chair. 'There's a shower just down the hall,' he said, pointing towards the stern. Vick was quickest to react and disappeared through the door, grabbing a towel on the way.

'Do you think it's a good idea to be taking her along?' Hughes asked when Vick was out of earshot.

'If you think you can talk her out of it, be my guest,' Gray said.

'Stubborn?'

'She'd prefer "tenacious".'

'Then she's in for quite a trip,' Hughes said. 'I've told the captain to head to Port Kelang in Malaysia so I can introduce you to Arnold Tang. He specializes in getting people into the UK.'

'A people smuggler? Nice company you keep.'

'He's actually a respectable businessman. He just happens to have his fingers in lots of pies.'

'How long will it take to get there?' Smart asked.

'About fourteen hours,' Hughes said. 'This little beauty will do sixty knots without breaking sweat.'

'No, I don't mean how long to Port Kelang. I mean how long will it take to get to the UK?'

'Ah,' Hughes said, finally understanding the question. 'That, I don't know. I'm sure Arnold will let you know tomorrow.'

'More importantly, how much is it going to cost us?' Gray asked.

'I'll get mates-rates, but it'll still be pushing seventy thousand for the four of you.'

Gray explained his cash situation, but Timmy wasn't concerned. 'Once you get this all sorted, you should be able to get access to your money. You can pay me back when you do.' Hughes rose from his seat and opened a small safe built into the wall. He handed an envelope to Gray.

'Here's five grand. That should keep you going once you get back to the UK.'

'I don't know how to thank you,' Gray said. 'I really appreciate it.'

'You could thank me by taking a shower before you mess up the sheets in your cabin,' Hughes smiled.

Vick entered the cabin, wearing nothing but her towel. All heads turned, and Gray's remained fixed on her. She may have looked good in the jungle, but having scrubbed up, she had the presence and beauty of a movie star. Her damp blonde hair fell about her shoulders, and she smiled at Gray.

'Shower's free,' she said. Gray simply nodded, struck dumb by the vision in front of him. It took him a moment to realise that he was staring.

'I'll go next,' he said, averting his gaze.

As he picked up a towel, Sonny offered some friendly advice, accompanied by a huge grin.

'Better make it a cold one.'

Gray shot him a look before disappearing down the hallway. The bathroom was not as large as he'd expected, but it had a spacious shower stall. He climbed in and turned on the water, letting it soak him for a few minutes while the heat took some of the stress out of his muscles. By the time he had washed and shampooed his hair, his body felt relaxed for the first time in days.

He returned to the main cabin to find that Vick was no longer there.

'She's gone to bed,' Smart said when he saw Gray. 'Timmy told her where to find some clothes, and she turned in.'

'I could do with some myself,' Gray said, and Hughes told him to help himself from the closet in the master bedroom. After saying his goodnights, Gray went in search of some shorts and a T-shirt to wear in the morning, then found the cabin Timmy had assigned him.

He climbed into the bed naked, and within moments the rhythmic bobbing of the boat began rocking him to sleep. What seemed like seconds later, he felt the bed covers move and he sat bolt upright, fully awake. Lying next to him on the bed was Vick, wearing just a T-shirt which barely extended below her hips. She smiled at Gray and put an arm around his neck, pulling his head towards hers. The kiss was long, their tongues exploring deeply. The love-making that followed was gentle, unrushed, and afterwards Gray collapsed next to her, spent. Vick placed her head on his shoulder and ran her finger lazily across his chest. He made to say something, but Vick placed a finger on his lips, relishing the silence.

Within a few minutes he heard the change in her breathing which signaled the transition to sleep, and he wasn't long in following her.

Chapter Two

Sunday, 22 April 2012

Tom Gray woke to find himself alone in the bed, and for a fleeting moment he wondered if he had dreamed the events of the previous evening. Those fears were allayed when Vick opened the cabin door, clearly fresh from the shower and again wearing nothing but a towel. She stooped and kissed him on the cheek.

'Good morning. Sleep well?' she asked.

'Like a log. What time is it?'

'Two o'clock. Timmy says we should be in port by eight this evening.'

Gray ran a hand up her leg but she swatted it away. 'Later,' she said with a smile. 'I'm starving.'

Vick slipped into a T-shirt and shorts and brushed her wet hair. Even without any make-up Gray thought she looked beautiful, her tanned skin perfectly complementing her blonde hair.

'Don't be long,' she said as she left the cabin in search of food, and Gray realised just how hungry he was. After a quick shower he wandered on deck, where he found everyone sitting round a fully laden table. He took a seat, said his good mornings and dived into a plate of sausages and eggs.

'So how is your friend going to get us to the UK?' Gray asked Hughes.

'I don't know the details of the entire route, but I expect entry through the port will be in the back of a truck.'

'That's not a guaranteed way in,' Sonny said, concerned. 'I've seen the documentaries on the telly, and there are lots of ways of detecting stowaways. They can detect minute concentrations of carbon dioxide in the back of the trucks, and that's just for starters.'

'He has a very high success rate,' Hughes said. 'I'm sure he's got everything covered.'

Gray hoped his friend was right; otherwise, the closest he would get to redemption would be Dover.

It was five hours later when they cruised up the narrow channel, passing a jungle-covered island on the left and industrial units on the right. As they pulled up to the dock, Gray saw a black SUV with tinted windows parked up, and as the gangway was lowered, one of the rear doors opened.

The melon-shaped passenger who climbed out weighed around two hundred and fifty pounds and was wearing smart trousers and a white shirt. By the time he climbed the gangway, circles of sweat had appeared around his armpits.

Hughes was waiting to welcome him aboard. 'Arnold, thank you so much for coming.'

'Not at all,' Tang Ben Lee smiled. He'd adopted the name Arnold and told anyone who asked that it gave him what he liked to call 'international appeal'. In actual fact, it was due to ignorant foreigners reading his name as they would in the West and addressing him as Mr. Lee, which was his given name. His contempt for Westerners came despite having studied at Oxford University, which was where he'd acquired his accent.

Hughes led him to the stern, where the others were sitting at the table, the onboard lights illuminating them as the sun began to sink below the horizon. He made the introductions before placing a glass of expensive cognac in front of Tang. The Remy Martin Louis XIII cost upwards of fifteen hundred dollars a bottle and was reserved for a select number of guests.

'I understand you want help with transporting some goods to England,' Tang said.

Hughes gestured to his four companions. 'That's right, Arnold.'

'These people?' Tang asked. 'What's wrong with Malaysian Airlines?'

'They lost their passports,' Hughes said with a smile, but Tang didn't reciprocate.

'I'm not happy with this situation, Timmy,' Tang said. 'I don't usually meet the cargo, for obvious reasons.'

'Don't worry, Arnold, I can vouch for them. I trust them enough to pay for their trip.'

Tang let his displeasure show on his face as he mulled it over. If he allowed these people to travel through his network, there was a chance that they might expose his role should they ever get caught. But then again, they *already* knew about his involvement.

On the flip side, there was a lot of money to be made from this shipment, and Arnold Tang knew how to have his cake and eat it. An idea came into his head, one that would solve the problem, and he pulled out his phone before speaking quickly in Cantonese. The conversation lasted just a few seconds.

'The initial part of the journey will be by boat,' he told the group at the table, 'which leaves in eighteen hours. It will be two weeks before you reach South Africa, so make sure you bring enough clothes and food for your journey. You'll be fed on the ship, but I can't guarantee the quality of the cuisine. Once you reach Durban you will be taken by cargo plane to northern Africa and across Europe by truck. You should reach the UK in three weeks.'

'We have concerns about crossing the border,' Gray said. 'How do we get around their detection methods? I understand they can detect even the smallest concentration of carbon dioxide. Is that true?'

'The vehicle you will be travelling in is equipped with CO_2 re-breathers that direct the exhaled gasses through a filter canister containing a carbon dioxide absorbent, in this case a form of soda lime. Even the most accurate probe placed next to the filter gives inconclusive results.'

That went some way towards allaying their fears, but the questions kept coming. 'How do we fly from South Africa to North Africa without passports?' Sonny asked.

'You do not need to worry about the logistics,' Tang said. 'I have people in place all along the route to ensure you reach your destination, and my delivery rate is unparalleled. All you need to do is follow instructions until you reach England. Once you get there, you are on your own.'

He turned to Hughes. 'The fee will be one hundred and twenty thousand.'

'That's a lot of money, Arnold. I thought perhaps ...'

'It is one hundred and twenty thousand because you put me in this awkward position. Just be grateful I am willing to help you.'

Hughes considered the options, and after a glance at Gray he agreed to pay the money. 'Okay, I'll transfer it once my friends reach their destination.'

Tang's face lost what few signs of geniality remained. 'I want the money within three days or your friends will never see England again.'

'Arnold, I am laying out a lot of money which my friend here is going to repay once he gets home. If you are confident enough to guarantee his arrival, what is the harm in waiting until delivery is complete?' Hughes sat back in his chair and took a sip from his beer. 'On the other hand, if you can't be sure he'll get there, I will have to take my business elsewhere.'

Tang was beside himself with anger. No one dictated terms to him, not even his own mother, because she knew what it meant for a Chinese person to lose face. Just a few moments earlier he had planned to have the four passengers thrown overboard once the money had been transferred, but now he would have to guarantee their safe passage lest this *gweilo* insult him further by going to a competitor. He took a few deep breaths to disperse the adrenalin coursing through his body before replying.

'Once they reach the UK, they will call you to confirm their arrival. You will then transfer the money.'

'Deal,' Hughes smiled, offering his hand to shake on it, but Tang ignored the gesture.

'If the money isn't in my account an hour after that phone call, you'd better pray that you're already dead.'

While Hughes digested the threat, Tang rose from his seat and polished off his brandy. 'The ship leaves at three tomorrow afternoon. It is the *Huang Zhen* on dock C6.'

With that, he took his large frame down the gangway and climbed back into his vehicle, which left immediately.

'Nice chap,' Len said sardonically.

'I didn't realise it was going to take so long to get home,' Vick said, not relishing a fortnight on board a ship. Having gone from sleeping in the jungle to the comparative luxury of Hughes's boat, she was reluctant to endure any further hardship, but there was no way she was letting Tom Gray out of her sights.

'It'll give us a chance to come up with a plan,' Gray said.

'So what do we take with us?' Vick asked. 'I don't want to sound stereotypical, but I've got literally nothing to wear.'

'I'll send the skipper into KL first thing in the morning,' Hughes said. 'Let me know what you need, and he can pick it up.'

'KL?' Len asked.

'Kuala Lumpur,' Hughes explained. 'It's about thirty miles from here.'

Vick began scribbling a list while Sonny passed the beers around. 'We might as well enjoy these while we can.'

Arnold Tang sat in the back of the SUV, his anger growing with every passing second. Having built up a small empire both at home and abroad, the last thing he needed was for it all to come crashing down, which is what would happen if anyone found out about any of his less than legitimate enterprises.

He pulled his backup mobile phone from his pocket and inserted a SIM card with one hundred Ringgit of prepaid credit. He then looked up a number on his main phone and dialled. When the connection was made, he was very brief, speaking in his native language.

'A consignment of four will be delivered in three weeks. Once they arrive, give them a phone and make them call this number.' Tang read off Hughes's mobile number and got the recipient to read it back.

'After they make the call, get rid of them.' He turned the phone off and removed the SIM card before opening the window and throwing it into the street. As for Hughes, he would wait until the money was transferred before deciding the man's fate.

James Farrar was in the middle of preparing his Sunday roast when his mobile rang. He wiped his hands and checked the display, which told him it was Todd Hamilton, head of the team watching Carl Levine.

'What is it?' Farrar asked, although the weekend interruption suggested it wasn't good news.

'They've gone,' Hamilton said.

'Who's gone?'

'Levine and his family. We saw no sign of them this morning, so we sent a couple of team members in with Watchtower brochures. There was no answer.'

Farrar was puzzled, a feeling of dread beginning to build in the pit of his stomach. 'Have a poke around, make sure they're gone.'

'We've been all around the ground floor and checked through the windows. There's no sign of any activity in the lower rooms, and they never sleep this late.'

Farrar put him on hold and wondered what the hell could have spooked Levine and caused him to up sticks during the night. He checked the call log with GCHQ and was told that, as requested, they had been looking for contacts from the Philippines. There had been no calls or emails originating from that country. As they reiterated the criteria he had specified, the thought struck him that he hadn't updated the monitoring information following Gray's disappearance. All he had been expecting over the last year was for Gray to contact his old friends from his new home in Manila, but now that he was on the run he could be anywhere in the region.

'Alter the search to check for any and all calls, regardless of origin.'

It was a few moments later when he got the bad news. 'There was a call on Friday the twentieth to Levine from Singapore.'

As the number was read out, Farrar was already moving to the living room. He sat down at his laptop and entered his password before loading the file belonging to Timmy Hughes. The number he'd just been given matched the one on record.

Damn!

He asked about all calls to Jeff Campbell, and his Sunday got a whole lot worse.

Farrar ended the call and took Hamilton off hold. 'What about Campbell? Have you been in touch with the other team?'

'Not yet,' was the reply, and it wasn't the one Farrar wanted to hear. He hit the 'End' button and found Matt Baker's number.

'What's the situation with Campbell and his family?' Farrar asked once the call was answered.

'All quiet here,' Baker said nonchalantly.

Farrar was furious at the man's casual attitude to the situation, despite Baker not being aware of all the facts.

'Where exactly are you now?' he asked as calmly as he could.

'I'm parked at the end of their street. I can see the house from here.'

'I want you to go to the house and make sure they are still inside,' Farrar said.

The phone went quiet for a while before Baker's voice said, 'Just did a walk-past and I can't see any movement in the house.'

'I didn't ask for a fucking walk-past! I want to know, in the next two minutes, if there is anyone in that house!'

Baker began spluttering, but Farrar cut him off. 'I don't care how you do it: just find out if they are home. Knock and ask for a cup of sugar, try to sell them double-glazing—just *let me know if they're still there!*'

At times he regretted having made Baker a team leader. The man was young and keen, never shirking his duty, and he executed the end game skilfully. It was just a shame that he often focused all of his efforts on the kill at the expense of the operational fundamentals.

Baker was back on the line ninety seconds later. 'There's no answer,' he said.

'Did you try the windows?'

'I looked through but couldn't see anyone. No sound from the TV or radio, either.'

Farrar couldn't believe what he was hearing. Just a few days earlier he'd been looking to wrap up the operation by the end of the month, and now he had five fugitives and no idea where to start looking.

He told Baker to remain where he was and report in if the family came back, but he wasn't holding out much hope. A year ago Levine and Campbell had managed to evade the authorities despite a nationwide search, and Farrar had just six men under his immediate control. It was nowhere near enough, and his options were limited. There was one person who could help, but it was a phone call he didn't want to make.

He paced the room, trying to come up with an alternative, but there was nobody else who had the infrastructure he needed. Reluctantly, he picked up the phone and dialled her number.

Veronica Ellis concluded the meeting and sent the staff on their way. She was sitting at the head of the conference table, contemplating the notes she'd taken, when her cell phone rang and she looked at the caller ID.

It was the last person she'd expected a call from.

'Hello, James. To what do I owe the pleasure?'

Their break-up two years earlier hadn't been the most amicable. The relationship had been deteriorating for some time, each blaming the other for focusing more on work than the other. However, the clincher for Ellis was finding Farrar in bed with one of his interns.

'I need access to one of your resources,' Farrar said.

'Yes, I'm fine,' she said sarcastically. 'Thanks for asking.'

'Veronica, this is a professional call on an urgent matter. I need help in finding two individuals and their families.'

Same old James Farrar, Ellis thought. What she ever saw in the man, God only knew. Still, it made her response all the more satisfying.

'Impossible. We are stretched as it is, and we have more work coming in every day. Why else do you think I'm in the office on a Sunday?'

'Veronica, either you find someone to help in my search or I get the home secretary to order you to assign someone. It makes no difference to me, but I'd prefer this to be handled in the spirit of cooperation.'

Ellis was not normally one to succumb to threats, but she knew that Farrar had access to the minister and would use that influence if necessary. Having taken over from John Hammond as assistant director general of MI5, following the Tom Gray fiasco, she was well aware that the service was still under the microscope. The last thing she needed was more scrutiny from the upper echelon.

'I can give you one man—that's it.'

'That's all I'm asking for,' Farrar said, his voice more pleasant now that he had gotten his way.

'Send me the details, and I'll get someone to work it up. What's the rush, anyway? Is it something we should know about?'

'It's nothing to concern you or your department. I just need information as to their whereabouts. We know they were in London in the last twenty-four hours.'

Ellis knew she wasn't going to get anything more from him, so she ended the call without a goodbye and dialled Andrew Harvey's internal number.

'My office,' she said when the call was answered, and set off to meet him.

Harvey had been the section lead when Hammond had handed in his resignation, taking full responsibility for the service's failure to end the Gray saga in a manner which put the government in a good light. She had stepped into the hole that had been left at the top of the organisation, on what was supposed to be an interim basis, but her ambitions reached beyond being a stop-gap.

Her first act had been to deal with the others responsible for the debacle, and while there was no evidence of Andrew Harvey, Diane Lane, or Hamad Farsi being guilty of negligence at the disciplinary hearings, Ellis was quick to ensure they were never given anything more important than analysis work for a while. This hadn't sat well with Lane, who resigned within a few weeks, but Harvey and Farsi still reported to their desks dutifully each morning. Ellis knew that they were very capable operatives, as their performance over the subsequent months proved. There did, however, seem to be some resentment towards her, as if it were her fault that Hammond was ousted. It wasn't something that concerned her, though. Adding yet another string to her considerable bow was far more important than making friends with the staff.

This latest request had piqued her interest, though, and if anyone could dig deep enough to get to the real story it was these two.

Harvey knocked on the door and walked in when called, standing at ease in front of her desk.

'What's your workload like at the moment?' Ellis asked.

'Manageable,' he replied.

'Good. I have something extra for you. We need to locate a couple of people.'

'What are their names?' Harvey asked.

'We don't know yet. The details will be with us shortly and I'll pass them on to you.'

'What's the urgency?' Harvey persisted.

'I don't know that, either. I'll pass the information on as soon as it arrives.'

Harvey nodded, her last statement telling him that this was an external request. He left the office wondering why she had bothered asking about the amount of work he currently had assigned to him. Normally she would just dump things in his lap regardless of his other commitments, and this suggested the new task needed someone's full attention.

He resumed his seat, and from the opposite desk Hamad Farsi asked why he had been summoned.

'The Oberstgruppenführer wants me to find two people.'

'Who?'

Harvey gave a replay of the brief conversation and asked for his colleague's opinion.

'Sounds very strange,' Farsi said, but clammed up when he saw Ellis approaching with a printout in her hand. She asked them to follow her as she passed their table, and led them into the conference room, closing the door behind them.

'I've just been told who you're looking for,' she said. 'It has come through as eyes only, so it doesn't go beyond the three of us.'

She placed the sheet of paper on the desk, and Harvey read the names before passing it to Farsi.

'I know these people,' he said. 'I interviewed them after the attack last year.'

'Yes, they jumped out at me, too,' Ellis admitted.

Farsi studied the names. 'You just want us to find them?' he asked.

Ellis's eyes betrayed a conspiratorial glint. 'That's the request that came in, but I'd like to know *why* someone wants them found. I don't like being kept out of the loop, and if these people are involved in something, I think we should know about it.'

'So let's start with who made the request,' Harvey said.

'His name is James Farrar,' Ellis said. 'I don't know who he works for, though.'

'Yet you're granting his request for information? Isn't that contrary to every protocol we have?'

Sharing her past with her subordinates was not something Ellis was comfortable with, but she had little choice if she wanted their help in getting some answers.

'We used to work together over the river,' she said, referring to the Secret Intelligence Service building on the opposite bank of the Thames. 'We were ... *involved* for some time, but shortly after we broke up, he left Six to join another organisation. Our paths have crossed a few times since, but he'd never tell me who he is working for now.'

'And you want us to find out?' Farsi asked.

'Discreetly,' Ellis confirmed.

Chapter Three

Monday, 23 April 2012

It was just after ten in the evening when Timmy Hughes walked down the gangway of the Sterling Lines and through the Saf Yacht Club to his waiting Bentley. The ten-mile drive south took a leisurely twenty minutes, and he parked in the Atrium car park just a couple of hundred yards from his apartment right off Orchard Road.

The streets were still alive despite the hour, with the majority of the reveller tourists taking in as much of the city as they could manage in a single day. As he neared the apartment building, the throng had thinned out to just a few locals. He was digging for the keys to the lobby when he felt a dig in his back, and a figure appeared next to him, a sports jacket draped over his right hand.

'Hello, Timmy,' the stranger said. Hughes didn't recognise him, but the accent was from his own neck of the woods, just north of London. A second dig in the ribs told him that the man was carrying more than just a Carl Gross coat.

'You know the drill. Nice and cool, stay calm and follow me to my car.'

The hire car was waiting just around the corner, and Hughes was told to drop his bag and get into the front passenger seat.

'Roll down the window. There's a set of cuffs under the seat. Put them on your right hand.'

Hughes again complied and was then told to thread the other cuff through the door handle and attach it to his left hand. After checking it was tight, the stranger climbed into the driver's seat and set off through the light traffic.

It was a forty-minute drive to the Sungei Buloh Wetland Reserve in the Lin Chu Kang area, and they made the journey in silence after it became clear to Hughes that his questions were going to go unanswered.

When they reached their destination, Ben Palmer handed Hughes the keys to the cuffs, told him to get out and then followed him through the passenger-side door. Hughes found himself in an industrial estate, deserted because of the late hour.

'Move,' Palmer said, indicating with his silenced pistol that they should head into the darkness. They walked for a minute before Palmer told Hughes to stop and get down on his knees.

Hughes refused. Instead, he turned and faced the gunman. If this man wanted him dead, it would have happened by now, which meant he needed something from him. That gave him the advantage.

'Care to tell me why you're going to kill me?'

Palmer had the gun pointed at centre mass. 'On your knees,' he repeated.

Hughes was five yards from him and moved closer, hoping to cut the distance in half so that he would have a chance to go hand-to-hand, but Palmer put his left hand behind his back and grabbed the Taser tucked into his waistband. He hit Hughes in the chest with the barbed dart and kept his finger on the trigger, delivering fifty thousand volts down the thin wire. Hughes dropped to the floor, and Palmer gave him another jolt for good measure.

'It's much easier if you do as you're told,' he said, standing over Hughes. 'Now, tell me where Len Smart is.'

'Never heard of him.'

Palmer delivered another shock to jog his memory. 'I don't like it when people lie to me,' he said calmly. 'You've been in contact with Smart and Simon Baines. Where are they?'

'Go fuck yourself.'

Palmer brought the pistol up and shot the prostrate man in the kneecap. When Hughes screamed and reached for the wound, Palmer kicked him in the temple, knocking him out cold.

Hughes regained consciousness a few minutes later and immediately reached for the wound, but his arms wouldn't obey the command. He lay there helpless, staring up at the night sky, the stars magnificent in the cloudless night.

For the first time in his life, Timmy Hughes felt truly frightened.

Palmer could see it in his face and welcomed the sight.

'I'm not gonna bullshit you, Timmy. You're gonna die. It's just a matter of how long it takes, and that's up to you. Now, where are Baines and Smart?'

He removed the tape covering Hughes's mouth and got a face full of spittle in response.

Palmer wiped it away. 'Okay, have it your way.' He pulled a small bottle from his jacket pocket and unscrewed the lid carefully before pouring a couple of drops on his victim's hand. The sodium hydroxide solution immediately began to burn through the skin, and Hughes screwed up his face as he fought to battle the pain.

Palmer gave him a few moments to consider just how much suffering was still to come.

'It's going to hurt a whole lot more when I put it on your knee,' Palmer said, holding the bottle over the open wound. 'After that I'll do your eyes, one at a time.'

Hughes knew there was nothing he could do except hope for a swift end. He wasn't afraid of death, and he knew that there was little point in delaying the inevitable, but he wasn't about to give up his old friends so easily.

'They've gone,' he said.

'Where?'

'Home. Back to the UK.'

Palmer considered this for a moment. If the British security services were after these people, it was unlikely that they'd be on a commercial flight. 'How are they getting there?'

'I don't know.'

Palmer poured a quarter of the solution into the hole made by the bullet and Hughes screamed with every ounce of breath in his lungs, but the hand placed over his mouth stopped the noise travelling. Palmer waited until there was nothing left but whimpering and tears.

'Let's try again. How are they getting back to England?'

'I don't know,' Hughes whispered, and Palmer shook his head, positioning the bottle above his left eye.

'No, wait! Wait! Sammy Li!'

Palmer moved the bottle and looked into Hughes's eyes. 'Tell me more.'

'I handed them over to Sammy Li in Malaysia. He said he would get them home.'

'Who's Sammy Li? Where do I find him?'

'I don't know where he lives, but he is a regular at the Atlanta Club in Kuala Lumpur.'

Hughes prayed that this stranger would fall for his ruse and end up searching for a fictitious target. Unfortunately for him, Palmer wasn't about to take his word for it. He took out his phone and hit a pre-programmed number.

'It's me. I need information about a Sammy Li from Malaysia. He might be involved in people smuggling.'

He turned to Hughes. 'I have access to several security services throughout the world. If you are lying to me ...'

He returned his attention to the call, listening intently before thanking the other party and hanging up.

'Sammy Li comes up blank, but I was given another name. Care to guess what it is?'

Hughes knew the game was up, and any more procrastinating would only lead to more pain. He felt bad for letting his friends down, but this man would get the information out of him eventually. Besides, their boat had already set sail, and the chances of this man getting through Tang's security screen and having enough time to question him seemed remote at best.

'Arnold Tang,' he said and closed his eyes, waiting for the bullet. He felt the tape being placed over his mouth, but the shot didn't come. Instead, Palmer emptied the bottle onto his exposed throat and stood back quickly.

Hughes began gagging and spluttering, trying his best to expel the corrosive solution, but Palmer had mixed it at such a high concentration that it burnt through the skin in seconds and poured into his larynx. Screaming was impossible with his voice box destroyed, and moments later his heart gave out under the overwhelming assault on his nervous system.

'That's for lying to me,' Palmer said and strolled back to his car. Once inside he pulled out his phone and dialed the number he had called earlier.

'You were right, it's Arnold Tang. Tell me about him.'

———

Farrar looked at the screen, and what he saw wasn't encouraging. Arnold Tang had long been suspected of being involved in a variety of illegal activities, but there had never been enough evidence to bring a prosecution. From gambling dens to fraud, the accusations had been levelled and immediately withdrawn, mainly due to his powerful connections.

It was also reported that Tang had two personal bodyguards who travelled everywhere with him, meaning it wouldn't be easy for Palmer to get in close enough to do what he did best, and he said as much to the contractor.

'What about posing as a customer?' Farrar suggested.

The line went silent while Palmer considered the suggestion. The reply wasn't what Farrar wanted to hear.

'I don't do undercover. You hired me for my skill set, and I don't go outside my comfort zone. That's how mistakes happen. Just give me the names of some known associates, and I'll have a quiet word with them.'

Farrar looked through Tang's profile and found two men suspected of being heavily involved in the trafficking operation. He started to read out the details, but Palmer cut him off.

'From now on, no details over the phone. Go to the website and enter this code.'

He read off a series of numbers and got Farrar to repeat them.

'Leave a message and I'll call you tomorrow,' Palmer said and hung up.

Farrar did as instructed and gave the names and addresses of Tang's men. He ended the note with instructions for when Palmer located his targets:

When you find Baines and Smart, find out what 'Saturday the ninth of April, option three' means. It is vital, repeat, vital that you get this information.

Farrar hit the 'Send' button and then called Veronica Ellis for an update. He found her in a less than accommodating mood.

'We just started looking yesterday,' she said when he asked how things were progressing. 'You have to realise that last year they managed to evade a countrywide manhunt when every police force in the nation was looking for them. If these people don't want to be found, it will be almost impossible with such limited resources.'

Farrar knew that her point was valid, but he wasn't about to cut her any slack. 'Can't you draft anyone else in to help?' he asked.

'In order to fund some extra overtime I would need to know more about the operation; otherwise, I can't justify it.'

'It's beyond your pay grade, that's all you need to know.'

The statement didn't sit well with Ellis, but Farrar's next words almost had her screaming venomously down the phone.

'If you can't get this done with the resources you have, I'll send over the names of six of my operatives. You can set them up with accounts and give them grade one access.'

Ellis took a few deep breaths as she formulated an appropriate response—one that didn't require Farrar to go and fuck himself. She knew that denying him access to the network would simply send him scurrying to the home secretary, but the more she considered the request, the more she could see it work in her favour.

'I guess that's the only way we're going to find them,' she said, feigning disappointment. 'Email the names; I'll fill out the paperwork and have the accounts set up within the hour.'

'No!' Farrar said a little too quickly. If the accounts were set up through the proper channels, it was possible that his bosses might find out about them and start asking some awkward questions. The last thing he wanted to do was alert them to the fact that Campbell and Levine had skipped town from under his nose. Even worse was the fact that he now needed to bring MI5 into the mix. Despite his earlier bluff about making a complaint to the home secretary, that was the last thing he wanted to do.

His men weren't really cut out for this kind of work, but he wanted to have something in place, just in case Palmer failed to deliver.

'Just ... keep this below the radar. I don't want other agencies interfering with this case.'

Intrigued, Ellis promised to do all she could, but made it clear that his latest request meant it might take some time to put things in place.

Farrar thanked her and hung up, and Ellis went straight to Gerald Small's office, grabbing Harvey and Farsi on the way. They found the technician tucking into a sandwich in front of a bank of monitors, each one displaying network activity.

'Busy?' Ellis asked.

Small pulled his feet off the desk and scrambled into a proper sitting position.

'I ... er, was just ... someone was trying to hack the network. I was just running a trace.'

'Calm down. I'm not the posture police. I need you to come with me,' Ellis said, and the head of the Technical Operations Department dutifully followed her to the conference room, throwing Harvey a look that asked what was going on. He got a shrug in response.

Once inside, and with the door closed, Ellis explained the situation.

'I need you to create six new network accounts, all with grade one access.'

'Sure,' Small said, wondering why this couldn't have been done in his office. 'Just send me the requisition forms and I'll set them up.'

'It's not quite that simple,' Ellis said. She was worried that too many people were being dragged into her little conspiracy, but she had no choice but to involve Small: without him, she had little chance of discovering what Farrar was up to.

She gave Small a summary of recent events, including Farrar's request to find Campbell and Levine, his reticence in sharing any further details, and the request for network access.

'Am I right in thinking that every request, every search made through our accounts, is audited and reports made available to the JIC?'

Small confirmed that she was correct. Every database search and VOIP—or voice over IP—telephone call was recorded, and the Joint Intelligence Committee had access to these reports. It was a way of ensuring that the information held on their systems was not abused in any way.

'Is there a way to spoof an identity so that their searches appear under someone else's name?'

Small thought about it for what seemed an age. 'I suppose it *could* be done,' he eventually said, 'but it would take a couple of days to set up.'

'What will it involve?' Ellis asked.

'I'll have to create a virtual server and route their requests through it. I'll also need to write a Windows service that intercepts the request. At that point I can switch principal identities.'

'Before you forward the request with the new identity, can you make a note of every search they make?' Ellis pressed.

'That shouldn't be too hard,' Small said. 'I can set up a separate database to record everything they are looking at. You'll want to view the results real time, I suppose?'

'If you can, that would be great.'

'No problem. I should have it all in place by Thursday morning.'

With that matter dealt with, Ellis asked Harvey for an update on the search.

'When they went into hiding last year, they had friends pay for everything so that they couldn't be traced,' he explained. 'That doesn't seem to be the case this time. None of their known acquaintances have any credit or debit card payments that suggest a planned disappearance.'

'Are you saying they haven't left a single trace?'

'No, we have the use of their debit cards at an ATM, but that was late on the evening before the search started, and it was at South Mimms services on the M25. It's at the junction with the A1, which means they could be anywhere north of London by now.'

'If they actually headed north,' Farsi pointed out. 'Let's assume they know the card transactions will be picked up: Do you think they'd use an ATM on their actual route?'

Harvey had to concede that his colleague was right. 'Then they could have headed in any direction, which gives us even less to go on than we had a minute ago.'

Ellis knew that with a cold trail it would be almost impossible to locate their quarry. 'What about phone conversations? They must have spoken to someone in the last few days.'

'That's where it gets interesting,' Harvey said. 'We asked GCHQ for a list of all calls to and from their known numbers in the last two weeks and got a couple of interesting hits.'

'Interesting how?'

'Most of the calls in the preceding days were mundane, but Levine got one at midday the day before they disappeared. The number was an unregistered mobile originating from Singapore. A minute later Levine called Campbell, and that was the last call either of them made.'

'Do we have transcripts?' Ellis asked.

'They came through this morning and we've been working up a lead,' Farsi said. 'The call from Singapore was brief. The caller introduced himself as Timmy and said he had a message from the Sarge.'

'The Sarge?' Ellis asked.

'We're working that up, just waiting for the MoD to get back to us,' Harvey said.

'What was the message?'

'That's the interesting bit. All he said was "Saturday the ninth of April, option three."'

'That was just a couple of weeks ago,' Ellis said. 'What's the significance?'

'Actually, the ninth of April this year was a Monday. We think he was referring to the same date last year.'

Ellis couldn't make the connection and asked them to spell it out.

'That was the day Tom Gray's eight associates went into hiding, and five days later his website went live,' Farsi explained.

'So this Timmy has told them to do what they did a year ago, which is disappear. Could option three be an alternate hideaway they were planning to use?'

'It could be,' Harvey admitted. 'Unfortunately, we expected Tom Gray's death to be the end of the matter, and no one thought to question them about any other preparations they'd made.'

Ellis thought for a moment. 'So we don't yet know where they are, but someone has told them to go into hiding. Have you checked the whereabouts of the other four members of Tom Gray's team?'

'Paul Bennett was killed in a road traffic accident at the start of the year, and Tristram Barker-Fink died while on a security detail in Iraq. Phone records suggest the remaining two, Baines and Smart, took a contract job in Manila last Monday. We checked the number they were called from and it's no longer in use, so we've asked the British Embassy to check it out for us.'

'Have you got a recording?' she asked.

'Not available, according to GCHQ, though they did send over the auto-transcript. The contact in Manila was someone called James, no surname mentioned.'

'If we find Baines and Smart, they should be able to tell us what option three was,' Ellis pointed out.

'It could be our best chance of finding Levine and Campbell,' Farsi agreed.

'Then let's concentrate on the leads we have,' Ellis said. 'Find out all you can about Timmy and the Sarge, and track down Baines and Smart.'

Chapter Four

Monday, 30 April 2012

Vick woke once more to the smell of body odour and curry and began having second thoughts about tagging along with Tom Gray. Oh, for a hot shower and a soft comfortable bed rather than a stinking mattress on the floor of the cargo container they shared with more than a dozen others. Even an hour in the sun would have been appreciated, but the captain had made it clear that anyone sticking their head above deck would be dealt with severely, and she suspected that in the people-smuggling trade, severely often meant permanently. That meant two weeks in the lower hold and goodbye to her tan. At least there was a chiller unit pumping cold air into the compartment; otherwise, the heat would have quickly become unbearable—perhaps even fatal—given the temperature in the Indian Ocean, especially during the earlier part of the journey.

She looked down at Gray, who was still sleeping, as were most others in the cramped container. She ran her finger over the crescent-shaped scar on his cheek and tried to imagine what it must have been like to be in that building when it blew up around him.

Vick had asked Gray to share the whole story with her, from the death of his son to his arrival on Basilan. He had tried to gloss over certain events, but she'd insisted on hearing all of the details, even from Sonny's and Len's perspectives. It had certainly passed the time, but with another week to go until they reached Africa she was beginning to wonder if she'd made the right decision. There had been nothing to stop her from just going to the British embassy in Singapore, explaining her story and getting a flight home, but her heart had told her to stick with Tom.

After a quick visit to the toilet, a Portacabin-like structure located just outside the container, Vick returned and rummaged through one of their bags to find something to eat. They were served hot food twice a day, but there was a limit to the amount of curry she could eat, so she found a tin of ham and tucked in.

Gray woke next to her and yawned, immediately regretting the action.

'Christ, it stinks in here.'

'You've just noticed?' Vick asked, trying to ignore the smell as she chewed.

Gray ignored the jibe and went to relieve himself. When he returned, he grabbed a fork and helped Vick finish off the cold meat.

'Last night I thought of a way we could locate Farrar, but it's a risk,' Gray said.

'What's your plan?'

'We need someone on the inside, and I think I may have just the person.'

'Anyone I know?'

Gray shook his head. 'An old adversary.'

'Then yes, it does sound risky. Care to tell me more?'

'I met him for just a few moments, but something about him told me he was honest and could be trusted,' Gray said.

'How do you know he isn't involved in the whole thing?' Vick persisted. 'What if he just turns you all in?'

'It was something Farrar told me last year. I remember he said something disparaging about MI5, which suggests they weren't involved in all this.'

Vick wasn't convinced, but it was Gray's call, and he had made a few good ones in the last couple of weeks. Having said that, she'd have been a lot happier if Gray had packed an air freshener, and she told him as much.

'Yeah, I never have one when I need one,' he sighed.

Azhar Al-Asiri prepared for one of his infrequent jaunts into the outside world. As always, he strapped on the bulletproof vest, and over that went the padding to add the appearance that he weighed a hundred pounds more than he actually did. The ensemble was completed by the full-length black *burqa*, transforming him from Al-Qaeda leader to humble wife.

Outside, the vehicle was waiting. The Toyota Land Cruiser appeared to be ancient, but under the hood was a finely tuned V10 engine, and the side panels were armour plated. Al-Asiri stepped out into the street for the first time in weeks and made the short walk to the car, looking to any casual observer like a harmless octogenarian. He took a seat in the back and cranked the window a little: not so much that he would be exposed to any incoming small-arms fire, which the bulletproof glass could easily handle.

The drive was a short one, and within ten minutes they arrived at the hotel, where his fellow passenger helped him out and escorted him through the lobby to the small elevator. They rode in silence up to the third floor, and when the doors parted, Al-Asiri waited until his bodyguard checked the hallway for danger. After getting the all-clear, Al-Asiri followed him to room 317, where they found two men, one sitting on the bed, the other on a chair.

Al-Asiri recognised one of them as part of his security detail, which meant the balding man in his fifties had to be Professor Munawar Uddin. Although he'd never met the man, Al-Asiri had been financing his work for the past five years, and as reports suggested the project was almost complete, he wanted to get the latest update in person.

He removed the *burqa* and waited for the shock to pass from Uddin's face.

The professor had been told nothing about the purpose of his visit, just that he would be away from his facility for as short a time as possible. The last thing he'd ever expected was to meet the leader himself.

Al-Asiri offered his greetings, dismissed the escorts and took a seat in the chair opposite the professor.

'I understand the project is nearing completion,' he said when they were alone in the room. 'Tell me about the latest test results.'

Uddin took a moment to gather himself before explaining that the experiments carried out on bonobo —once known as the pygmy chimpanzee—had shown a 93 per cent success rate.

'The virus we have developed successfully targeted the male Y chromosome in all of the test subjects. A few suffered testicular azoospermia, which is a complete lack of sperm in the semen, while the majority suffered a highly reduced Y chromosome sperm count, roughly two per cent of all sperm produced.'

Al-Asiri was pleased with the update, but wasn't about to celebrate a victory quite yet. 'What are the chances of similar results in humans?' he asked.

'The genetic differences between the two species are negligible, and the process of spermatocytogenesis is virtually identical.'

The look Al-Asiri gave Uddin suggested a simplified explanation might be in order. 'The formation of sperm starts with cells called spermatogonia. The spermatogonium splits to form two spermatocytes, which in turn split to become spermatids. These spermatids mature to become the spermatozoa.'

Al-Asiri nodded for him to continue, though he didn't pretend to understand the whole process.

'Consider the spermatogonia to be templates: they are not in infinite supply, and so when they split, some remain in the basal compartment to create further spermatogonia, while the others move to the adluminal compartment to enter the spermatidogenesis stage, the next step in the production of the spermatozoa.'

'At what stage do the subjects become affected?' Al-Asiri asked, beginning to grow impatient.

'W-well,' Uddin stammered, acutely aware of the need to get his point across, 'at the initial spermatocytogenesis stage we have found a way to latch on the spermatogonia containing the Y chromosome, which produces male offspring. The virus destroys these cells, leaving just the female X chromosome spermatogonia. Eventually, only X chromosome sperm will be produced by the subjects, which means all offspring will be born female.'

'How soon is "eventually"?'

Uddin swallowed, knowing the answer was not going to be accepted with good cheer.

'It could take months, perhaps a year,' he said, awaiting the backlash.

None came. Instead, Al-Asiri seemed quite happy with the time frame.

'What about delivery methods?' the head of Al-Qaeda asked.

Uddin was happy for the subject to be changed and breathed a sigh. 'The virus is a hybrid of Influenza A and so can be passed from person to person through airborne transfer. The lifespan outside of the host is an impressive one hour in the air, with a reduced period of around thirty minutes on door handles, work surfaces and other nonporous surfaces. On contact with skin and other porous surfaces, such as paper, the virus will die within a few minutes, but if anyone comes into contact with an infected surface and then touches their eyes, nose, or mouth, they will be susceptible.'

'What about introducing it into the water supply?' Al-Asiri suggested. 'Surely, that would have the greatest reach?'

'From the very start of the project, the delivery method was a primary consideration. Your idea was one of the first we looked at, but investigations showed that most modern water purification processes use ultraviolet light to eliminate bacteria, viruses and mold from the sewage. Our virus would not be able to withstand such exposure to the UV radiation.'

'Then what do you propose?'

Uddin explained that the virus had an incubation period of four to five days, following which the subject would experience mild flu-like symptoms which would last two, perhaps three, days at the most.

'Introducing the virus into a densely populated area would have the maximum effect. Perhaps you could send infected subjects onto the London underground to spend the rush hour riding the tube, or have them attend an indoor concert.'

Al-Asiri filed the suggestions away for later consideration, but he had a more pressing concern. 'What about the selectivity issue?' he asked. 'Can you guarantee that only Westerners will be affected?'

'There are no guarantees, but the differential allelic gene expression resulting from X-chromosome—'

'Enough!' Al-Asiri said, his patience worn thin. 'Just give me a number. Are you one hundred per cent sure that it will affect only Westerners, or just ten per cent?'

Uddin considered his answer carefully. While there had been extensive research in this area, it had yet to be proven conclusively that a particular race could be identified—never mind targeted— at the genome level. Nevertheless, his work with a variety of cell samples had managed to produce the desired results in 77 per cent of trials, a figure he shared with Al-Asiri.

The response was quiet contemplation for a few moments before Al-Asiri declared the number high enough for the project to go ahead.

'Prepare as much as you can over the next ten days,' he said, rising from his seat. 'I will be in touch with you after I have made other preparations.'

He made sure his disguise was in place before leaving the scientist in the hotel room and making his way back to the car. Once settled, he reflected on how far things had come in the last few years, and how close their biggest victory now appeared.

It was a shame that they would never be able to claim responsibility for it.

⎯⎯⎯⎯

Veronica Ellis strode purposefully into the Technical Operations office, her mood destroyed by yet another phone conversation with James Farrar.

'Any idea when it will be ready?' she asked Gerald Small, her tone a little harsher than she normally used on the staff.

The technician continued tapping away on his keyboard.

'Almost there.'

Another few keystrokes and he declared the job done.

'The next time he logs on to his computer, his account profile will be pulled from the central server. When this happens, the key-logging application will extract itself and begin running. I'll place an icon on your desktop that gives you a breakdown of every key he presses in real time.'

Ellis thanked him and apologised for her abrupt manner. The thrice-daily calls from Farrar were beginning to grate on her nerves, especially as he now had three times the manpower working on the search.

The accounts he'd requested had been set up a few days earlier, and she had been through their searches only to find that they were simply duplicating much of the work her team had already done. None of their network activity had given any clues as to who they were working for, which was why she had requested that the key-logging software be installed on their workstations. Unfortunately, it wasn't standard software in the MI5 inventory, and so she'd asked Small to code it up himself. Being more of an infrastructure specialist than a developer, it had taken Small a couple of days to get a working version ready to deploy.

'Please let me know once it's activated,' she said as she left the office.

Her next port of call was Andrew Harvey's station, where she found him involved in a heated phone call. She waited for him to finish and then asked for an update on the two men they were concentrating on: the Sarge and Timmy.

'We've been through the records of all eight men involved in the Tom Gray episode, and between them they served under five sergeants in the SAS. So far we've had no luck with four of them.'

'What about the other one?' Ellis asked.

'The other one was Tom Gray himself,' Farsi said, from the opposite desk, 'so we kinda ruled him out, with him being dead and all.'

Ellis conceded that it was a fair call. 'What about Timmy? Did you manage to identify him?'

'We've had seven hits and we're working through them now,' Harvey told her.

'Diplomatically, I hope,' she said, recalling the conversation he was having when she arrived at his desk.

It took Harvey a moment to realise what she was referring to. 'Oh, that. Just some dickhead at the British Embassy in Manila. I've been waiting for news about Knight Logistics Management, the company Smart and Baines were supposed to be working for. I sent the request in over a week ago, and he's still dragging his feet.'

'Want me to have a word with them?' Ellis asked.

'No, it's okay. I've put a flea in his ear, and he promised to get back in touch later today.'

'So how long before we can identify Timmy?'

'We've eliminated four so far,' Farsi told her. 'Of the other three, one left the country a few years ago, and we think he might be the one we're looking for. His name is Timothy Hughes, and he served with Levine eight years ago.'

'Who was his sergeant at the time?' Ellis asked, hoping the pieces would just drop into place.

Her momentary excitement evaporated when Farsi told her that it had been Tom Gray.

'Any idea where Hughes is now?'

'We already sent out a request to the British High Commission in Singapore,' Harvey said. 'They came back with an address, and I've asked them for all information they have on him.'

'Let's hope they don't take as long as Manila,' Ellis said.

Harvey was about to respond when his phone rang. He took the call and indicated for Ellis to hang around. After a minute he asked the caller for all phone records and emails for the last month and hung up.

'That was the Commission in Singapore,' he said. 'The good news is they've found Timmy Hughes.'

'And the bad news ... ?'

'He's in the morgue. It looks like a professional hit.'

James Farrar rubbed his temples as he digested the news he'd just received from the British Embassy in Manila. Why hadn't he considered the fact that MI5 might make a connection between Levine and Campbell and tie them to Baines and Smart?

Yet another sleepless night was beginning to take its toll, and he'd been unable to come up with a quick and satisfying answer, instead telling the attaché to just stall any further requests for the time being.

The last thing he needed was Ellis and her team poking around in his operation, and he decided to nip that activity in the bud.

'Veronica,' he said with his most pleasant voice when she answered his call, 'I understand you are doing some investigation into Simon Baines and Len Smart.'

'And just how would you know that, James?' Ellis asked, her curiosity aroused.

'Well … obviously … I want to be kept abreast of developments, and as you haven't done a very good job of finding my two fugitives, I decided to look through the logs to see what your team had been doing all this time.'

Farrar was relieved at having come up with such a good excuse, yet angry for leaving himself wide open like that. In the future he would think it through before calling Ellis: she was nobody's fool, and one day he was going to dig himself a hole too deep to climb out of.

'We've been doing what you asked,' Ellis said, indignation in her voice. 'We know there is an obvious link between all four men and we want to—'

'Forget about them,' he interrupted. 'Baines and Smart have nothing to do with this case, so stop wasting valuable time on them and concentrate your efforts on finding Levine and Campbell.'

'James, we have to investigate all possibilities if—'

'Veronica, I want you to *drop it!*' he shouted. *'Now!'*

Farrar took a few moments to calm himself, the phone shaking in his hand. 'I'm sorry,' he eventually said. 'This whole case is being closely watched by the home secretary, and he wants results sooner rather than later. I can't have you sending your people on wild goose chases when resources are so limited.'

It was Ellis's turn to pause, and for a moment Farrar thought she'd already hung up. Her voice came back, the tone one he recognised from their time together: compliant, but not wilful. 'Okay, James, we'll ignore Baines and Smart and concentrate on your two suspects.'

Farrar started to thank her but found himself talking to a dial tone.

Great, he thought. *Just when the day couldn't get any worse, a quick chat with Veronica and it turns to complete shit.* He was wondering for the umpteenth time how they'd managed to stay together for so long when his phone rang. The caller simply gave him a twelve-digit number before hanging up.

Farrar recognised Palmer's voice and logged onto his computer, then brought up the website he had used earlier in the week. After entering the code he was redirected to a page with a short message that improved his mood a little:

Sorry about the delay in replying, was waiting for the right moment. Spoke to subject 1 yesterday. Knows that they travelled by boat (Huang Zhen) to Durban, but no onward itinerary available. Subject 2 confirmed same. Additional: there are now 4 (four) passengers heading your way. Names unknown.

Farrar wondered where the hell this fourth person had come from, but the more pressing issue was how to track them once they reached South Africa. He opened a new browser window and searched for a website offering shipping itineraries. Once he found one, he entered the name *Huang Zhen* and found that it was due in to Durban on the seventh of May, a week from today. That was plenty of time for Palmer to get to South Africa and head them off.

He wrote a quick note in reply to the message and hit the 'Send' button.

⎯⎯⎯⎯⎯

Ellis was still fuming when Small knocked and entered her office. Before she could even begin to complain about the intrusion, he gave her some much-needed good news.

'Farrar logged on, and the software has been activated.'

He hit a couple of keys on her laptop to minimise the open files and clicked the icon he had placed on her desktop. A new window filled the screen, and Ellis soon found some human-readable data.

'What are these other characters?' she asked Small, pointing to what appeared to be random keystrokes. He told her that they were non-alphanumeric keys, such as 'Backspace' or 'Shift'.

'I can filter them out if you like, but it will take time and you'll have to wait until he logs out and back in again.'

'Never mind,' she said. 'I can make it out.'

Near the top of the screen, she saw what looked like a website URL suffix, but the random characters before it didn't look like any Internet address she'd ever seen, and she dismissed it as a coincidence. Small, however, had found it more curious. He grabbed the mouse and highlighted a series of characters.

'This is the first website he visited after logging on,' Small explained. 'I've been there and found just a textbox and a "Submit" button.' He moved down the screen and selected a twelve-digit number. 'It looks like this was his log-in. I tried entering the same code, but it simply redirected me to a porn site.'

'Do you think that was Farrar's intended destination?' Ellis asked.

'I shouldn't think so,' Small said. 'After logging in he went to another website and did a search for "*Huang Zhen*". I retraced his steps and saw the itinerary for a cargo ship.'

'Is he expecting a delivery?' Ellis asked.

Small nodded and pointed to a section of text further down the screen:

Passengers arriving Durban May 7th, 3 PM. Meet them, get the information and ensure no onward journey.

Ellis read the succinct message a few times, and a couple of questions popped into her head: Who were the passengers, and who was being sent to meet them?

'Any idea who's behind the website?' she asked.

Small shook his head. 'First thing we tried, but whoever it is, they know how to cover their tracks. I've got one of my guys working on it, but I'm not hopeful.'

'Then we need to know who these passengers are. What was the port of origin for the *Huang Zhen*?'

'Port Kelang in Malaysia,' Small told her. 'It left there last Monday.'

South-East Asia again, Ellis thought. First there was Timmy Hughes in Singapore, then Baines and Smart in Manila. Now Farrar seemed to be tracking some people who'd recently departed from Malaysia, and all this in the last couple of weeks.

She called Harvey and asked him to bring Farsi to her office. When they arrived, she also told them about Farrar's request to stop searching for Baines and Smart.

'And you're going to do as he says?' Farsi asked.

'Of course not,' Ellis said. 'Those two are the key to finding the others. What we must do is try to keep any searches off the record.'

The operatives nodded, and Ellis gave them a rundown of the information gleaned from Farrar's computer and laid out her findings.

'It could be just a coincidence,' Harvey said. 'Maybe Farrar has more than one thing on the go.'

'I agree,' Farsi said. 'There was that terrorist attack in the southern Philippines last week. Maybe he's working that up.'

The attack on Jolo had slipped Ellis's mind. Although it had been flagged to her department and was being investigated, there was nothing to suggest a threat to Britain. It was the CIA's jurisdiction, and they'd shared some of their data—it had, after all, been an American base which had come under attack—and her team of analysts had created a summary report for her. It suggested Abdul Mansour had been responsible for the attack, although there was no concrete evidence—just an eyewitness statement, but they were working hard to confirm his location with several other agencies around the world.

Ellis conceded that Farrar might be working a different case, but it couldn't hurt to go over the Jolo data one more time.

'Andrew, get over to the Asia desk and have them send everything we have relating to the attack on Camp Bautista. Once that's organised, contact our friends across the pond and ask them for the very latest information. The stuff we have is at least three days old.'

Harvey nodded and left to carry out her orders.

'Hamad,' Ellis said, turning to the other operative, 'get a manifest of the *Huang Zhen* and see if you can find a connection with anyone we have on our radar.'

Farsi followed Harvey out of the room, leaving Gerald Small alone with the boss.

'One thing puzzles me,' he said, his eyes still on the short message Farrar had sent. 'If he has his own team, why isn't he communicating with them through normal channels? Why go through the trouble of setting up an untraceable website?'

Ellis hadn't picked up on that fact, but the more she thought about it, the more intriguing she found it. 'An outsider,' she said and began pacing the room, throwing ideas around in her mind. Why would he use an outside contractor? Whoever it was, they were interested in some people originating from Malaysia, which placed them in the same area as Timmy Hughes. And the fact that Hughes was linked to Levine and Campbell meant that whoever had taken him out could well be looking for them, too. It could, of course, be a coincidence that Hughes was taken out by a professional just a few days after contacting Levine, but the more she thought about it, the more unlikely it seemed.

Ellis knew that in order to confirm her suspicions, she had to discover who Farrar was in contact with. 'You said that whoever created the website covered their tracks: Does that make finding them impossible, or just very difficult?'

'As I said, I have someone working on it. We might get lucky if the host has been careless, but at this moment in time I wouldn't hold my breath.'

It wasn't what Ellis wanted to hear, but she was determined to either verify the connection or dismiss it as an avenue of investigation.

'How about gaining access to Farrar's files? Would you be able to do that undetected?'

Small thought about it for a moment, not wanting to offer hope if there was none. He knew the network inside out, but as several agencies had access to the core functionality, a lot of it was compartmentalised. Gaining access to a subnet would be no easy task, but as he'd never even explored the idea before, it didn't mean it would be impossible.

'I can try,' he said, the excitement of the challenge plain to see.

'Go for it,' Ellis smiled.

Chapter Five

Tuesday, 1 May 2012

Ben Palmer's Emirates flight touched down at King Shaka International Airport just after five in the afternoon. An hour later, he climbed into an airport taxi which ferried him twenty-two miles to the Alteron hotel, a three-star establishment a couple of miles from the container port. A larger, more opulent choice of accommodation was available to him, but he preferred the low-key lifestyle while working. His cover as a British businessman would probably stand up to close scrutiny in one of the four- or five-star establishments dotted around the city, but he much preferred to be off the radar.

The hotel had been booked in advance, and after signing in at reception he took the stairs to the second floor and found the single room was as pleasant as could be expected for the price. He dropped his baggage on the bed and took a quick shower before opening his laptop and logging in.

The first thing he did was to visit the proxy server. As he was using the hotel's Internet connection, he couldn't be sure that they weren't logging every website he visited. To be on the safe side, he routed all requests through the proxy, so as far as any snoopers were concerned he would only appear to have visited one website.

Once signed in, Palmer went straight to his own website and composed a short email, which was encrypted and sent to a friend named Carl Gordon. Palmer's knowledge of computers was limited to the end-user experience, while his profession required a deeper understanding and ability. Knowing at an early stage that he wouldn't be able to learn enough to work alone, he had recruited a student a few years earlier. He'd scoured the Web for court schedules, looking for anyone facing charges under the Computer Misuse Act 1990. Gordon had been caught hacking into the servers of a utility company threatening to cut the power to his shared accommodation and had been slapped with a hefty fine. Palmer had been in court listening to the case, and afterwards he met up with Gordon and agreed to pay the fine in exchange for some well-paid ad hoc work in the future. The kid had jumped at the chance and they had worked together ever since, although Gordon had never discovered Palmer's real name. All subsequent communications had simply been signed 'B.'

An hour later he received a text message which simply said: 'Hi, Billy. Fancy a drink later?'

It was Gordon's signal to say the work had been completed. Palmer replied, saying he would try to meet up but wasn't making any promises. What he was actually saying was that Gordon's fee would be transferred to the usual account within the hour.

Palmer logged into his own website and looked at the information his specialist had managed to find in the shipping port's system. He had requested the manifest for the *Huang Zhen* as well as the name of the haulage company that was scheduled to collect the container, and he found everything he needed on the screen.

After searching for the website of Wenban Freight Management, he made a mental note of the livery, glad to see that the dark-blue cab with lightning strikes on each door would be easy to recognise. It wasn't a large company, and there was no online freight tracking system, which suggested their paperwork would be hosted internally rather than on a server Gordon could get access to. That meant he had the choice of either visiting the office to see where the container would be heading next or simply following the truck to see where it dropped it off.

With six days to go before the ship arrived, there was more than enough time to check out the setup at Wenban.

He also had plenty of time to find a place to dispose of his targets.

———

Andrew Harvey was ploughing through the raw data the CIA had sent over and he had the feeling it was going to be a long day. The vast majority of the reports had already been couriered to Thames House a few days earlier and compiled into the summary which had been presented to Ellis, but he had to go through each one, just in case a relevant slice of information had been missed. It was the report highlighting the sighting of Abdul Mansour that got his attention.

A statement from the Special Operations Division commander, Travis Dane, mentioned that one of three Western prisoners had claimed to have seen Mansour in a local Abu Sayyaf camp the day prior to the attack. There were no further details as to who the prisoners were, and the summary had assumed that they had escaped from Abu Sayyaf.

Having not heard of any hostages being taken in recent months, he did a search for known abductions in the region and found three, two British and one American. *They could be the prisoners in the statement,* he thought, but as he read more the timings seemed off. Two of the prisoners had been strapped to the attacking vehicles, suggesting they couldn't have fingered Mansour the previous day. That left one—Victoria Phillips—but despite a thorough search he found no mention of her in the CIA documents.

Harvey put in a call to the British Embassy in Manila, though he wasn't expecting a whole lot more cooperation than he'd previously received. His heart sank further when the familiar voice came over the phone, but he kept his composure and politely asked if there was any information available about her disappearance and release.

'I can confirm that we were informed of her disappearance at the start of the year,' the attaché admitted. 'I haven't been informed about her release, though. She certainly hasn't been in touch with us.'

'Are you sure?' Harvey asked, astonished. If he'd been held by terrorists, the first thing he'd want to do was get to British soil, and that would require a passport.

'Positive,' came the reply, along with a little indignation. 'If she contacted the embassy, I would know about it.'

'If you say so,' Harvey said. 'What about the other matter, the one I called about last week?'

'I've got someone working on it,' the attaché said, 'but things work a little slowly around here. Once I have something, I'll be in touch.'

The phone went dead and Harvey wished the same on the attaché.

His next call was to the American Embassy, where he was put through to his CIA counterpart, Doug Wallis.

'Andy, how are you?'

Harvey didn't usually take kindly to people shortening his name, but Wallis was such an affable character, and when seeking information it was a good idea to let the little things slide.

'Good, thanks, Doug. How's the family?'

Wallis gave him the usual sob story about how his wife just couldn't get settled in England, no matter how much shopping she did. Harvey knew the story could go on indefinitely so he cut his friend short.

'I'm just looking for some information about the attack on Jolo last week.'

'We sent that over yesterday,' Wallis said. 'Didn't you get it?'

'Yeah, we got it, but I'd like to know more about the prisoners. We can't seem to locate one of them, a woman named Victoria Phillips.'

'I don't recall any of them being female,' Wallis said, sounding confused.

'Are you sure?'

'Positive. There was certainly no one named Victoria, anyway.'

Harvey rifled through the papers on his desk. 'I can't see any reference to the prisoners anywhere,' he said. 'Are you sure you sent that information over?'

'No, they won't be on anything we passed to you,' Wallis said casually. 'That report was classified Internal Eyes Only.'

'Any particular reason?' Harvey asked, curious as to why the identities should have been withheld.

'No idea,' Wallis told him. 'That's what we got from Langley, no explanation as to why.'

It wasn't unusual for agencies to withhold certain sensitive information from each other, but it seemed strange that the names of three people rescued from terrorists should be considered classified, especially if two of them were British.

'Is there any chance you can tell me the names?' Harvey asked, knowing what the answer would be. He had, however, planted the seed.

'Sorry, pal, no can do.'

'That's okay, Doug, I understand. Hey, fancy a beer later?'

The question was a signal they both used when they wanted something off the record, and Harvey was relieved when Doug agreed to meet up later that evening. He was, however, slightly frustrated that he would have to wait another few hours to get the information.

He walked round to Farsi's desk to see how he was getting on with the analysis of the *Huang Zhen* manifest. His colleague had been compiling a list of companies that had used the ship to transport their goods abroad. Once finalised, each company would be run through the internal search engine to find matches to persons of known interest.

'Anything yet?' Harvey asked, but a shake of the head told him all he needed to know.

'Nothing so far, but I've only been through a quarter of the companies. The *Huang Zhen* is a ULCV, or Ultra Large Container Vessel. This beast is carrying close to two thousand containers for just over twelve hundred companies. It's going to take some time to get through them all.'

Harvey sympathised with his friend. *If only investigations were like the movies,* he thought, *we'd just have to wait for that one clue to drop into our laps and the mystery would be solved.* Back in the real world, it was relentless hours of data analysis which usually won the day. It was just a shame the men in power didn't appreciate that fact; otherwise, they would provide more people to get the job done. As it was, the vast majority of staff had been assigned to identifying threats associated with the upcoming Olympics, which left Harvey and Farsi doing work the analysts would normally power through in a few hours.

To make matters worse, the equally undermanned UK Border Agency was forcing staff to take holidays in the months leading up to London 2012 so that they would have all hands on deck for the games. It meant queues would be shorter during July and August, but it left them woefully short-staffed in the lead-up, something that had been flagged up on several occasions. The politicians, however, refused to believe that anyone posing a threat to the UK would turn up prior to the games, instead expecting them to arrive when they were in full flow.

This short-sightedness was a constant thorn in the security services' sides, but it was something they'd learned to live with.

The culmination of this was that resources were stretched in just about every critical service, and all of the major newspapers had picked up on the fact. Their coverage, in Harvey's eyes, was an open invitation to attack the country, and he was one of the few people who could do anything about it.

Harvey shook the thought off and went back to his desk, where he found an internal message which informed him that a secure fax had been received.

He took a walk down to the communications office and handed over his identity card, despite knowing the receptionist and her recognising him from multiple previous visits. The rule was simple and rigorously enforced: no valid current ID, no entry.

After a quick inspection of his card he was given a smile and offered a seat while the receptionist placed a call through to the inner office. A moment later a junior clerk appeared and handed over the communication.

Harvey saw that it was the call records he'd requested from the High Commission in Singapore. As well as a list of calls made to and from Hughes's registered mobile number, there was a handwritten note at the bottom of the page:

A second mobile was found on the body, unregistered. Here is a list of calls we extracted from the SIM:

There were just four entries underneath the note, and Harvey had a feeling that one of them would be significant. He rushed back to his office and compared the numbers with those of Carl Levine and found a match on the last entry. The mobile number Hughes had called from also matched the incoming phone records they held for Levine.

Any suspicions they had that this was the Timmy they were looking for were now confirmed, and he asked Farsi to cross each of the company owners with the names on Hughes's call log.

'I know it's a major pain, but if we can tie Hughes to that ship somehow ...'

'Then what?' Farsi asked.

'I'm not sure,' Harvey admitted. 'But I have a feeling there's a lot more to Farrar's request for help than just finding Levine and Campbell.'

———

People were beginning to drift out of the office and a glance at the clock told Harvey that it was almost six thirty in the evening. He'd taken half of the manifest from Farsi and was also running company names through the computer, but for the last few hours he had come up empty.

When he met Wallis, it was usually at seven in Armando's restaurant a few streets away, which meant he'd have to make a move soon. He locked his half of the manifest in a drawer and grabbed his jacket as he headed for Ellis's office to deliver his end-of-shift report. He found her gazing intently at her monitor.

'I'm done for the day,' he said when Ellis looked up. 'We haven't been able to come up with anything that says the *Huang Zhen* is linked to Levine and Campbell, but we still have a lot of companies to go through.'

Ellis stretched and stifled a yawn. 'Nothing coming from Farrar, either,' she said. 'It's as if he's given up the search.'

'Should we do likewise?' Harvey asked, hoping for—and getting—a negative response.

'No, we carry on. There's a link in Asia, I'm certain of it. That was Abdul Mansour's last known location, and now Al-Qaeda chatter has gone off the charts.'

'As happened just before 9/11,' Harvey mused.

'Exactly,' Ellis said. 'A lot of it is rubbish—a smokescreen—but the sheer volume makes it near impossible to pick out the relevant stuff.'

She rubbed her temples and let out a sigh. Harvey could see she was under an enormous amount of pressure, as were they all, but as head of the organisation she bore the brunt. He wanted to cheer her up by letting her know about the meeting with Wallis, but if he mentioned it she would no doubt ask what information he had shared in the past. That wasn't a conversation he wanted to get into right now.

'I'm heading home,' he said, and Ellis nodded as he made for the exit.

Outside, the sky had clouded over once more, heralding yet more rain in what had already been the wettest May in recent years. It was only a ten-minute walk to Armando's, and he arrived just as the heavens opened. Inside, he found a table near the back, and the drinks arrived just as Wallis dashed through the door.

'I'm beginning to see why my wife wants to go home,' he said, bringing a smile to Harvey's face. He knew that Doug loved his current assignment, and the more his wife complained, the more determined he was to stay.

Wallis hung his coat on a stand and sat opposite Harvey. They enjoyed their drinks in silence for a moment, Wallis favouring a pint of bitter to Harvey's lager.

'So what have you got for me, Doug?'

Wallis savoured his beer before putting the glass on the table and leaning closer to Harvey.

'The order to keep it under wraps came from the home secretary himself,' Wallis said and saw the expected surprise on his friend's face. It quickly turned to curiosity.

'So who were the prisoners?'

'The one he was concerned about was Sam Grant.'

Harvey made the quick transition from curious to confused. He'd never heard the name, and was certain he hadn't seen it in any recent reports.

'Who is this Grant guy?'

'We don't know. Colonel Travis Dane, commander of the Special Activities Division on Jolo sent his picture over to Langley, and all they got back was the name and an order not to share with anyone, not even you guys.'

Harvey wondered why the minister would want to withhold information from his own security services, and the obvious answer was that it wasn't an operation that he wanted the Intelligence Services Commissioner to know about. The commissioner is responsible for service oversight and can visit any of the security services at his discretion, requesting documents or information relating to any case. Each year he reports his findings direct to the prime minister. This report is then laid before parliament and subsequently published.

If the home secretary didn't want this case becoming public knowledge, it could only mean one thing. But who would carry out such an operation? It would have to be someone with access to the system. He made a mental note to check with Gerald Small to see if any of the subnets fit the bill, but one leaped immediately to mind.

Farrar.

Ellis had said that even she didn't know who he worked for, which pointed to his role being covert. And if it *was* Farrar, did this mean that this Sam Grant was one of the passengers he was expecting?

'Who were the other prisoners?' he asked.

'Simon Baines and Len Smart,' Wallis said.

'Are you sure?' Harvey asked, a little louder than he intended.

Wallis nodded. 'I read through the report just before I left the office. According to Dane, one of his troops caught three armed men wandering around the jungle and brought them in for questioning.

They wouldn't talk, so Dane sent their pictures to Langley, who sent back the details. All they got for Sam Grant was a name, a photo, and that's it.'

'Do you have the report with you?' Harvey asked, more in hope than expectation.

'Sorry, buddy. You know the deal, completely off the record, and that means no hard copies.'

Harvey understood. 'So what happened to the prisoners? Where are they now?'

'Dane said the three of them went missing during the attack. The guard house was hit, and they must have escaped. Apparently, your people were pissed when they turned up to collect them.'

'*My* people?' Harvey asked, once more confused. 'Are you sure they were from Five?'

'Langley assumed they were, but the look on your face tells me otherwise.'

'They certainly weren't sent by anyone I know,' Harvey said, but he didn't add that it once again pointed to James Farrar.

He recalled that the *Huang Zhen* had left Malaysia on Monday the 23rd, while the attack on the base had taken place just three days earlier. That meant Baines and Smart would have had three days to travel to Port Kelang. His search through Hughes's file had shown that he owned a yacht, but could it make the journey in that time? He'd have to wait until he got back to the office to work that one out, and the introduction of the mysterious Sam Grant into the mix meant he wasn't prepared to wait until the morning.

'I have to go and check a few things out,' he said as he rose. 'Thanks for the info, Doug. I owe you one.'

'Big time,' Wallis agreed.

It took Harvey less than five minutes to jog back to Thames House, and once in the office he went straight to his desk and logged onto his computer. He was waiting for the security settings to synch when Ellis approached him.

'I thought you'd gone home,' she said.

'I've got some new information,' Harvey told her. 'I need to do a search for Sam Grant.'

The welcome screen appeared, and he began typing into the internal search engine.

'Where did you get the name?' she asked as they waited for the results to come back.

'A completely anonymous and deniable source,' Harvey told her with a smile. 'I could tell you, but then I'd have to kill myself.'

The screen showed six results, and they went through each one, Harvey looking for anything that could link him to the current investigation. The first four were quickly dismissed, but when trying to open the fifth record, he was shown a dialog box which requested a password. He entered his account login, and a flashing message filled the screen: 'Access Denied.'

'Okay,' Ellis said, looking at Harvey. 'You got my attention. Who is this guy?'

'I've got no idea. However, find Sam Grant and we find Baines and Smart.'

He gave her a breakdown of the information he'd got from Wallis, but stopped short of revealing his identity, despite Ellis asking more than once. She suggested they try to access the file using her credentials, which had a higher level of access. When they got to her office and repeated the process, the outcome was the same.

'If the home secretary personally gave the order to withhold Grant's file from the CIA—and from his own people—then it smells of black ops to me,' Harvey said. 'That means we're dealing with a team who have the minister's ear, a team who are off the official grid but still have access. And if Grant was with Baines and Smart on Jolo, that team would not want you looking for that particular pair, even if they were solid leads to finding Levine and Campbell.'

He looked Ellis in the eye. 'So who does that sound like?'

Ellis had to agree that it pointed the finger fair and square in Farrar's direction, but it wasn't conclusive.

'We need to pin this to him,' she said, rubbing her palms together as she concentrated.

'Then what?' Harvey asked.

It was a very good question, one she hadn't got round to considering. If the passengers were in fact the mysterious Grant and the two men Farrar didn't want her searching for, what was she to do about it? If she interfered in an order signed by the minister himself, she knew she could kiss her career goodbye. On the flip side, she had proof that Farrar had ordered someone to intercept them, and the phrase 'ensure no onward journey' sounded very much like a kill order. If these people were who she thought they were, could she stand idly by and allow a state-sanctioned hit on British citizens? She knew she wouldn't allow another nation to get away with it, so why shouldn't those same standards apply to her own government?

'First we confirm that Farrar is behind this,' she said.

Harvey nodded. 'How do we do that? If Farrar is involved, he'll just deny any knowledge of Sam Grant.'

Ellis smiled. 'To catch a rat, you have to become a rat.'

James Farrar was wading through the reports his team had produced. So far they had checked hundreds of bed and breakfast establishments for cash-paying families checking in on the 22nd of April, but there were still thousands to be done. There were also numerous camp sites, caravan parks and boat rentals to be eliminated, and all of this in the next few days. At the current rate, his targets would die of old age before he found them.

He wished he could bring in the police, but that was out of the question. The last thing he wanted was this hitting the newspapers, and all it would take would be one loose-lipped copper opening his mouth to the wrong person.

He was still fumbling for ideas when his mobile rang. The display told him it was Ellis, and he prayed that she had some good news. He answered using the most pleasant voice he could muster.

'Veronica, how are you?'

'Tired,' Ellis said wearily.

You and me both, Farrar thought, though he didn't say as much. 'I hope you're calling to let me know you've found what I'm looking for,' he said, not wanting to be too specific over an unsecure line.

'Not yet, but we have been given a lead, a name. Trouble is, we can't follow it up.'

'Why the hell not?' Farrar asked, dropping the pretence of amiability.

'I can't access his file,' Ellis said. 'It's password protected. I was calling to ask if you could have a word with the home secretary and persuade him to release it to me.'

'Whose file is it?' Farrar asked as he prepared to enter the name into the search engine.

'Sam Grant,' she said, and Farrar almost dropped the phone. Where the hell did she get that name from?

'Are you there, James?'

'Uh ... yeah, just doing a search now.' He brought the screen up as he tried to figure out who the hell knew about Grant. He did, of course, and the home secretary. Besides them, there was the request from the CIA a few weeks earlier. Farrar had been on a plane back from Manila when the request had come in; otherwise, he would have handled it himself and sent them a completely different name. In his absence, all they had been given was a photo, which was what they had in the first place. Giving them the name should have been no big deal, either: it was a fictitious name in a sealed file that was only accessible to a handful of people, and the CIA had been given explicit instructions not to share with anyone. Unfortunately, it seemed that the Americans hadn't been as tight-mouthed as they should have been.

'I'm getting a password prompt, too,' he said. 'Looks like I'll have to ask the minister for access. I can't promise anything, though. If I can't see the file, there must be a good reason.'

Ellis sounded disappointed as she asked Farrar to do his best.

'I will,' he assured her, 'but I need to know what information you have about this man. If it can lead us to Levine and Campbell, I can put that forward as a case for releasing the file.'

'Nothing beyond the name,' Ellis told him.

'Okay, then who gave you the name?' he asked, hoping to confirm that it had come from the CIA.

'One of my operatives got it from an undisclosed source.'

'Which operative?' Farrar pressed.

'That's not important, James. Please just let me know when you've spoken to the home secretary.'

The phone went dead in his hand, and Farrar swore half a dozen times before typing his password into the box.

Whatever was in this file, he had to find it quickly.

⁓

Ellis still had her hand on the receiver when the key logger began spitting out new characters. She copied and pasted them into the password dialog before hitting the 'Enter' key. A moment later a picture appeared, underneath which was the name Sam Grant.

'James Farrar, you're a lying shit!'

They read through the brief biography and found nothing out of the ordinary. In fact, it appeared decidedly sterile. Born in London during the early seventies, worked for a few small companies after leaving school, single, no driving licence, lived in rented accommodation until his sudden move to Manila a year earlier.

'It looks like a legend,' Ellis commented.

'And a poor one at that,' Harvey confirmed. 'I'll have someone check these firms, but I'll bet they're no longer trading, if they ever existed in the first place.'

Legends are cover stories created when an intelligence operative is required to go undercover. It creates a believable personal background should anyone do any checks into the operative's history.

Ellis nodded and scrolled down through the entries. If the bio was brief, the last entry was even more succinct: 'Deceased.'

The entry was dated Thursday the 19th of April, 2012, a day before the attack on Camp Bautista. Harvey wondered how that could be: according to Wallis, the three prisoners had escaped during the attack, and he told Ellis as much.

'Then to paraphrase Mark Twain,' Ellis said, 'it looks like reports of his death have been grossly exaggerated.'

Harvey studied the picture, which also appeared to be contrived. It was like a collage of facial elements, with a large flat nose that didn't seem to naturally fit with the size of the face. Despite this, there was something familiar…

The image disappeared as Ellis clicked the 'History' link to see who had been responsible for each of the entries. The last recorded user, the person who had declared Grant dead, was none other than James Farrar.

'So Farrar thinks Grant is dead, but when the CIA requests his details, a team from the UK is sent to pick up him and his friends. We know that team wasn't one of ours, so I'm guessing Farrar is behind that, too.'

'It certainly looks like it,' Harvey agreed, 'which is why he doesn't want you looking for Baines and Smart. He already knows where they are and has someone waiting for them when they arrive in Durban.'

Ellis nodded, having come to the same conclusion. 'I want you to go out there,' she said. 'Find them and bring them home.'

Harvey told her that he was happy to oblige, but was also aware that there could be some serious fallout. 'I don't think the home secretary is going to be too happy if we interfere with one of his operations,' he warned her.

'I know,' Ellis said, 'but when I joined the service I vowed to protect Britain from all threats, foreign and domestic. We don't know why Farrar is looking for these people, but whatever it is they're supposed to have done, they are still entitled to a fair trial. It isn't up to the home secretary to decide who lives and dies.'

'Not even in the interest of national security?' Harvey asked.

'If it was national security, we'd have heard about it,' Ellis said indignantly.

Harvey suspected the real reason she was taking this course of action was that she had been left out of the loop by her superiors. She might also be looking to settle an old score with Farrar, but whatever her motive, they were reading from the same page.

'I'm going to need some help over there,' he said. 'We don't know if it's just one man or a whole team waiting for the *Huang Zhen* to arrive. The only thing that we're certain of is that someone will be waiting to kill those passengers.'

'Then you'll need to establish that as your priority. You'll be looking for someone who's just entered the country and is booked into accommodation until the seventh of May. Cross-reference flights from Malaysia with hotel reservations, and run any matches through the system.'

Ellis brought up a new screen and searched for information on their people in South Africa. She was rewarded with the bio for Dennis Owen, whose cover was that of a senior advisor in the UK Trade & Investment Department.

'I'll let him know you're coming,' she said. 'Draw up a list of anything you're going to need, and choose your legend. Farrar may be watching the airport departure lists, and I don't want to have to explain what you're doing over there.'

Harvey nodded and went to his station to book his flight. He chose one the following evening to give himself time to try to discover just who was waiting for Baines and Smart in Durban. He was too pumped up to sleep and knew an all-nighter was on the cards, so he set the search running and grabbed his jacket before heading out of the building. He was back twenty minutes later with a large coffee, two sandwiches and a selection of chocolate bars, once again thankful that there was no one waiting for him at home.

The list of passengers was ready and waiting for him, and he immediately filtered out those who were in transit as well as all South African nationals. It was entirely possible that whoever he was looking for could be a resident, but he had to focus on the leads he had. If Farrar was using a contractor, it was highly likely that person would be British.

The filtered list contained just over seventy promising matches and Harvey began the process of comparing them, one by one, with names held on their system.

Tom Gray stared at the ceiling of the container and for the umpteenth time he wondered what he was going to do to James Farrar once he got his hands on him. Vick was having yet another nap, while Baines was busy cheating at a game of patience and Smart was once again engrossed in the new Kindle he'd purchased in Kuala Lumpur.

'What are you reading now?' Sonny asked.

'*The Bones Of The Earth* by Scott Bury. It's a historical fantasy.'

'Sounds good.'

'I'd say it was closer to exceptional,' Smart said and returned to his book.

Vick woke and stretched, doing her best to stifle a yawn in case she breathed in too much of the fetid air. She got up to get the circulation moving in her legs before sitting back down and rummaging in the bag for some food.

'What time is it?' she asked.

'Three in the morning,' Sonny told her. 'That means about a hundred and thirty-something hours until we get to Durban, so go easy on the food.'

Vick soon realised what he meant. They had brought along enough tins and drinks to last them well beyond the two-week journey, but boredom had seen her snacking constantly, and there was barely enough left for the next couple of days. Despite this, she broke open a tin of peach slices and tucked in with a fork.

Her actions hadn't gone unnoticed by one of her fellow passengers. A young Chinese man stood and walked over to her, gesturing at the food and pointing towards his own chest. Vick instinctively cradled the food close while turning her back on him. This did nothing to dissuade the man, and he began to raise his voice, gesturing towards the bag.

'What's he saying?' Grant asked Sonny.

'How the hell should I know?'

'I thought you took language lessons in the Regiment. I know I signed off at least three of your requests.'

'That was because the teacher was so pretty. During the lessons I only picked up the most important phrases.'

'Which were?' Len asked.

'"Give me a beer", obviously.' This brought appreciative nods from the other two former soldiers. 'There was also "fancy a shag", and of course, "kill him".'

'Why do you need to say that in other languages?' Vick asked.

Sonny grinned: 'I don't. I just need to know when someone is saying it in my presence.'

Their idle chit-chat was beginning to incense the Chinese passenger, and he stepped in among the group and reached down into the bag. Baines grabbed the man's wrist and pulled it towards him while getting to his feet, twisting the arm as he did so. The hungry stranger lost his battle with gravity and landed on his back, and Baines was on him in an instant. He put one knee on the man's chest and grabbed him around the throat.

'That's not very polite,' Baines said as he squeezed with just enough force to bring some colour to the face.

A howl erupted behind Baines, and Gray touched him on the arm, motioning towards a woman who was quite clearly pregnant. 'Let him go, Sonny.'

Baines hesitated for a moment but then climbed off. Gray handed the man a tin of Spam and gestured for him to disappear.

'Wonderful,' Baines said. 'That takes us about ten hours closer to starvation.'

'Don't be daft,' Smart said, his eyes still focused on his book. 'They'll be serving breakfast in a few hours.'

'Don't get me wrong, but while highly original, curry for breakfast does lose its appeal after a while. I'd rather eat a Pot Noodle.'

To change the subject, Smart put down his Kindle and asked Gray if he'd decided on a plan of action.

'I'm still torn between two options, but I'm swinging towards public exposure.'

'We dismissed that idea a couple of weeks ago,' Baines pointed out. 'They'll have DA-Notices out, and no paper would dare run the story.'

'I agree that if we just called the BBC or a newspaper, they wouldn't run the story, but there are other ways.'

Gray explained what he had in mind, but the others were not totally convinced that his plan would work. However, they'd had the same reservations a year and a half earlier but had come so close to pulling off a masterful plan.

'I know it's risky, but the alternative doesn't guarantee results, either.'

Plan B was to gain control of a television news studio and tell the world what James Farrar had been up to on behalf of the government. However, they would eventually have to hand themselves in, and they couldn't be sure they would be allowed to see the light of day again.

The others agreed with him, and so they spent the next few hours developing Gray's favoured option, suggesting and dismissing ideas until they had what they thought was a workable solution to their problems.

'It all hinges on you convincing your man to help us,' Smart pointed out. 'Fail to do that and we fall at the first hurdle.'

Gray was well aware that the initial plea for help was crucial to their success. If he couldn't pull it off, there would be no option but to revert to the backup plan. 'Then I'd best be at my most persuasive,' he said, determination in his eyes.

Chapter Six

Thursday, 3 May 2012

Ben Palmer crept through the darkness towards the chain link fence surrounding the Wenban Freight Management compound, even though he knew there was no camera coverage to record his approach.

His initial recce the previous day—a drive-by followed by a walk-past—had revealed just three CCTV cameras covering the vehicle park, all static. Negotiating them wouldn't be a challenge, but he had no idea what kind of security they had in place to protect the main office building. To get to the office, he first had to get through the fence. It wasn't particularly high but was topped with razor wire, so going through seemed the most prudent option.

A quick look around showed no sign of life, either from the tyre yard thirty yards to his left or the warehouse on the other side of the road, which looked like it had long been abandoned.

He pulled a pair of cutters from his jacket and began snipping away at the wire next to a supporting post, starting at the bottom of the fence and working his way upwards until he had created a twelve-inch gap. He put the cutters aside and pulled the broken part of the fence towards him so that he could squeeze underneath. He stopped when he heard a sound close by and strained to detect the direction it had come from. A glance to either side showed no signs of movement, but he waited a couple of minutes, just to be sure.

The compound was quite a distance from the nearest populated town, so he assumed the noise was probably some kind of nocturnal animal scratching around for food. He turned his attention back to the fence and was beginning to roll it upwards when a hundred and seventy pounds of Boerboel came bounding towards the fence, barking for all it was worth. Palmer barely had time to roll the fence back into place before the guard dog began clawing at his fingers, shredding the skin and destroying his surgical gloves.

Palmer fell on his backside and used his feet to prevent the dog from crawling through the gap he'd created, at the same time reaching for his Taser. By this time, the hound had managed to get its head through the small gap and was attacking Palmer's feet, though the thick rubber soles of his boots prevented any serious injury. The animal still came at him, inching through the hole while snapping and snarling, saliva dripping from its mouth.

Palmer finally managed to get the Taser free and fired into the dog's shoulder, delivering a charge which at first appeared to have no effect but which eventually brought it to the ground. He kept his finger on the trigger while he extracted a syringe, and he cut the charge just before he stabbed it into the back of the dog's neck with shaking hands.

With the animal incapacitated, he lay on the ground to catch his breath, wondering where the hell it had come from. He'd looked for a kennel during his earlier observations, but there had been nothing whatsoever to point to a guard dog patrolling the compound. The manager must have kept it inside during the day, probably to stop it attacking the staff, judging by its demeanour.

Palmer decided to keep the Taser handy, just in case there were any more surprises. He also had to get the dog back inside the compound so that his little visit went unnoticed. He moved the animal aside and crawled through the gap he'd made, and it took some considerable effort to pull the mutt through after him. He eventually got it clear of the hole and dragged it behind a stack of pallets, then used his feet to obliterate the trail leading to his entry point.

With the dog hidden, Palmer wiped the sweat from his face and neck, and then pulled out his lock-picking tools. The main office was bathed in darkness, and he stepped carefully, listening intently for the slightest sound that could indicate another dog, or even a night watchman, though the latter seemed unlikely given the amount of barking the dog had done.

He reached the door and found that his first hurdle was a padlock which secured a deadbolt just above the door handle. It took less than fifteen seconds to defeat it, and another thirty to open the Yale lock. He eased the door open gently, looking for any sign of an alarm but finding none.

Once inside the wooden structure, he found a couple of untidy desks, both with computers at least a dozen years old. He ignored those, instead looking for hard copies of movement schedules. He found these in the single filing cabinet, and using a small torch with a green filter over the glass to diffuse the beam, he flicked through the records searching for anything relating to the seventh of May. He was thankful that the operation was small, with less than a dozen vehicles, which meant he was able to find what he was looking for within a minute.

There were just seven entries for the coming Monday, and two of them were pickups for Arnold Tang's company. His little chat with Tang's lieutenant hadn't revealed the fact that there would be more than one consignment arriving, which left Palmer having to decide which container his targets were likely to be in. The first one was a standard forty-foot-high cube container with a declared gross weight of forty-five thousand pounds, while the second was half the size and lighter by around 70 per cent.

Palmer knew that his targets were just four of twenty people making the journey to the UK, so he discounted the smaller container and checked the details of the other one. It was due to be offloaded just before seven in the evening, with delivery to an import/export company the following morning. This suggested that the container would be parked up overnight, most probably within the compound.

After taking snaps of both records with a compact digital camera, he carefully placed all of the documents back in their respective folders and closed the cabinet, wiping down any surfaces he had touched. At the door he did the same before closing it quietly and reattaching the padlock. The dog was still where he had left it, and he was pleased to see that it was still breathing; the last thing he needed was a dead dog broadcasting his incursion.

At the fence he smoothed out the soil around the gap and pulled a pallet up to the post before squeezing through the hole. He then moved the pallet over the hole to prevent the dog from scratching around and bringing it to anyone's attention. He then used small lengths of wire to fasten the fence back to the post as best he could. It wasn't a permanent solution, but if it prevented detection for just a few days, it would serve its purpose.

He made his way back to the main road and waited until there was no traffic in sight before sprinting to the main entrance, where he quickly checked the condition of the security. A large, rust-free chain and combination lock secured the two metal gates, and he made a mental note to add industrial-strength bolt cutters to his ever-growing shopping list.

Palmer ran back to his car, which he'd parked behind the tyre yard, then drove back into town, stopping off at a bar to grab a beer. He stayed there for just ten minutes, and once he reached his hotel, he made a point of getting close enough to the receptionist that she could smell his breath as he asked for a morning wake-up call. This helped keep up the pretence of the travelling salesman out enjoying the local nightlife.

When he got to his room, he booted his laptop and logged into his proxy server before searching his contact list for the number of an old friend. He called using an unregistered prepaid phone he'd bought earlier in the day.

'Sean,' he said when the connection was made, 'it's Ben. I was in town and thought I'd look you up.'

'Hey, it's good to hear your voice, man.'

They chewed the fat for a couple of minutes before Palmer explained that he needed to do some shopping while he was in town.

'No problem,' Sean said. 'I'm having a *braai* this weekend. Wanna join me?'

'Just like old times. Sure, sounds great.'

They arranged to meet at the farm just after midday on Saturday, and Palmer ended the call. He spent the next thirty minutes finding a van rental company with a vehicle large enough for his purposes, before turning the lights out and grabbing some sleep.

———

Andrew Harvey's KLM flight touched down just after nine thirty in the evening, and an hour later he was met in the arrivals lounge by a man wearing a suit despite the temperature being close to eighty degrees Fahrenheit.

Dennis Owen was in his early thirties and had the bearing of a man who did more in life than simply offer advice on trade and industry matters. His hidden remit was to get detailed background information on companies looking to invest in the UK in order to ensure there were no skeletons in closets that might embarrass the country. The last thing the government needed was a repeat of the Quatromain fiasco a few years earlier. It transpired that the money men behind that corporation were subsequently prosecuted for drug trafficking, which was a particular embarrassment for the secretary of state for business, innovation and skills, who had personally signed off the deal.

Owen offered Harvey a confident handshake. 'Welcome to South Africa.'

'Thanks,' Harvey said, stifling a yawn. The twenty-hour journey had taken a lot out of him, despite his managing to grab some sleep on the flight following the two-hour stopover in Amsterdam's Schiphol Airport. 'Did you have any luck with the seven names I sent you?'

'I've got a friend in the local police force who did some checking, but none of them have any records here at all,' Owen said as he led Harvey out of the airport terminal in the direction of the car park. He stopped at a BMW saloon and, once inside, handed a printed sheet to Harvey. 'These are the supposed itineraries of your suspects. I also got the name of the haulage company collecting the containers you're interested in. They're a small firm called Wenban Freight Management.'

Hamad Farsi's efforts had paid off. He'd made the connection between Timmy Hughes and Arnold Tang, which in turn led to the discovery that one of Tang's companies had two consignments on the *Huang Zhen*. They hadn't yet been able to get into the Durban Port Authority computers to find out who was collecting the containers, which was why they'd asked Owen to get the information. Although they now knew who would be collecting the consignments, they still had no idea where they were going to be dropped off.

'What about the company?' Harvey asked. 'Any ties to Arnold Tang?'

'None that we could find. It looks like your typical small business. They've been in operation for six years and grown from a couple of vehicles to ten during that time. Tax records and company accounts suggest this expansion has been financed using their own capital, and their income is consistent with a haulage company of that size.'

'That's good. They should have no problems cooperating with us.'

'You'd think so, but we spoke to them this afternoon, and the owner is reluctant to give us any information about his customers, without a warrant.'

'Fine, so get one,' Harvey said.

'Not so easy,' Owen told him. 'I asked my friend, but he said the police will want documented evidence before they apply to the courts. We might have better luck with customs, though. If we let them know the container might contain illegal immigrants, they could check it at the port.'

Harvey thought about it, but soon dismissed the idea. 'If we do that, we lose whoever's here to meet them,' he said. If he was going to play his part in disrupting Farrar's plans, he wanted concrete evidence of his involvement in any wrongdoing, and having the person or persons sent to carry out the kill order would be a good start.

It was forty-five minutes later when they arrived at the hotel, and Owen dropped Harvey off outside.

'I'll be back for you at seven in the morning; then I'll drive you down to Durban. Your room is booked and paid for.'

Harvey thanked him and dragged his suitcase into the foyer. It was aesthetically mundane, though that mattered little to Harvey, as he planned to do nothing more than sleep for the next six hours.

Azhar Al-Asiri threw open his arms to welcome his young general home.

'*Salam alaikum!*'

Abdul Mansour returned the greeting and took a seat at the small table. It was the first time he had been to Al-Asiri's home, and the humble surroundings were exactly as he would have fashioned for himself.

'How was your journey?'

'Fine,' Mansour said as he accepted the offer of tea, though 'fine' was being generous. Once he'd received news that his lieutenant, Nabil Shah, had been killed on Jolo, Mansour had made his way home from Indonesia. He had spent most of the journey on a fishing vessel, and it had been several days before he'd stopped throwing up. Even now he wondered if the smell would ever leave him.

'I am glad you are back, my friend. Tell me about your latest mission.'

Mansour explained how he'd delivered the weapons and money to the Abu Sayyaf leader and provided training in their use, but as for the attack itself, he only knew what the television and newspapers had reported. Over a hundred American and Filipino soldiers had been killed in the firefight at Camp Bautista, although Abu Sayyaf had lost a couple of hundred men in a reprisal attack immediately afterwards.

As for the overall mission, he had convinced the leaders of Jemaah Islamiyah—Abu Sayyaf's Indonesian counterparts—to enter into talks aimed at creating a Muslim alliance. The promise of more weapons and money had been extended to the Indonesians, with a view to them controlling most of maritime South-East Asia.

'You have done Allah a great service,' Al-Asiri told him. 'However, the fight must continue at pace. Tell me, how would you feel about going back to England one last time?'

'I will go wherever you ask,' Mansour said with heartfelt conviction.

'As I thought.' His master smiled as he leaned back into his chair. 'Your mission will be to simply provide training to a new group of martyrs. You will not be exposed to danger yourself.'

'What do they need to know?'

'You will show them how to create explosive devices. These are young men who have not come under the scrutiny of the security services, and to use the Internet for their research would be to wave a red flag at a bull.'

'How can we be sure that they are not being watched?' Mansour asked. 'The last thing we should do is underestimate our enemies.'

'I have people with access to this information,' Al-Asiri said confidently. To his lasting regret, he hadn't been able to get anyone into the security services themselves, but there were other agencies that were party to certain information, and airline no-fly and watch lists were just two ways of knowing if MI5 were interested in an individual.

'What would you have them attack?'

'There are multiple targets across the UK,' Al-Asiri told him. 'In addition, coordinated attacks will take place in the US and Canada. Timing will be of the utmost importance.'

'Are these military targets, or infrastructure?' Mansour asked, intrigued.

'Sperm banks,' Al-Asiri said and smiled at Mansour's confused expression.

'I'm sorry, I do not understand. How will this further the cause?'

Al-Asiri explained how his research team had developed a virus that would kill off Y chromosome sperm, and spelled out his vision for the future. 'The next generation of British and American children will be predominately female, which in years to come will reduce their fighting capability. The small percentage of males born will carry the new gene, which means the cycle continues in ever decreasing circles. The only chance to produce male offspring is through interracial breeding.'

Mansour looked at Al-Asiri and did well to hide his true feelings. His facial expression portrayed fascination, but inside he began to wonder if the old man had gone completely mad.

'You plan to breed them out of existence?'

'Exactly,' Al-Asiri told him. 'In a hundred years, America and Britain as we know them will be nothing more than a page in the history books. Our Muslim influence will spread throughout their lands until ultimately the whole world kneels before Allah!'

Mansour had to marvel at the audacity of the plan, but it was flawed on so many fundamental levels.

'How many sperm banks are there in the UK and US?' he asked, hoping his master would recognise the scale of the operation he was proposing.

'Many hundreds,' Al-Asiri told him, 'but we do not need to destroy them all. We have a website ready to go live, and it will proclaim the formation of the Campaign for Natural Birth. It is a fictitious Christian organisation seeking the abolition of medically assisted pregnancy on the grounds that it is God alone who decides the birth of every child.

'We will bomb a small number of sperm banks in each country and CNB will claim responsibility for these actions, warning that more attacks will come unless they are closed down. They will also claim that anyone donating to one of these banks makes themselves a viable target.'

Mansour could see the sense in that approach, and if nothing else it would tie up the security services in both countries for quite some time. Nevertheless, he still had major concerns about the overall plan, and he wasn't sure how much criticism he could level at his master's idea.

'That still leaves them with a very large stockpile. I'm not sure these efforts will deliver the results you are looking for. I am also concerned that the bombers will give away the fact that a Christian group wasn't actually behind the attacks.'

'That is why you are here,' Al-Asiri told him, his demeanour a lot less convivial than moments earlier. 'I have given you the tools and explained the effect I wish to achieve. It is now up to you to make it work.'

Mansour sat in silence, the enormity of the task weighing heavily on his shoulders. His rise through the Al-Qaeda ranks had been meteoric, but fail this mission and all of his efforts would have been in vain.

Al-Asiri saw the blank, almost pained expression on his general's face and offered a powerful incentive. 'As you know, since the Sheik died and I took over his mantle, I delayed in filling the vacant place on the inner council. There was a reason for this. I have been watching you develop over the years, and your commitment to the cause, your courage and skill all point to you one day making a great leader.'

Al-Asiri paused to let the words sink in. 'Complete this mission and take your place on the council.'

Mansour's excitement was tempered by his concerns over Al-Asiri's mental state. He had hoped to one day become a regional commander, but he'd envisaged that being many years in the future. To have it handed to him on a plate at such a tender age was a blessing from Allah himself, though it meant being led by a man who was obviously cartwheeling towards senility.

The seed of a plan popped into Mansour's head, one that would need to be nurtured, but for the time being he gave his leader the reaction he desired.

'Of course I will take on the challenge,' he smiled. 'Tell me what plans you already have in place.'

Chapter Seven

Friday, 4 May 2012

'I'm bored!'

Alana Levine sat with her arms folded, staring at the caravan floor. 'Wish I could have brought my iPhone.'

Her father was drying dishes in the tiny kitchen area, and he slammed down the cup in his hand, smashing it into a dozen pieces. 'How many times do I have to tell you?' he snarled.

Sandra Levine grabbed her husband by the arm. 'Carl, leave her alone. What do you expect from a thirteen-year-old?'

Carl Levine took a couple of deep breaths before gathering up the shards of porcelain and dumping them in the trash. After getting a look from his wife, he went to sit next to his daughter and put an arm around her shoulder.

'I'm sorry, darling, but we couldn't bring anything that could be traced. I told you that.'

'I know, but I could use it to just play games,' Alana pouted, bottom lip thrust out like a diving board.

Levine sighed. He had been through this a dozen times, explaining how SIM cards could be tracked even when the phone was not in use, and that even without the card it might be possible for those with the right technology to locate the device.

'I'll make it up to you when this is all over, I promise.'

'But when will that be?' she asked.

Carl Levine didn't have an answer to that one. A year earlier he had a schedule to keep to, but this time it was simply a case of waiting to hear from his friends. He didn't have any way of communicating with the outside world, and all the money they had was being spent on food and fuel. Although they still had a few hundred pounds between them, the money wasn't going to last forever. It was a blessing that the caravan they were staying in was owned outright by Tom Gray's solicitor and the ground rent was being paid by direct debit; otherwise, their finances would be stretched even further.

'Hopefully, not too long,' Levine said.

'Is it going to be like last time, with the reporters hanging round the house and school?'

Levine promised her that it wouldn't be a repeat of the previous year, when the press had camped outside their house for a fortnight in the hope of a story. They had even tried to interview his daughter as she entered the school grounds, and the following day he had escorted her to the entrance of the school building. On leaving the playground, he'd stopped to speak to the press, but not to give them the story they'd hoped for. Reading from a prepared statement, he'd given them what he considered their final warning.

'Yesterday, several members of the press tried to manhandle and harass my daughter into giving them an interview, something I, as her father, find deeply offensive. I reported this matter to the police and asked them to provide her with an escort every day, but they say they don't have the resources, despite my insisting that adults were laying their hands on my vulnerable child.

'As the police refuse to do anything about this situation, I will be forced to take the matter into my own hands should anyone try to interfere with my daughter on her way to or from school, using all force necessary to protect my child.'

Levine smiled as he remembered that statement going out on all the news channels, with commentators asking why the police were leaving a twelve-year-old girl to the mercy of a mob of reporters, and the anchors quick to point out that none of the reporters worked for their particular franchise. Within a few hours a police escort was arranged for the next few days until the media eventually gave up their efforts.

'I'm sure it won't be like last time,' he told her, even though he himself had no idea how it was going to play out. He kissed his daughter on the head and went back to his kitchen duties.

'I think she's missing her friends,' his wife said, and Levine could quite understand. It wasn't easy for him, sharing a small space with not only his wife and daughter but Jeff Campbell and his wife, too. For Alana, it must be doubly difficult, especially with no company her own age to keep her occupied.

He once again hoped that whatever was happening, it would be over soon, for his daughter's sake if nothing else. When the call had come, the last thing on his mind had been creature comforts, and he certainly hadn't been expecting to be holed up in this tiny box for more than a couple of days. It was now approaching two weeks, and he still no idea why they had been told to go into hiding.

Campbell was just as concerned, highlighting the fact that during their enforced holiday they hadn't been mentioned on the BBC news channel. That suggested the police weren't the ones they were hiding from, but if not the police, then who?

Following the attack a year earlier, and with Tom Gray lying critically injured in hospital, they had been briefed by a representative of the Home Office. He'd explained that the knowledge they had regarding the whole affair—the fact that no bomb existed and that Tom Gray hadn't actually killed any of his hostages—could be highly embarrassing to the government if it were ever leaked. In return for their silence, the government would allow Tom Gray to be spirited away with a new identity, and the six survivors would face no criminal proceedings.

Levine and the others had been given a few minutes to consider the proposal, and on face value it seemed an acceptable offer. It meant staying out of prison, and keeping their mouths shut was second nature to members of Two-Two Regiment.

It wasn't until a couple of days later that they had gotten together and discussed some of the less favourable scenarios, and it was then that they realised what they had signed up for. The knowledge they held was always going to be damaging, be it to the current government or future ones, and all that stood between complete secrecy and a national security fiasco was their individual integrity.

In effect, they were relying on the government to trust six men who had only a few days earlier held the country to ransom.

Following that epiphany they had promised each other that if one of them were to disappear or die under suspicious circumstances, the others would take their stories to every available media outlet. The death of Tristram Barker-Fink in Iraq had been a shock to them all, but there was no way they could blame that on anyone but the terrorists who took out the convoy he was travelling in. A few weeks after Tristram's death, Paul Bennett's followed, crashing his motorbike at high speed. Independent witnesses saw his tyre explode while he doing more than eighty miles per hour, with no other cars within fifty feet of him. The police report also cited mechanical failure as the reason for the crash, the tyre having blown out.

Both of these losses were put down to misfortune, but since they got the call to go into hiding, they were beginning to have second thoughts.

Levine went to sit next to Campbell. 'It's been a while since we heard from anyone,' he said quietly. 'What if we're the only ones left?'

'I was thinking the same thing,' Campbell agreed, 'but there's no way of knowing. I also don't like the idea of being in the same place for so long.'

'Me neither. The longer we stay in the same place, the easier it will be to track us down.'

Both men thought about their predicament, with their focus being on the other family members.

'We could send the girls away and wait it out,' Campbell suggested, and Levine liked the idea, though he had concerns as to where they would be safe. Hotels and guest houses were out of the question, and there was no way to get them out of the country.

'We could get them a tent and they could stay in a field close by,' Campbell offered, and Levine concurred.

'I think that might be the best option. I also think that any threat will come at night, so the girls can stay here during the day and slip out when it gets dark.'

'Sounds good to me,' Campbell said. 'I'll send the missus into town to buy a tent, and they can start using it tonight.'

While the men broke the news to their wives, Alana resumed her ritual of staring out of the window. For the first time, she noticed movement in the next caravan and saw that a family estate car was parked next to it. A young boy, no older than seven, was helping his parents unload bags and boxes and take them inside, but it was the sight of the girl that caught her attention. She was roughly the same age as Alana, and rather than helping her family, she was leaning against the car, her attention focused solely on her mobile phone.

⌣

Andrew Harvey sipped his mineral water in the hotel bar and looked at the photo in his hand.

He'd arrived in Durban after a six-and-a-half-hour drive and gone straight to the address of the first person on his list.

Gerry Ainsworth, forty-six years of age, served in Northern Ireland as an eighteen-year-old Green Jacket, left the Army five years later, and had various jobs since, mostly in sales. He was currently running his own business, which purported to sell diving equipment.

After grabbing a sandwich, Harvey had parked himself in the bar while he waited for Ainsworth to return from a day of canvassing potential clients, and it was just after six in the evening when his target finally walked through the lobby.

Harvey was disappointed to see that the man had gained at least forty pounds since his passport photograph had been taken, and he wheezed under the weight of the sample bags he was carrying. There was simply no way Ainsworth could be the hit man he was looking for.

With one name eliminated, he asked the receptionist to call him a taxi to take him to a local bar, and while he waited, he called Owen to see how he was getting on with his suspects.

'Nothing from the first one,' Owen told him. 'I asked his hotel receptionist where he might be, and she said he'd taken a taxi to the International Convention Centre. I checked that he'd signed in and watched him come out about an hour ago. Looks like he's really here for the gardening exhibition.'

Harvey agreed to meet up with Owen for dinner at the hotel of suspect number three and hung up. His taxi arrived a few minutes later, and he told the driver to forget about the bar and just to take him to the Fairview Hotel. When he arrived at his destination, he found Owen waiting for him in the bar, with two cold beers sitting in front of him. He took a seat that gave him a good view of the entrance.

'It's not going to be easy to check the others out now that the weekend has arrived,' Owen noted.

Harvey had been thinking the same. If their suspects were here to ply their trades, they would be unlikely to do so over the weekend, and Harvey explained that probably meant him and Owen spending the next two days shadowing each one in the hope of finding something out of the ordinary.

'Are you ready to tell me who's arriving on Monday?' Owen asked.

It was a question which had come up during their drive from Johannesburg earlier that day, but Harvey had simply explained that some British subjects were arriving on the seventh and that persons unknown were waiting to intercept them. He hadn't said who was on the ship, for fear of opening a can of worms: if word spread that he was looking for Baines and Smart, it could eventually reach the wrong ears, and the fewer people who knew he was about to crash a government-sanctioned party, the longer his career was likely to last.

However, he had been so preoccupied with keeping them from Farrar's clutches that he hadn't considered how he was going to get them back to the UK, and for that he knew he was going to need Owen's help.

'Does the name Tom Gray ring any bells?'

'Are you kidding?' Owen laughed. 'I'm hardly likely to forget him.' He looked Harvey in the eye, his tone more serious. 'You're not going to tell me he's on the ship, are you?'

It was Harvey's turn to offer a smile. 'No, but he did have some help, remember?'

'Yeah, a few of his Army buddies were involved, weren't they?'

'That's right,' Harvey said, 'and two of them are on their way here.'

He gave Owen a rundown of events over the last two weeks, starting with the request for help in finding Levine and Campbell, and all the way up to the discovery that James Farrar was looking for two of the men on the ship, too.

'This Farrar, is he looking for the rest of Gray's team?'

'These *are* the rest of the team,' Harvey explained. 'Two were killed in the attack last year, and two have died since.'

Owen thought about this for a moment. 'Sounds like this Farrar is looking to eliminate the whole team.'

'That's the conclusion we came to.'

'Do you know why?' Owen asked.

'That's what I plan to ask Baines and Smart.'

Owen tapped him on the arm and nodded towards the door. 'How do you want to do this?'

Harvey watched Alan Skinner enter the bar and order a Southern Comfort, then browse a menu as he waited for the barman to pour the drink.

'You keep him occupied,' Harvey whispered as he stood, 'and I'll check his room.'

He left the bar as Owen took a seat next to their target and struck up a conversation. Harvey knew Skinner's room was on the second floor, and he was glad to see that the hotel hadn't upgraded to key cards. He had the lock open in seconds and slipped into the room, searching for anything out of the ordinary. He found a diary and flicked through it, only to find appointments with various companies around the world. The suitcase, cupboards and drawers offered nothing to contradict the suggestion that Skinner was anything other than a travelling salesman, and he headed back downstairs, a frustrated figure.

As he walked past the entrance to the bar, he paused and waited for Owen to notice him, and when he did so, Harvey offered a quick shake of the head and disappeared towards the entrance. His companion followed a minute later.

'It's not our guy,' Owen said, preempting Harvey, who concurred.

'Let's call it a day and pick them up first thing,' Harvey suggested. 'If we get to their hotels early enough, we can catch them before they go out.'

'You don't sound convinced,' Owen said, detecting a note of dejection in Harvey's voice.

'I'm not. These are the best leads we have, but what if the one waiting for the ship to arrive isn't using the same passport for the hotel as they did for the flight? What if they have more than one identity?'

'That's what I'd be inclined to do.'

Harvey knew there was no point trying to investigate the other sixty-something people on his list. There simply wasn't time, and besides, none of them had been flagged on the system as being of any interest.

'Want me to drop you at your hotel?' Owen asked as they climbed into his BMW.

'Later. First I want to take a look at Wenban Freight Management.'

Chapter Eight

Saturday, 5 May 2012

Ben Palmer steered the rented Mercedes Sprinter van down the dusty trail towards the remote building, his back taking a pounding from the rough ride over potholes and ruts.

Sean Littlefield's place was a farm in name only. It had been years since any animal or crop had been within a few miles, as Littlefield made his living from a completely different source. He was standing at the door when Palmer's van pulled up to the house, a pair of tongs in his hand.

'How's you?' He smiled.

'I'm good, Sean. Jeez, can't you get yourself a place near a decent road?'

Littlefield slapped him on the back and led him through the entrance. 'This place is perfect, man. I can see people coming from miles around in any direction.'

Having once been a prominent member of the Afrikaner Weerstandsbeweging under the leadership of Eugène Terre'Blanche was reason enough to be prudent when it came to unannounced visitors. His activities during the apartheid years—being suspected of attacks and murders against non-whites—was another.

Inside, the house looked just like Palmer remembered it, except that the antique furniture had gathered an extra layer of dust.

'Still no woman in your life?' he asked, but Littlefield waved him away. At close to sixty, he had long since abandoned the idea of sharing his remaining days with anyone but himself.

The barbeque was already going, and a couple of huge steaks were sizzling away nicely. Palmer took a seat and accepted a cold beer while Littlefield prepared a salad.

'So what brings you here?' the host asked, and Palmer explained the need for a few sensitive items. Littlefield rubbed the stubble on his chin as he went through the list.

'Sounds like you're planning a party,' he smiled. 'The gun is no problem, but I'll need to visit a friend for the rest.'

'Can you get them by tomorrow night?' Palmer asked, and Littlefield assured him he could.

With business out of the way, Palmer was able to relax. He polished off his beer and accepted another, and they spent the next two hours swapping stories of their exploits since they'd last met. More accurately, Palmer told the stories while his friend listened intently, his days of action far behind, though the desire still burned inside.

'So what's the latest job?' Littlefield asked as he tidied up the dinner plates.

'More of the same, really. Just gotta get some information from a couple of ex-soldiers and their two friends, then dispose of them.'

It didn't sound all that exciting, but it was more action than the old man had seen in a few years.

'Need a hand?' he asked. 'I mean, it's not going to be straightforward with four people to control.'

Palmer smiled. 'You pining for the old days, Sean?'

'You know it.'

The old man has a point, Palmer thought. He may not be able to outsprint a fleeing fugitive as he used to during his days in the South African Police, but the years hadn't robbed him of his mean streak. Palmer preferred to work alone, but he knew it would be handy to have someone on lookout, or a second gun should it come to that. Help with carrying four lifeless bodies wouldn't go amiss, either.

'I can't promise you any fireworks, Sean, but you're welcome to tag along.'

Abdul Mansour had done nothing but think in the two days since his meeting with Azhar Al-Asiri. This very evening his new position would be announced to the whole of the organisation, and coupled with the mission he had been given, he had seen the opportunity to elevate himself to greatness beyond his wildest expectations.

Once, he would have been satisfied to have his loyalty and dedication recognised by his elders, but as his reputation grew, so did his aspirations. Becoming a general had been a magnificent honour, but it was just another step on his path to ultimate glory. His sights had then been set on the rank of regional commander, which also meant a place on the council, allowing him the chance to share in the highest level of decision making.

However, one goal reached simply meant a new one to strive for, and following his promotion that meant only one thing.

Azhar Al-Asiri, still in his early fifties, was not an old man by any means. He could carry on as their glorious leader for another thirty years if Allah wished it, but Abdul Mansour wasn't prepared to wait that long. He'd asked to meet the scientist to gather more information, such as a suitable alternative method of delivery and any conditions which would lessen the effect of the virus. This meticulous attention to detail had pleased Al-Asiri, and he'd readily agreed, unaware of Mansour's true motive.

As they drew near the building, it looked just like the grain wholesaler the sign above the entrance proclaimed it to be. Sacks of maize were piled up beside the main door, and local vendors were busy bartering for their stock for the coming week.

Mansour was driven round the back of the large building—more a warehouse than a shop—and found the rear entrance open, a man waiting for him. Mansour climbed from the vehicle, and when the driver made to follow him, he signalled that he would go in alone.

Inside, all he could see was the silhouette of the man leading him down the narrow corridor. His guide suddenly stopped and fumbled against the wall, and Mansour heard a faint click as a chink of light appeared through a door off to his left.

Mansour stepped through and found himself in an antechamber. Through toughened glass he could see people inside the laboratory, wearing protective suits complete with breathing apparatus. One of them noticed his presence and entered an inner door into a chamber, where jets of what looked to Mansour like steam filled the small area for a few seconds. Extractors sucked the vapour from the air, and moments later Professor Uddin emerged and removed his headgear.

'Thank you for taking time to see me,' Mansour said after greeting him. 'I appreciate that you are very busy.'

Uddin assured him that it was no inconvenience, and Mansour noted how nervous the scientist was. Al-Asiri had told him that Uddin had been like a lamb in a lion's den when they'd met at the hotel, and Mansour was glad to see the same reaction.

'The Emir tells me you are doing some fine work here,' Mansour said as Uddin led him to a small office. 'He is delighted with the progress you have made.'

Uddin seemed to relax a little at the praise, but Mansour soon took the smile off his face. 'However, he would prefer you to do more testing on the virus before we unleash it on the world. He is not completely satisfied with the figures you presented to him.'

'We ... er ...'

Mansour waved off any attempt at an excuse. 'I spoke to the Emir, and we agreed that this operation should only go ahead when we are completely confident of success. As that isn't currently the case, we are going to postpone it while you conduct further tests.'

Uddin looked worried, but Mansour allayed his fears. 'The Emir is not angry with you, but he does think it prudent to wait. He had wanted to use an upcoming window of opportunity, but others will come along.'

The professor let out a sigh, grateful that he hadn't incurred Al-Asiri's wrath.

'Despite this, the window remains open, and the Emir wants to make full use of it. Tell me about the other variants you and your team have been working on.'

Uddin explained that the vast majority of time had been spent on Al-Asiri's pet project, but they did have another strain of the virus that was much more aggressive.

'It is a natural variant of Reston Ebolavirus, which originated in the Philippines. Reston has been found in several indigenous animals, from crab-eating macaques to pigs, although as yet it hasn't claimed any human lives. Our strain has been genetically modified to enhance the cytopathic effect—the breaking down of cellular tissue.'

'Why not just use Ebola itself?' Mansour wondered aloud.

'Governments from all over the world—governments with much better resources than we have here—have been trying to find a cure for Ebola Zaire since it was first discovered in 1976. They have tried and failed, and only recently the US military cut funding to two private companies searching for an effective antidote.

'If they cannot find it, there is very little chance of us stumbling across the answer. Even with our own creation, we are not yet able to reverse the effects.'

'What does it do to those exposed to it?' Mansour asked.

'It causes irreparable damage to the liver and kidneys,' Uddin told him. 'Failure takes place just forty-eight hours after infection, leading to major haemorrhaging and eventually death within the next twenty-four hours.'

'What about an antidote?'

'We have been unable to prevent death once the subject has become infected,' Uddin said. 'Those subjects who were given the vaccination prior to infection did survive, but they suffered severe damage to their organs. We need to do a lot more work on this before we can be confident it is ready for use.'

'It seems to me that it is ready now,' Mansour smiled.

'I agree it has the effect we were looking for,' Uddin said, 'but until we are able to control it, we cannot consider using it. With international travel so common, a strain this virulent could reach almost every major population before it was ever discovered. It would create a pandemic within weeks.'

Mansour was impressed with the projected reach, but the target he had in mind would only claim around a thousand lives. Al-Asiri's vision of breeding Westerners out of existence was flawed at even the most fundamental level: it wasn't the people that were the issue; it was the people leading them, the policymakers who determined which countries were to be invaded, which villages were to be bombed. He had no real issues with the people of Britain or the United States: they simply followed their leaders like sheep. No—more like lambs being led to the slaughter by warmongers fuelled by greed. They dressed it up as a crusade to rid the world of tyrants, but their sole agenda was to get cheap access to the Arab world's oil supply.

The internal conflicts in Libya and Syria epitomised this. When Tripoli used deadly force to put down the uprising, the US and Britain mobilised troops immediately and were instrumental in the fall of Gaddafi. Yet the troubles in Syria started at around the same time, and eighteen months later the UN were still dithering and threatening worthless sanctions. Russia and China were the major suppliers of arms to Damascus and were vetoing any resolutions at the UN, and the Western powers conveniently used this as the main reason they couldn't take any decisive action to stop the massacres. Mansour knew that even if the Eastern superpowers voted in favour of military action, the cost of an invasion would greatly outweigh the financial gain to the likes of Britain and America. They would continue with the rhetoric while waiting for the next oil-rich country to implode.

'My target is a building which is protected against chemical and biological attacks. However, they would be expecting an attack to come from the outside, not within the building itself. If it were released in such a place, would it be able to escape?'

Uddin admitted that without schematics of the defences, he couldn't offer any guarantees, but he did think the efficacy of the virus would be severely diminished. 'The air within such a building would most likely be filtered through sophisticated scrubbers, ultraviolet lights and a host of other defences. It could be destroyed within minutes.'

'What if the filtration system was inactive during the initial release and no one was allowed to leave the building. Would that make a difference?'

'It certainly would, but it would depend on the size of the building and the number of people within it. The more people, the less effective the defences would become, but eventually the virus would become so prevalent that everyone within the building would succumb.'

The news was exactly what Mansour wanted to hear, and he instructed the professor to prepare as much of the virus as possible within the next few days. 'I will also need a way of transporting it via aeroplane and through customs without arousing suspicion. What would you suggest?'

The professor looked nervous. 'I have to reiterate that this virus is not ready to be used. If just one person were to get out of the contaminated area, there is no telling how fast it could spread. The incubation period—the delay before the onset of symptoms—is two days, but the virus can be passed to others within a few hours through close contact. I really think you should reconsider, at least until we have a working antivirus.'

Mansour's glare told Uddin that any further dissension would not be tolerated, and the professor reluctantly stood and picked up an inhaler from a shelf. 'This is capable of storing the virus for seventy-two hours,' he said, his voice edgy. 'If you press here, it works just as it should.'

As promised, a small cloud of mist shot out when the cartridge was pushed into the device. 'When you first insert a new canister, it breaks the initial seal and works like a normal inhaler. However, if you were to hold it pressed in for a count of ten, you activate a second valve which releases the entire contents of a hidden compartment in one continuous burst.'

'You mean it can be activated and left unattended?' Mansour asked, and Uddin nodded.

'We tried to design it with built-in latency to give the person activating it a chance to clear the area,' Uddin told him, 'but that introduced too many extra components which would show up on security scanners, such as airport X-ray machines.'

Mansour liked the simplicity, and it should easily pass a cursory inspection at any border. The fact that it required someone to sacrifice their life to deliver the virus was not a problem: there were plenty of true believers willing to take on the task in the name of Allah.

'What kind of coverage will I get from one canister?' Mansour asked.

Uddin thought about it for a moment, searching for a suitable comparison. 'If you were to activate one canister in a large airport baggage hall, it would infect everyone in a ten-metre radius in moments, and it would travel to all adjoining areas within five minutes. It would take less than an hour for the entire airport to become contaminated.'

The projection once again pleased Mansour, especially as the target he had in mind was similar in size to a major airport terminal. 'How many of these canisters can you provide in the next twenty-four hours?' he asked.

Uddin did a quick mental calculation. 'We can have two, perhaps three, capsules ready,' he replied.

'Two will suffice,' Mansour told him. 'Taking any more than that through Heathrow's customs channels could arouse suspicion, but carrying your inhaler and a spare would be seen as normal for most travellers.'

He rose from his chair. 'I will return in two days. Please have them ready when I arrive.'

The professor considered one more attempt at dissuading Mansour from this course of action, but instead he held his tongue and assured him that everything he needed would be waiting on his return. Mansour paused at the door. 'This goes no further than the two of us,' he warned. 'As far as your team are concerned, you are going to deliver the original virus as planned. Do you understand?'

Uddin nodded meekly and Mansour left.

Once alone in the office, Uddin slumped in his chair and wiped the sweat from his forehead. Designing the virus for use on their enemies was something he was comfortable with: whether they died from a bomb, bullet or bug was immaterial. What he couldn't accept was the possibility that his creation might be unleashed on the entire world. It would not differentiate between Muslim and Christian, Hindu or Buddhist; it would simply strike down everyone it touched.

Could it be contained within the building Mansour was targeting? Without knowing the layout of the building, the intended release point and the number of exits, he simply couldn't say. Even the counter-biological defences Mansour mentioned could prove to be inadequate, but he couldn't be certain unless he had the chance to look at the specifications.

Uddin wrestled with his conscience for some time, but he knew that if he didn't fulfil Mansour's wish, the only thing he could look forward to would be death. Not just for him, but for his entire family, too. And it wouldn't be as quick as a bullet to the brain. He was certain that he would be made to watch his family die before he himself was killed, and the thought sent a shiver through his body.

With a heavy heart he stood and slowly walked back to the laboratory, suddenly feeling a lot older than his fifty-eight years.

Chapter Nine

Sunday, 6 May 2012

'We've got the location of the website!'

Veronica Ellis was in the middle of weeding her garden when the call from Gerald Small came through to her mobile, and she was glad of the interruption.

'Where is it?'

'A flat, here in London. Hamad's preparing to take a team to the location.'

'I want you to go with them,' Ellis said and hung up. She tapped the phone against her temple as she absorbed the new information, and after a couple of minutes she called Hamad Farsi.

'I don't want you bringing anyone in,' she said when the intelligence officer answered. 'The person we are after is in South Africa, so anyone manning the equipment has to be an associate.'

'Makes sense,' Farsi agreed. 'What's the plan?'

'Find out if the flats in the building are connected to the gas network. If they are, pretend there's a leak and clear the street, but when you get to the target flat, I want you to secure it and keep the occupants there. We don't want whoever is in Durban to know they've been compromised.'

The phone went silent as Farsi relayed the instructions, and a minute later he told Ellis that gas was supplied to the entire street.

'Okay, so that's your cover. I want you to take Gerald along to analyse the setup and confirm that we have the right people.'

Farsi confirmed the order, and Ellis told him to forward all the information they had to her laptop. Gardening forgotten, she went into the house to get changed. Once suitably attired for a day in the office, she found the details she'd requested waiting for her.

The council-owned flat was being rented by Carl Gordon, and his record showed one previous conviction for a computer-related offence. He certainly sounded like their man.

She packed her laptop into her briefcase and drove the twenty-minute journey to Thames House, arriving just as Farsi and his team were getting ready to leave the office.

'Gordon's file says he lives alone,' Hamad told her as he donned his reflective jacket, 'so we don't expect to encounter much resistance.'

'Perhaps, but don't go rushing in and spooking the guy. We need his equipment intact.' This was directed at Small. 'I need you to make sure comms stay open with whoever's in Durban. Do what you need to do to convince Gordon to help you.'

The team headed down to the car park and climbed into the van. During the thirty-minute journey, Farsi used his phone to get an overhead view of the target building. Gordon lived in a side street off the main road, which would make evacuation a lot easier, and as his building was towards the end of the street, they wouldn't have to clear too many homes.

His team consisted of surveillance specialists, and he briefed them on the mission.

'The building in question is number twenty-seven, and we're after the occupants of flat three.' He selected two of the team and gave them the job of cordoning off each end of the street and preventing people from entering the area. 'If anyone asks, an automated system in the pipeline detected a leak beneath number twenty-seven. That should satisfy them if they start wondering who called us in.'

He instructed the other three members of the team to go from house to house and clear them.

'Two houses either side should be enough,' he told Rob Zimmerman, the surveillance team leader. 'Once they're empty, converge on the target. We'll leave his flat until last.'

Everyone acknowledged their roles, and they did a quick comms check before they arrived in Mercia Road.

Carl Gordon saw the British Gas van arrive on his monitor, but it held his attention for nothing more than a few seconds. He'd installed the CCTV camera to spot the police arriving, not utility vehicles, and he returned to his attention to the website he was working on.

His attempts to sort out an issue with a troublesome Web control were interrupted again as another flash of yellow moved across the monitor, and on closer examination he now saw a man in a high-visibility jacket shepherding people towards the end of the road.

Gordon moved from his office to the living room and looked out of the window, where he saw yet another figure extending a roll of tape across the entrance to the street where temporary barriers were already in place. Below him, two more people were heading towards the entrance to his building.

It was obvious to Gordon that the street was being evacuated, and his first concern was his equipment. His office was a small second bedroom, and one wall was dedicated to servers, which he kept on a purpose-built air-cooled rack. The metal frame of the rack was wired up to a capacitor which could send a massive electric current through every box, frying the hard drives instantly.

It would mean thousands of pounds of equipment would be rendered useless, but it was rather that than incriminating evidence falling into the hands of the police.

He hit a few keys to save his recent work to an online storage system before priming the anti-intruder device, something he did every time he left the apartment. Once he closed the door to the office, the device was activated: the next person to enter the room would have just ten seconds to hit the 'Cancel' switch, and they could only do that if they knew about it and could find it.

He walked back to the window in time to see his ground-floor neighbour carrying her two cats towards the cordon, and from behind him came a loud banging on the door.

'British Gas! We've got an emergency and need you to leave the building!'

Gordon grabbed his coat and opened the door, but through habit he left the chain on.

'Got any ID?' he asked through the small gap.

The man in the hallway seemed unimpressed with the request, but he held up the card hanging around his neck. Gordon was satisfied with the comparison, but his attention was drawn to the other man in the hallway, who had his finger on an earpiece which fed down into his collar. At that moment he realised he was facing more than utility workers and he tried to slam the door closed.

It barely moved.

Hamad Farsi had seen the look of panic suddenly appear on Gordon's face and had stuck his steel toe-capped boot into the gap, quickly bringing up the bolt cutters he'd placed beside the door. The thin chain offered no resistance and Farsi shoved his way into the room, drawing his Taser as he moved. His target hesitated in the middle of the room for a second before heading at speed for a door off to his right-hand side.

The electric barb hit Gordon in the thigh just as he reached for the handle, and his legs gave way beneath him. He tried to raise his arms to protect his face, but they reacted like jelly, and he smashed into the door nose first, leaving a trail of blood as he slid to the floor.

Farsi pulled out a pair of plasticuffs and secured the prisoner's hands and feet, then dragged him onto a sofa. Two members of the team began securing the tiny flat, one taking the kitchen and bathroom, while the other started a search in the main bedroom.

'Now why would anyone react like that to the gas man?' Farsi asked, but Gordon just looked at the three men standing in his living room, his gaze shifting from one to the other. Zimmerman had his Beretta drawn and ready, and Gerald Small stood still next to the wall. This was only his second field assignment, but he knew to keep out of the way and not touch anything until he was needed.

Farsi noticed Gordon glancing at the bloodstained door and indicated for the surveillance officer to take a look. Zimmerman nodded, and he had his hand poised on the handle when Small told him to stop.

'He *wants* you to go in there,' Small said, having noticed the faintest of smiles forming on Gordon's face. Zimmerman took a couple of steps back and aimed at the door, ready to deal with anyone who came out, while Farsi stood over the prisoner.

'Who's in there?' he asked.

'I want a solicitor.'

'I said who's in there?' Farsi repeated.

'You broke my nose.'

Farsi grabbed Gordon's hair and pulled his head back, examining the man's face. 'Hmm, looks okay to me.' He suddenly raised his arm and brought the side of his hand crashing down on the bridge of Gordon's nose. The distinct crack was drowned out by the prisoner's yelp.

'Yeah, you're right, it is broken,' Farsi said, less amiably. 'Now tell me who's in that room.'

'No one!' Gordon spat, blood spraying from his mouth. 'Open it and see for yourself.'

The two men finished up clearing the other rooms and emerged shaking their heads.

'Where's your computer?' Farsi asked, and Gordon nodded towards the bloodstained door. 'In there. Help yourself.'

'Thanks, but I'd rather trust my colleague.' Farsi looked over at Small. 'What do you think?'

'I think we should stick a fibre-optic camera in there first.'

Farsi agreed and sent one of his men down to the van to get one. While he was waiting, he decided to make Gordon as uncomfortable as possible.

'I find it reassuring that the first words out of your mouth were to demand a solicitor,' he said. 'Most people would have asked what the fuck we were doing in their home, but you seem to have been expecting us to call round at some point.'

Gordon said nothing, but his expression told Farsi he'd hit the mark. He let the prisoner stew for a couple of minutes until the surveillance device arrived. Small took it and unravelled the flexible cable, then checked the screen to make sure he had a good image. Satisfied that all was working, he hit the 'Record' button and played the cable under the door.

'No sign of anyone,' he said as the tiny camera snaked along the floor. 'He's got some serious hardware in there, though.'

Small used two dials to control the direction of the camera, and as he moved it to the base of the rack he saw the capacitor tucked away on the bottom shelf. The cable wasn't long enough to get in any closer, but he knew what he was looking at.

'Where did you get the capacitor?' he asked Gordon.

'It was here when I moved in.'

Unlikely, Small thought. 'Okay, what are you using it for?' he asked, although he was certain he already knew the answer.

Gordon ignored him, and Farsi seemed confused and asked what the capacitor could be used for.

'Think of it as a kind of rechargeable battery,' Small explained, 'but rather than releasing its energy at a constant rate, it purges instantly. They are used on a much bigger scale to replicate lightning strikes.'

'How big is this one?' Farsi asked.

'It's not huge, but my guess is that as soon as you open that door, everything in the room gets hit by a couple of thousand volts. Forensics might be able to salvage some of the data on the hard drives, but if he's using SSDs, everything will be wiped instantly.'

'SSDs?'

'Solid-state drives,' Small said. 'Normal hard drives store data on rotating metal disks, but SSDs are more like chips or RAM, with no moving parts. They are more resistant to shock, such as being dropped, but they are susceptible to power surges. Zap one with a capacitor and you lose everything.'

Farsi looked at the prisoner. 'Do you think you can wriggle out of this if you destroy the evidence?'

Gordon suddenly found some bravado, more in desperation than anything. 'I want to see the search warrant.'

'We're here under the Terrorism Act 2000. We don't need a warrant. All that's required is for me to suspect that you're a terrorist, simple as that. No warrant, no solicitor, no bail, and we can hold you as long as we like. How does that sound?'

Gordon's eyes grew wide with shock. 'I'm not a terrorist!'

'Perhaps not, but while we suspect you are, you're royally screwed. I guess the only way you can prove us wrong is to give us access to your computers.'

Gordon's eyes darted around the room, searching for a way out of the situation. He'd thought they were there because of the hacking he'd done on behalf of his benefactor, the man he knew only as B, but as far as he was aware he hadn't accessed any networks that were so sensitive that his actions could be labelled terrorism. There had been a few individuals' computers and perhaps a dozen companies', but none of them were risks to national security.

This led him to wonder just what they were planning to charge him with.

'What is it that I'm supposed to have done?'

'Collection of information of a kind likely to be useful to a person committing or preparing an act of terrorism,' Farsi replied. 'We know you host a website for someone we're looking for, so you can add helping in the preparing or commissioning of a terrorist act, too.'

'That's got nothing to do with me!' Gordon shouted. 'I just host the site, that's all. There's no law against it.'

'You must have known he was up to no good,' Small jumped in. 'Otherwise, you wouldn't have hidden behind a dozen relay servers.'

The prisoner bit his lip as he stared once more at his office door.

'If you've got any booby traps in there, I suggest you disarm them now.' Farsi said. 'You're looking at a long time in prison, so don't add further charges by destroying any evidence. We already have proof that the website is being run from this flat, and that will be enough to convict you. However, if you play nicely, we might be able to convince the judge that your cooperation helped our investigation. You might get away with five years.'

The prospect of a long sentence was the final straw. He was built to manipulate ones and zeros, not fight for survival in a prison environment.

'I want immunity from prosecution,' Gordon whined. 'I can't go to prison. I wouldn't last a week.'

'Not going to happen. We might be able to push for three years, and you'll serve just eighteen months, with half of that out on licence.'

Nine months was still a long, long time, and if word got out that his sentence had been reduced because he'd given evidence against someone else, his cards would be marked.

There was also the backlash from B to consider. He'd met the man just twice: the first time outside the court when he'd offered Gordon work, and the second when he'd turned up with his first cash payment. On that occasion his new employer hadn't been as cordial. He'd explained what he needed and asked if Gordon could provide it. The answer had been an easy 'Yes'. He already had a server relay in place for his own file-sharing site, and setting up another would be a piece of cake. Finding ways into other people's computers wouldn't be too challenging either, Gordon had promised—though it obviously depended on the nature of the information. He could get into the telephone networks or National Health Service in seconds, but banks and government networks were out: their firewalls and intrusion-detection systems were simply too advanced.

B hadn't needed anything that secure, and the partnership had been sealed with the handing over of the money and delivery of the caveat: 'When you take this money, you're in for good. There's no walking away when you get bored, and you never tell anyone about me. If I find out you've opened your mouth, I'll hunt you down, and trust me, you don't want that to happen.'

With his contact book containing zero entries, Gordon had no qualms on that score, and the weight of the envelope had felt good in his hands. The money would enable him to buy some of the equipment he'd only been able to dream about, and the threat was soon forgotten.

Until now.

Whether he gave up his employer or not, he was facing jail, and that didn't make for an easy decision.

Jeff Campbell helped his wife, Anne, prepare the evening meal while the Levines dealt with yet another teenage tantrum. Alana was facing her third night in the tent and wasn't about to go quietly.

'I hate it in there,' she pouted, arms firmly crossed against her chest. 'There isn't even a toilet.'

Carl Levine sympathised with her, having spent countless evenings sleeping rough during his time in the Army, but she had a roof over her head to keep the rain out, and the inconvenience of having to squat behind a bush just didn't rank very highly in his book.

'It won't be for much longer,' he told her for the hundredth time, but when pressed for a firm date, he admitted he had no idea. All he could do was reiterate the offer to make amends once things were back to normal.

Alana noticed movement outside the window and suddenly her demeanour changed.

'Okay, but I want a new laptop when we get back home.'

'Deal,' her father said, glad that there wasn't going to be a scene.

'Can I just go for a little walk?' Alana asked in her sweetest voice, and Levine nodded, but not before reminding her of the rules.

'Your name is Alice and we're here on holiday from Essex, okay?'

'I know, Dad.'

She was up and out the door before Levine could say anything else, and his wife took the vacant seat.

'Are you sure about all this?' she asked her husband. 'There hasn't been anything about us on the news, and no one seems to be looking for us. Is there a chance you've misinterpreted the message?'

Carl wondered if it was possible. Had he turned their lives upside down for no reason? Alana had missed over two weeks of school, and the authorities would soon be taking an interest—if they weren't already. On top of that, his wife, Sandra, hadn't told her employers that she would be taking time off, which meant she would probably find herself out of work once the situation was resolved. Finding another job at her age—given the current economic climate—would be no easy task.

If he'd got the message wrong, this whole mess could have been avoided, but in his heart he knew he was doing the right thing.

'I know it seems strange that no one appears to be looking for us, but I'd much rather be safe than sorry.'

Sandra wasn't about to argue with her husband. She might have if Alana weren't a consideration, but her daughter was her whole life, and she wasn't about to let anything happen to her.

Levine took her hand in his. 'We'll have a family holiday when this is over,' he told her. 'Somewhere nice and sunny, just the three of us.'

'As long as it isn't camping,' Sandra said with a hint of a smile.

While the Levines discussed possible destinations, Alana struck up a conversation with the girl from the adjacent caravan.

'You look like you're enjoying this as much as me,' she said.

The girl rolled her eyes. 'I can't believe they call this a holiday. I'd rather be at school.'

'I wouldn't go that far!' Alana laughed, and got a smile in return.

'I'm Melissa,' the girl said.

'Alice,' she replied, remembering her father's instructions. 'So why *aren't* you in school?'

'My dad works away most of the year,' Melissa said, 'and he's only back for, like, two weeks. I can't believe we have to spend it here, though.'

'Yeah, same here. Dad disappears for months at a time, but I'd rather stay at home than go camping. It sucks big time.'

Alana looked at the girl's handset. 'What phone have you got?'

Melissa handed it over. 'It's the new Samsung.'

'I prefer the iPhone,' Alana said, though the one in Melissa's hand was very similar. 'Would it be okay to text my boyfriend? My dad forgot to pack the chargers, so all our phones have run flat. I haven't had contact with the real world for days.'

Melissa said it was no problem, and Alana tapped out a quick message:

Hi Sam. Hope 2 b back soon. Luv U & miss U. No need 2 reply. A.

She hit the 'Send' button, waited for confirmation and handed the phone back. 'Thanks.'

'That's okay. I get, like, five hundred free texts a month, so you can use it any time.'

They chatted for a few minutes about music and Facebook before Sandra called her in for her dinner.

'I gotta go,' Alana said. 'See you later.'

'See ya.'

Alana trudged back inside, the thrill of her communication fix wearing off quickly, replaced by the dread of another night under the stars.

———⌣———

'We've got our man,' Farsi said over the phone, 'but his equipment is booby-trapped. He'll only give us access if we offer immunity from prosecution and give him a change of identity.'

'What about Gerald?' Veronica Ellis asked. 'Can't he get access?'

'If we open the door to the room, it triggers a device which wipes the hard drives. He said he has a similar detector on the windows, though we haven't been able to check that yet.'

'Then go through the wall,' Ellis said sternly. 'I haven't got the power to authorise immunity. That's down to the CPS, and I wouldn't build his hopes up.'

Ellis knew that the Crown Prosecution Service *could* offer Gordon the deal he wanted, but there were no guarantees. They had famously done so with Bertie Smalls back in the 1970s after the armed robber offered to give evidence against over twenty others in return for his freedom and the chance to keep what was left of his ill-gotten gains. The men Smalls helped to prosecute were given a combined total of over three hundred years in prison, but with Gordon it was unlikely that the catch would be so big, meaning the director of public prosecutions would have little incentive to let him walk away a free man.

There was also the fiasco of the previous year to consider. Even though Tom Gray had died, his associates—the very men they were looking for—had been released without charge, following a deal done with the home secretary. That had come back to bite him on the arse at the subsequent general election, and there was no way the incumbent minister was going to be handing out get-out-of-jail-free cards any time soon.

'If we go through the wall, we still need him to log on to his computer,' Farsi told her. 'He claims to have encrypted his disks, and if we get the password wrong three times or remove the disks from their housings, they get wiped. Gerald confirmed that this is easy enough to do.'

'You're the lead officer on the ground, Hamad. Do *whatever* you need to do,' Ellis stressed, 'but get him to cooperate. We need to let Andrew know what he's up against.'

The phone went dead in Farsi's hand, and he stuck it back in his pocket.

'No promises,' he told Gordon, 'but we'll do everything we can.'

Gordon thought long and hard about his prospects, and eventually nodded in resignation. He pointed towards the door. 'I'll let you in.'

Farsi told Zimmerman to remove the cuffs and stayed close as Gordon made his way to his office.

'Wait here,' he said. 'Once I get inside, I have a few things to do. I can't disarm it if the room is full of people getting in my way.'

Farsi nodded to the others to hang back, and Gordon opened the door. Once inside, he felt for the top of the frame and then walked to the desk, leaned over his chair and drummed out a command on the keyboard. Finally, he walked over to the rack and reached deep into a gap between two servers as if searching for something on the back wall. His shoulder was hard against the rack and he grabbed one of the metal uprights with his free hand.

The procedure had taken seven seconds.

'I can't go to prison,' Gordon repeated and screwed up his eyes in anticipation of the end.

Farsi saw what was about to happen but was too slow to react. He managed just one step into the room when the capacitor vented its charge, sending over a hundred megawatts through the prisoner. The discharge lasted a little over a microsecond, and Gordon was thrown across the room, slamming into the far wall with enough force to make a body-shaped dent in the plaster.

Farsi ran over and checked his pulse while Small headed to the computers. The mains electricity had tripped, and he sent someone to find the fuse box. In the meantime he unplugged one of the servers and took a screwdriver to the back.

'He's dead,' Farsi said.

'So is this,' Small said as he noticed the scorch marks on the hard drive. 'As I suspected, he was using SSDs. I doubt we'll get anything from them.'

'I want you to try,' Farsi said. 'Load everything into the van and search for any hard copies. Look for a notebook, backup drive, anything that might tell us who's on the other end of that site.'

He dug around in Gordon's pockets and found just a mobile phone and some loose change. The phone refused to turn on, obviously affected by either the impact or electrical surge. Farsi handed it to Small and told him to see what he could get off it, and then made two phone calls. The first was to call in a clean-up team, and the second was to break the news to his boss.

———————

'We've found them!'

The call from Todd Hamilton came through to Farrar as he was entertaining guests, and he excused himself, finding a quiet spot in his study.

'Where are they?' he asked.

'It looks like a caravan park in Dorset. We intercepted a text sent to the Levine kid's boyfriend and traced it back. She wasn't using her normal phone.'

'Can you pinpoint the caravan they're in?' Farrar asked.

'We narrowed it down to a thirty-metre radius, and slap-bang in the middle is one owned by Tom Gray's solicitor.'

'I told you to check connections to all friends and acquaintances,' Farrar said angrily. 'Why am I only hearing about this now?'

'It's registered at the camp in his wife's maiden name,' Hamilton said. 'We just hadn't dug that far.'

The phone went quiet for a while, and Hamilton took the opportunity to deflect some of the blame away from his team. 'If we'd drilled down to relatives of friends, where does it end? Relatives of relatives of friends? Friends of relatives of friends? We've had our hands full just looking at known contacts.'

Farrar knew he had a point, but wasn't about to let him off the hook so easily. 'I want this finished tonight. Get in touch with Matt Baker and work up a plan.'

'Baker's a liability,' Hamilton objected. 'My team can handle this.'

'He gets the job done,' Farrar replied, hoping the insult registered. 'It must look like an accident, you understand?'

'Got it.'

'Make no mistake: if you don't end this in the next six hours, you certainly will "get it"!'

Farrar killed the connection and put the phone back in his trouser pocket. His watch told him it was just after eight in the evening, which meant it would be a few hours before the team was in place. Despite this, he wanted to end the dinner party early so that he could get to the office to listen in to the takedown over a secure connection.

After dishing up the meal, he informed his guests that an emergency had come up at work, and he would have to disappear shortly after dessert. They made consoling noises, not envious of the hours he kept.

Throughout the meal, Farrar wondered whether or not to tell Palmer about the find. There was no longer a need to get the information from Baines and Smart, but it would be satisfying to have them go through one of Palmer's interrogations. Then again, Palmer was a valuable asset, and the men he would be going up against had proven themselves rather resourceful. It would be totally unprofessional to ask Palmer to take on these two as well as Gray when three bullets could solve the problem.

Actually, four bullets, he reminded himself. There was a fourth passenger on the ship, though he had no idea who the other might be. Whoever else was with Gray was obviously a fugitive; otherwise, they wouldn't be tagging along. That made them desperate and potentially dangerous.

Farrar decided that he would tell Palmer to simply kill the targets. However, he would wait until his team confirmed that Levine and Campbell were well and truly dead. Given the incompetence shown by his team in the last couple of weeks, he wasn't going to go as far as demanding heads on plates, but he did want to know that they were no longer breathing before signing the task off as complete.

Alana Levine muttered to herself as she angrily stuffed a change of clothes into her rucksack. Carl knew the night ahead wasn't going to be a pleasant one for his wife, and he apologised in advance, but Sandra ignored him. She wasn't too happy with the new sleeping arrangement, either, but she held her tongue as she finished making the last of the sandwiches.

Once the food was packed away, she called her daughter and Anne Campbell, telling them it was time to leave. The men had to forgo their goodnight kisses.

The girls left the men to their own devices and headed out into the night without another word. Carl Levine knew he was going to have to work damn hard to make things right, and he was working on a mental list of peace offerings when there was a knock on the door. Instinctively, he grabbed for the handle of the 9mm automatic pistol which was strapped to the underside of the table, but Campbell waved him off.

'It's just the kid from the next caravan.'

Campbell opened the door. 'Hi,' he smiled. 'What can I do for you?'

'Is Alice here?' the girl asked, holding up her phone. 'She got a text from her boyfriend.'

Campbell was about to say she must be mistaken when Levine joined him in the doorway.

'How did he get your number?' Levine asked, a little too harshly.

'Alice sent him a text,' Melissa said, taking a step backwards. 'She said her dad forgot the chargers for the phones, so I let her use mine.'

Levine did his best to keep his anger in check. 'When did she send the text?'

'I dunno. Couple of hours ago, maybe.'

Campbell moved past Levine. 'The girls have gone out for the evening,' he said, smiling. 'If you give me the message I can pass it on to Alice when she gets back.'

Melissa wasn't too keen on the idea. This was boyfriend–girlfriend stuff—definitely not the kind of thing you shared with parents.

'I think it's best if I give it to Alice,' she said and got no objections. Levine wasn't interested in the content of the message—just the fact that his daughter had disobeyed his instructions.

'No problem. She'll be back late, but I'll let her know and she can pop round in the morning.'

Melissa seemed happy with the arrangement and headed back to her own caravan, leaving the men to consider the implications of Alana's actions.

'What do you reckon?' Campbell asked once he'd closed the caravan door.

'If it *is* the government who are looking for us, they'll have traced either one or both of those text messages, and that means they'll probably be on their way.'

Campbell agreed. 'Let's grab the girls and go.'

'Not so fast,' Levine said. 'We still don't know for sure that anyone's actually looking for us. If we run now, we still won't know. I say we leave the girls where they are, find an OP close by and see if anyone knocks on the door.'

'And if someone does turn up?' Campbell asked.

'Then we'll know we're not being paranoid. I say we grab at least one of them and find out what they want.'

'Sounds fine if they send a small team, but what if they bring half the local police with them?'

'I very much doubt it,' Levine said. 'If the police were going to be involved, we'd have known about it by now.'

Campbell saw the wisdom in his friend's words, but he expressed his concerns for the safety of the women. 'I'd feel happier if they were out of the area. How about I drive them into the nearest town, park up out of sight and then tab back here?'

Levine asked why the women couldn't just drive themselves, and Campbell pointed out that they hadn't had the defensive and evasive driver training the men had been through in the regiment. 'If they're spotted en route, they'll have no chance. It would also be a good idea to change the plates on the car, and there's a Skoda showroom in town. I can swap the plates from a similar model, and that should give us enough time to get to where we're going.'

'Fair point,' Levine conceded. 'Let's load our gear before we fetch them.'

They grabbed what few belongings they had and stuffed them into holdalls, which went into the boot of the car. Campbell trotted off and was back within ten minutes, the three ladies in tow. Their mood hadn't changed in the last half hour, and Levine guessed his friend hadn't yet explained the situation.

'You have to go,' Levine said, opening the door to the car so that his wife could get into the front passenger seat.

'Why? What's going on?'

'Ask Alana,' Levine said and glared at his daughter.

'What have I done now?' Alana asked, full of indignation.

'Sam replied to the text message you sent him.'

'But I didn't use my own phone,' his daughter argued. 'You didn't say anything about using someone else's.'

There was no time to get into a fight, especially with such a head-strong teenager. 'Just get in,' Levine said. 'I'll deal with you later.'

Alana stamped her feet like a five-year-old as she trudged to the car, arms once again folded tightly across her chest. She climbed into the back seat and put her seatbelt on, her face still a picture of fury as she failed to comprehend the seriousness of her indiscretion.

'So what was Sam's message?' she pouted, and Levine just stared in disbelief. Her life was in danger, yet she was more interested in how her boyfriend was doing. He knew he would have to have a word about priorities when this was all over.

He turned his attention to his wife and spoke to her through the open window. 'Jeff's going to take you into town. I want you to stay in the car until we come and get you.' He looked over his wife's shoulder at his daughter. 'That means all of you.'

'How long will you be?' Sandra asked.

'I don't know. Maybe a few hours. Just sit tight until we come and get you.'

'But what if you don't come? How long should we wait?'

'If we're not there by six in the morning, just go. Drive north for a few hours and find a town with an Internet café, but stay off the main roads. I want you to contact the newspapers, BBC, Sky—anyone. Tell them who you are and what's happened, and see if you can arrange to meet up to give them the whole story.'

'Why can't you just come with us?' Anne Campbell pleaded with her husband. 'We're not cut out for this kind of thing.'

'We have to end it tonight,' Jeff said. 'If we don't make a stand, we'll be on the run forever.'

Anne looked pitiful, but Campbell wasn't going to be persuaded otherwise.

'You want things to go back to normal, don't you?'

His wife nodded, and Campbell kissed her on the forehead.

Levine said his own goodbyes as Campbell climbed into the driver seat.

'I'll be tabbing back over the fields and coming in from the east. See if you can find a suitable observation post while I'm gone.'

Levine nodded and watched as the car drove out of the caravan park and turned left on the country lane, its lights fading quickly. His watch told him it was nudging nine thirty in the evening, and anyone coming to pay them a visit could be in the area soon, if not already. He ducked into the caravan and turned the lights off. From the window he could see several of the other mobile homes were in darkness, so it wouldn't look too suspicious.

There were several good spots to set up the OP on the hill off to the north, but rather than just observe his visitors, he wanted to get up close and personal. Confirmation that they were being sought was one thing, but more important was the need to know who they were up against. At the moment they were running from shadows, but once they'd identified their adversary, they would at least know the magnitude of the battle they faced.

That was, if anyone actually turned up.

Levine left the caravan and locked the door, then looked round for a suitable place to lie up. The caravan was situated three yards from the four-foot-high privet hedge that ran around the perimeter of the camp. Cut into the hedge was a wooden stile, a small ladder that granted access to the public footpath in the adjoining field. Levine climbed over, stepping into the darkness.

Off to his right he could just make out the shape of the tent the ladies had been using for the last few days, and it was from that direction that Jeff would make his appearance. Levine turned to his left and followed the hedge, looking for a spot which would allow him a good view of the caravan while also shielding him from sight if anyone wandered too close. The best he could find was a small depression, but the view through the bottom of the hedge was obscured by another caravan, so he retraced his steps and climbed back over the stile and into the camp. Even on this side he could find no natural cover, so he would have to settle for squeezing underneath the people carrier parked behind his neighbours' accommodation.

He tried it out for size, and from the side of the vehicle his vision was obstructed by the gas canisters underneath the adjacent caravan. He adjusted his position, peering out between the front wheels. This was a much better view, allowing him to see the door to his caravan as well as the ten yards leading up to it. The moon was full, but Levine was grateful for the cloud cover which reduced its glare and would help to keep him concealed.

His only worry was if the unwanted guests brought night-vision goggles to the party. He knew he couldn't be seen with the naked eye, but he would stick out like a sore thumb to anyone with NVGs.

With one position sorted, Levine crawled out and headed towards the entrance to the camp. He walked nonchalantly, just another holidaymaker out for a late stroll. He saw a couple of others braving the mild evening, but most of the residents were settled in for the night.

The heavy main gate was attached to concrete posts on either side of the entrance, marking the end of the hedge, but once again there was little to offer in the way of cover. He wandered out into the country lane and looked at the hedgerow on the other side of the road. There would be no reason for anyone to approach the camp from that field, not when they could simply drive up to the gate or park up nearby, so it seemed a sensible enough hiding place. The gate to the field was just ten yards away, and Levine scrambled over it quickly.

The field had been left fallow the previous year, and long grass grew around the edges. This would help to break up his profile should anyone glance his way, and he lay down to see what the view was like. He had to crawl forward a few feet, but eventually he found the perfect spot, one that enabled him to see through the entrance all the way to their caravan.

Levine got up and made his way back to the road, checking both ways to make sure no one was in the area. The road was clear, and he strolled back into the camp, waving to one of the residents as he headed back to the caravan. Inside, he took the rounds from the magazine to let the spring relax while he stripped down his Browning and gave it a thorough clean: the last thing he wanted was the gun jamming on him if he came to need it. It took him just a few minutes to finish the job, and once it was reassembled he headed for the stile to keep an eye out for Campbell.

Jeff arrived at a trot just after ten thirty, barely breaking a sweat.

'You took your sweet time.'

'I did some shopping on the way back,' Campbell said, holding out a plastic bag. Levine took it and fished out a pair of pay-as-you-go phones.

'I figured we'd need some comms,' Campbell told him. 'They were the cheapest I could find, but they come with hands-free kits.'

'Good thinking. Let's get back inside and charge them up.'

While Campbell cleaned his own weapon, Levine charged the phones, turned the ringtones off and programmed the numbers into each other's speed-dial facility. He then ran through the sequence of commands to call the other phone until he knew which buttons to press with his eyes closed. Once he had the combination memorised and he was sure that Campbell had, too, he put electrical tape over the tiny displays so that the light from them wouldn't be visible when they got an incoming call. Campbell told him they only had twenty pounds of calling credit each, which wouldn't last forever, especially with mobile-to-mobile calls, so they agreed not to use the phones until the person observing the gate saw some activity.

'How do you think they'll play this out?' Campbell asked as he reassembled his pistol.

'If they're morons, they'll come in all guns blazing,' Levine said. 'I doubt we'll be that lucky, though. I expect they'll turn up in the dead hours, probably between one and four in the morning.'

Campbell concurred. 'We'll let the phones charge for another hour, then get in position.'

Levine described the locations he'd found and offered to take the spot under the vehicle. At just five feet nine he was the smaller of the two by six inches and had a slight build compared to Campbell's bear-like physique. It would be much easier for him to get out quickly when the time came.

'We'll need knives,' Levine said and went to the kitchen. In the drawer he found two which would serve their purpose, though their edges were rather dull. He found a honing steel and sat down to sharpen the blades.

They discussed tactics until a few minutes to midnight. By this time the phones both had a charge of over eighty per cent, which was plenty for the next few hours.

Levine pulled the corner of the curtain aside and looked out into the camp.

'Clear.'

They left the caravan, and Levine locked up before they parted without another word.

Ben Palmer glanced over at the clock on his bedside table as the monotonous chime of the mobile phone dragged him from his deep sleep.

'Palmer,' he said wearily, wondering what was so urgent that it meant calling at close to one in the morning.

'It's James,' the voice said. 'I was just—'

'Wait.' Palmer hit a couple of keys on the handset and brought up the next combination of numbers for his private web portal. He read them out, and once he had confirmation that Farrar had written them down correctly, he asked if the message was vitally important or if it could wait a few hours.

'There's no rush, but I need you to check your messages tomorrow. We've had a new development here, and in the next few hours there could be a change to your mission.'

Palmer was glad that they wouldn't have to discuss business over the phone. There was no Internet connection at the farm, so he would have to wait until they drove back to Durban the next afternoon. 'I'll be able to get to them in around twelve hours,' Palmer told him. 'Can it wait until then?'

'Just as long as you check them before you meet our friends, that's fine.'

Farrar hung up, and Palmer was suddenly wide awake. He had everything ready for the next evening's operation, and now Farrar wanted to change things at the eleventh hour. It was bad enough having to source a new weapon with every job, what with handguns being frowned upon by the customs people, but Sean had found him a beautiful piece. He'd spent the day sighting his new suppressed Sig P226 and adjusting the trigger tension until he had a weapon that reacted to his liking. In the meantime, Littlefield had gone out early to get the 3-methylfentanyl and flash-bangs.

Now, with his shopping list complete and the plan in place, Farrar wanted to move the goal posts.

Was he going to call the whole thing off? No, he'd mentioned a change to the mission rather than a termination. Even if Farrar *did* decide to pull the plug, there was no way he was getting a refund.

It could be that there would be more than four people to deal with, or Farrar might want more information from them. Either way, he had what he needed to take care of the situation. The 3-methylfentanyl he'd asked Sean for was an analogue fentanyl, an opioid analgesic similar to the one the Russians used to end the Moscow theatre siege in 2002, when it was delivered by aerosol into the auditorium. Palmer was sure that any container designed to hold people for weeks at a time would have air vents to allow them to breathe, and it was through these that he would administer the incapacitating agent. If there were no vents, he would open the door and throw in a couple of the flash-bangs, which produce a deafening noise and blinding flash and are designed to disorientate, but unlike conventional grenades, they don't produce the large amounts of deadly shrapnel. This would allow him to set the canister to auto-release and throw it in the container. By the time anyone came to their senses, it would be too late to stop the contents being dispersed, and with the dispersal mechanism being almost silent, it was doubtful that anyone would notice it even with perfect hearing. Everyone in the container would lose consciousness within a few moments, leaving him the simple task of dragging out the four non-Chinese occupants and loading them into his vehicle.

Satisfied that he wouldn't have to adapt this plan too much, no matter what Farrar had in mind, Palmer settled back to sleep.

Chapter Ten

Monday, 7 May 2012

Todd Hamilton pulled in behind Matt Baker's Skoda Transit at just after one in the morning and killed the engine. His colleague was already out of the van, weapon drawn and hanging loosely by his side.

'Put that away,' Hamilton hissed as he got out. 'We need to make this look like an accident.'

'I know!' Baker responded loudly, and Hamilton wondered how he'd ever made it to adulthood, never mind team leader. Perhaps it was the kill rate despite his tender years, or his willingness to take on any job. It certainly wasn't down to his tactical thinking.

'Keep your voice down, man.'

Two more occupants climbed out of the vehicles and into the brisk evening, doing up jackets to shield themselves from the wind that ran ahead of the rain clouds. A downpour was forecast for the early morning, yet another in what had already been a miserable spring.

Hamilton could have called on all eight members of their teams, but there was little need for that many bodies. It just meant more chance of detection. He'd have happily done it with just Paul Dougherty from his own team for company, but orders were orders.

Hamilton assumed command of the operation despite holding the same position as Baker. The personnel from both teams listened intently as he outlined his plan, happy that Baker wasn't leading the assault.

'I've got a canister of silane in the back of the car,' Hamilton said. 'We're going to put it inside the target caravan and release it.'

'What the hell's silane?' Baker asked.

'It reacts violently with air, causing small explosions.'

'Great!' Baker sneered. 'We're gonna give them a tiny, indoor fireworks show.'

Hamilton squared up to him, their faces almost touching. 'If you'd let me finish, I could explain that when it's dispensed at high velocity under pressure, it results in delayed combustion.'

Hamilton took a step to the side and addressed the others, not waiting for a reaction from Baker.

'By the time the canister is empty, the air inside will be soaked with silane. The resulting blast will blow the caravan to pieces. It should also breach their gas bottles, making it look like one of them failed and caused the explosion.'

'What about residue?' Baker asked. 'Fire investigators can spot an accelerant a mile away. What are they going to make of this?'

'According to the lab, the explosion and resultant fire should destroy all traces.'

'After we deploy, how long do we have before it goes up?' Andy Hill asked.

'We should have around three minutes to clear the area,' Hamilton told him. 'I've had a look at the overheads, and that's plenty of time to get out of the camp.'

'Sounds risky to me,' Baker said. 'How do we get your canister into the caravan?'

'I'll go in with Paul. He's the best lock pick we've got and can pop the front door for me. I only need to open it a few inches, so I can place the aerosol on the inner step and hit the "Release" button.'

'What if they're still awake?' Baker persisted.

'Then we come back and re-evaluate,' Hamilton said, becoming increasingly frustrated with his colleague's attitude. He went to the back of his car and returned with a large can with an air-freshener label.

'This should be destroyed in the explosion, but if it survives it isn't going to arouse any suspicion.'

Baker had to admit to himself that the idea was a good one, but was still pissed that he hadn't been included in the planning.

'So what are we supposed to do? Sit here with our thumbs up our arses?'

'Exactly,' Hamilton said. 'Sit tight, and I'll radio in once the job is completed.'

He held out his tablet PC, which showed an aerial photo of the camp. 'Their caravan is situated near the back, here. We're going to enter this adjoining field and follow the perimeter of the camp until we come to this gap in the hedge, here. That brings us into the camp just a few yards from the target. After I hit the "Release" button, we'll come back out the same way.'

'Why don't we just come with you?' Baker persisted.

'Because if they somehow manage to get away, they'll do so by car. They've got women and a child with them, so they're not going to make a dash for it across the fields. I've left the keys in mine, so if you don't hear from us within ten minutes, seal the entrance and do what you have to.'

'You mean clean up your mess,' Baker sneered, and Hamilton was tempted to wipe the smile off his face. In-fighting, however, wasn't going to get the job done.

'I told you to bring the van for just this reason,' Hamilton said as calmly as he could. 'These guys know their stuff, so don't under-estimate them. I'm not, and nor should you.'

Baker looked for signs of nervousness but saw none. Hamilton was simply stating an opinion, not making excuses. 'If we don't make it, get them in the van and dispose of them.'

Baker perked up at the thought of some action if it all went to shit.

'Comms check. Alpha one.'

'Delta one,' Baker replied.

'Alpha two.'

'Delta two.'

'Farrar. Are you in position?'

'Setting off now,' Hamilton told him, and with a final gesture for Baker to stay put, he jogged off down the road, Dougherty in tow.

'How long is this going to take?' Farrar asked. 'I plan on sleeping tonight.'

'It should all be over in ten minutes,' Hamilton told him as his eyes swept the side of the road for the entrance to the adjacent field. He saw it a hundred yards from the vehicles and led Dougherty over the gate and into the darkness.

A minute later he reached the hedge enclosing the camp and heard Farrar's voice in his ear.

'Where are you now, Todd?'

Hamilton replied with three clicks of the throat mic and continued onwards, bending at the waist to stay below the top of the hedge.

'Todd, talk to me.'

'He's gone silent,' Baker interjected. 'He's near the target and can't talk.'

'So how come you can? Where are you?'

'I'm three hundred yards away, guarding the vehicles.'

'What the hell for? Why aren't you in there getting the job done?'

'Todd's taken charge of the operation,' Baker said, ensuring his frustration was noted. 'He had it planned out before we even got here and doesn't want me to go along. He's taken Dougherty, that's it.'

Farrar went silent, and Baker knew from experience that this was usually the calm before the storm. He was proven correct moments later.

'You get in there and make sure this job is finished in the next few minutes,' Farrar snarled.

Two more clicks came over the air. 'That'll be a "No" from Todd,' Baker explained, 'and I agree. If he can't pull it off, we have a backup plan.'

One that Baker was looking forward to.

Hamilton's idea, even though it had been thrown together at the last minute, was sound on paper. If the targets were asleep, if Todd didn't wake them as he activated his device and if the gas worked as expected, then it would be job done. However, it didn't have the hands-on aspect that Baker really enjoyed. Given the nature of their work, it wasn't often that he got to look his victims in the eye as he brought their lives to an end, and so he was glad that the next few minutes held so many imponderables.

'I'll leave that call to you, Matt,' Farrar eventually said, 'but I want this finished tonight.'

Baker looked at his watch. 'You've got seven minutes, Todd.'

Seven minutes, and then Baker would know if the mission was over or if it was time to have some fun.

Campbell hit the 'Accept' button the second the phone in his hand vibrated.

'Movement,' said the whispered voice. 'Coming from the west, looks like two.'

Campbell looked up the road in the direction Levine had given, but saw nothing. Whoever was heading towards Carl must have transport nearby, though.

'Clear here. I'll head in that direction and see if I can spot their vehicle.'

There was no objection from Levine, so Campbell rose slowly and made his way towards the gate, pulling off his waterproof jacket as he went. It had served its purpose, and he didn't want to be sneaking up on someone wearing a coat that rustled every time he took a step.

There was no sign of anyone in the immediate area, and he dashed past the entrance to the field, choosing to remain inside rather than expose himself out on the road. He stopped every fifteen yards and had a look through the bottom of the hedge to see if he could spot anything, but all the night had to offer was darkness and the usual hoots and screeches as animals went about their nocturnal activities.

Campbell crossed into the adjoining field, taking care to find a gap big enough that it wouldn't create a lot of noise as he squeezed through. As he traversed the edge, he kept stopping, hoping to see a sign of life or hear a sound to indicate that he was getting close, but it wasn't until he crossed into the third field and rounded a bend in the road that he came across a likely looking pair.

The vehicles were parked up on the grass verge, and two men were behind the Transit van, one of them looking cold and bored, with his arms wrapped close to his body. The other looked more focused, leaning against the bonnet of the Skoda saloon as he stroked the silenced pistol in his right hand. Every few moments he would glance at his watch and then look in the direction of the camp.

'I've got a car and a van, about two hundred yards from you. I see two X-rays, one definitely armed. There could be more in the van, though.'

Campbell waited for a reply, and when none came he knew the two men Carl had heard were most probably too close for him to talk.

'I'm going to get round in front of them,' Campbell said quietly. 'If they make a move, I'll stop them.'

He slowly backtracked until he could no longer see his targets, then found a small gap in the hedge and squeezed through before dashing across the road. He cautiously made his way back towards the vehicles and stopped when the right-hand front wing of the Transit van was in view.

All he had to do now was await a signal from Levine.

It came moments later.

———⁀———

Carl Levine watched as the first pair of feet landed silently a few feet from the car he was sheltering under. Seconds later another person climbed over the stile, and both men made their way towards the target caravan. Levine watched as one of them expertly attacked the lock, and now that he knew they weren't just fellow campers returning from a night out, he edged out from underneath the car. As he did so, he saw the caravan door open and one of the men placed something inside, closing the door almost immediately.

The men had a quick look around and then started walking back towards the stile, but their progress was halted as Levine suddenly appeared in front of them, gesturing with his pistol that they should reach for the skies. Both men did as instructed, shocked at the sight of the man they were supposed to kill standing just yards away.

Levine pointed the pistol at Hamilton and made a gesture with his left arm. Hamilton understood and slowly unzipped his jacket, revealing a silenced Beretta in a shoulder holster. With another couple of signed instructions, Hamilton got the message to take the gun out with two fingers and toss it towards Levine.

Dougherty followed suit, his agitation showing as his glance shifted from Hamilton to the caravan, and Levine realised that they weren't comfortable being so close to the scene of their crime. They certainly hadn't come to deliver pizza, so whatever they had shoved inside the caravan had to be some kind of explosive device. He quickly gathered up the guns, and after checking there was a round in the chamber of the silenced pistol he adopted it as his own, pushing his own weapon and the spare pistol into the waistband of his jeans.

'Move!' he hissed, indicating towards the stile, and as the men walked, he took up position behind them, grabbing Hamilton by the collar and placing the suppressor into the base of his skull.

'How many, and where?'

Hamilton hesitated for a few seconds, trying to decide whether to bluff or fold. 'There's a dozen of us,' he lied. 'The rest are waiting in reserve just down the road. There's no way out.'

Levine cuffed him around the ear with the gun. 'Try again, and remember I've got another pair of eyes out there.'

'Four,' Hamilton said, his ear still ringing from the blow.

'I've got two secure,' Levine said softly into his hands-free mic. 'Bringing them out now. Looks like four in total.' He heard a faint 'Roger' in reply, and a glance at Hamilton's left ear confirmed that the man had his own comms.

'Tell your buddies you're pulling back,' Levine said, 'and don't even think about trying to warn them.'

Hamilton slowly moved his hand to his throat mic and clicked it on. 'The Semtex is in place. We're on our way back.'

'Semtex, eh? You guys weren't planning on taking any prisoners, were you?'

Hamilton ignored the rhetorical question and followed Dougherty over the stile, hoping Baker had understood the message. His colleague wasn't the brightest man on the planet, but surely he could spot a warning signal.

'How long until it blows?' Levine asked, and Hamilton told him they had little under a minute to get clear. He was about to tell them to pick up the pace when Campbell's voice came over the earpiece.

'Something's spooked these two. They're heading your way and not hanging around.'

Levine jerked Hamilton to a halt and shifted his aim. A single round spat from the gun and Dougherty dropped to the floor before he could make a sound, a small hole on his temple marking the entry point.

'You came here to kill not only me, but my family, too,' Levine said, the gun once again pressed against Hamilton's skull. 'Don't think I'll hesitate to kill you.'

There was a barely perceptible nod in reply, and Levine pulled his prisoner over to the side of the field and forced him down onto his knees. Levine got down on one knee a couple of yards behind him, pistol up and searching for targets.

He didn't have to wait long.

The first figure appeared in his sights just as the explosion lit up the sky off to his left, and it caught Levine off guard for just a second. That was long enough for Hamilton to grab the stone near his left leg and he spun, throwing the projectile as he turned. Levine saw it a split second before it hit, catching him on the bridge of the nose before he could swing the gun around. Hamilton was up instantly, kicking the gun hand away before landing a blow to Levine's head which sent him sprawling backwards. The air was knocked out of him as Hamilton landed on his chest with both knees, grabbing for the weapon in Levine's right hand. He resisted as much as he could, aiming punches at his assailant's kidneys with his left hand, but Hamilton ignored the blows. He pinned Levine's right arm to the ground and began pummelling his shoulder, hoping to dislocate it. After three attempts there was a satisfying crack and a howl from Levine.

Hamilton picked up the pistol that had fallen from Levine's grasp, and he placed it against Levine's chest while he retrieved the other two weapons from his waistband. He turned when he heard footsteps from behind and saw his colleagues approaching.

'Campbell's out there somewhere!' he told them.

'What happened to Paul?' Hill asked, standing over Dougherty's body.

'Levine killed him. Now go find Campbell!'

'Let's get this one in the van,' Baker said, 'then we can all look for him.'

Hamilton didn't see the point in all three escorting the prisoner to the van, especially in his current state. 'I'll deal with Levine,' he said. 'You take care of the other one, and make it quick. We'll have to come back for Paul's body.'

Baker didn't like the fact that Hamilton was still giving the orders despite his plan having gone to shit, but the prospect of spending a few minutes alone with Levine spurred him on. He and Hill retreated the way they'd come, weapons up in search of movement. They soon disappeared from view, and Hamilton ordered Levine to his feet.

'Fuck you!'

'I'll count to three,' Hamilton said.

'Don't bother, just give me the bad news.'

Hamilton was sorely tempted, but he needed to know where their spouses were, a fact not lost on Levine.

'There's no way in hell I'm giving up my family,' he said as he got up onto one knee, all the time cradling his useless right arm. Looking up at Hamilton, he let his left arm drop to his side.

'Do it,' he said, focusing his eyes on the gun pointing towards his head.

The park was now fully awake, with people shouting and several children screaming. An adjacent caravan, showered in flaming debris from the initial blast, began to burn, adding to the intensity as the fire crept higher into the night sky.

It was only a matter of time before the emergency services arrived, and Hamilton wanted to be clear of the area before that happened.

'Come on, you stubborn bastard...' He grabbed for Levine's collar, and the knife came up with such ferocity that he didn't even have time to register shock before it plunged into his throat and exited through the back of his neck, severing the spinal column on the way.

Levine eased the corpse to the ground and retrieved both the silenced pistol and his own weapon. He replaced his earpiece, which had fallen out during the struggle, then took the dead man's comms unit and placed the receiver in his right ear.

'These two are down, the other two are coming towards you now,' he said over the phone.

A quick search for ID produced nothing but a small amount of money. No driving licence or credit cards, not even a library card to put a name to the face. That wasn't too surprising, given the nature of their visit.

Leaving the dead where they'd fallen, Levine jogged towards the road. He slowed as he reached the trees lining the narrow country lane and peered through the foliage, cursing the flames from the camp for ruining his night vision. Shadows danced before him, and he knew he would have to break through the tree line and put it between himself and the fire in order to see anything.

He carefully climbed over the rickety wooden fence and sought cover behind the largest tree he could find. A glance around the thick trunk told him he was just a few yards from the road, but there were no signs of any vehicles. He guessed he was too close to the camp, so he headed away from it, taking care to mini-mise the sound of his footsteps.

The van came into view thirty yards ahead, and he could see Campbell kneeling next to it, a gun held to his head. He knew the other one had to be close by, and he realised just how close when the cold, hard steel of the suppressor jabbed him in the temple.

'Move,' Baker said, holding his hand out for Levine to surrender his weapons. Where the man had come from, Levine didn't know, but he'd been as silent as a cat. He gave up the guns and stood, receiving a shove in the back to urge him forward.

'Hamilton screwed up,' Baker said into his throat mic, 'but I've got things under control.'

'What do you mean, he screwed up?' Farrar asked.

'His bomb went off, but there was no one in the caravan. I've got the two men, and I'll make them take us to the women.'

'Hamilton, talk to me. What the hell is going on there?'

'Hamilton's dead,' Baker told him as he ushered Levine forward. 'So is Dougherty. I'll report back when we're done.'

Farrar wasn't happy that the mission hadn't been wrapped up, but he accepted that it might take a little time to break the ex-soldiers. He told Baker to call him as soon as the job was complete, then signed off comms.

When they reached the vehicles, Campbell offered Levine an apologetic look.

'Sorry, mate. They got the drop on me while I was trying to slash their tyres.'

'Shut it!' Hill hissed, giving Campbell a kick in the ribs.

Baker told Levine to lie on the floor and ordered Hill to cover them both while he fetched two pairs of plasticuffs from the van. He returned and went to work on Levine first, wrenching his injured shoulder and pleased to see the signs of discomfort. Levine clenched his teeth as the pain from his shoulder shot through his body, but Baker wasn't in the mood to be tender, and he gave the arm another tug for good measure.

When both prisoners had their hands secured behind their backs, Baker gestured for them to climb inside the van. Levine looked over to where Hill had Campbell by the scruff of the neck, and he moved towards the van, hesitating in front of the open door. Baker moved in to give him a shove and as soon as Levine felt the hand on his back, he made his move.

Placing one leg up onto the sill of the van, he pushed back with all his strength, swivelling in mid-air and coming down with an outstretched leg which caught Baker on the chin. The strike knocked the man backwards, and he fell against the bonnet of the Skoda but managed to squeeze off a round, which caught Levine in his good arm. The thud of the impact spun him for a second, but the adrenalin pumping through his body held the pain at bay. He kicked Baker's legs from under him, and as he hit the floor, Levine threw himself on top of him. He began using his forehead to pummel Baker's face, smashing the nose and sending blood spraying into the air.

Campbell took this as his cue and raked his heel down Hill's shin. While the man was stunned by the intense pain, he took a step away from him and tried to deliver a roundhouse kick, but Hill recovered just quickly enough to deflect the blow and he kicked out at Campbell's groin, knocking the wind out of him. Once he was on the ground, Hill gave him another kick to the head, then went to help his team leader.

Hill grabbed Levine's bloodstained arm and dragged him off Baker, and the resulting scream pierced the night. Baker sat up groggily and climbed unsteadily to his feet, his pistol swinging drunkenly by his side. He gingerly felt for the damage done to his face, and his hand came away a dark crimson in the faint moonlight.

With anger seeping from every pore, Baker approached Levine and pointed the pistol at his head.

'I thought you wanted them alive,' Hill said, having seen the look before.

Baker glanced over at Campbell and saw him sprawled out on the ground, alive but dazed.

'We only need one,' he snarled.

Carl Levine looked into the small hole of the suppressor and knew that death was an instant away. He'd always known it would come, and a bullet in the head was preferable to other ways of meeting one's end, such as drowning or the lingering agony of a terminal disease, but his thoughts turned to his family. Who would look after them once he was gone? How would—

The sound of the bullet echoed through the trees, and Levine flinched, but the anticipated darkness never came. Instead, Baker sank to his knees before collapsing forward onto his face. A stranger came into view with a pistol held in a two-handed grip and trained on Hill.

'Drop it,' the newcomer said with a hint of an accent. As he drew closer to pick up Hill's weapon, Levine could see that he was of Asian origin, perhaps from India or Pakistan. Another man appeared and quickly cuffed Hill before leading him back down the lane.

'Carl Levine, I presume.'

Levine said nothing. Although thankful to still be alive, he was too busy wondering what the hell was going on.

'I know this is going to sound corny,' the man standing over him said, 'but come with me if you want to live.'

Levine saw two more men appear. One came over and knelt down next to him, placed a first-aid kit on the ground and pulled out a bandage which he used to dress Levine's bullet wound. The other went over to Campbell and helped him to his feet.

'You mind telling me who you are, and who they are?' Levine asked, nodding towards Baker's corpse.

'We're Five,' the man told him. 'The name's Hamad. Hamad Farsi.'

Levine looked sceptical. 'If you're Five, who the hell are these guys?'

He winced as the medic tightened the bandage around his wound and declared him good to go before calling the other man over to help carry Baker's body. They dragged it to the van and unceremoniously threw it in.

'You'll find two more in the field,' Levine told them as he staggered to his feet. 'Head towards the fire, you can't miss them.'

The two men trotted off, and Farsi gestured for Levine to follow him. 'We need to get you to a proper doctor.'

Levine stood his ground. 'You still haven't told me what's going on. Who were those guys?'

'They work for the government, and we believe they're trying to eliminate everyone involved in the Tom Gray episode last year. Why, we don't know.'

Levine thought it was obvious, but he didn't let on. He wanted to speak to Jeff alone before he said anything else, so he followed Farsi down the road to where two saloons were parked. Campbell was already in the back seat of one, and Levine climbed in beside his friend.

Farsi climbed into the front passenger seat and turned to face them.

'Are your families close by?' he asked as the first of the emergency service vehicles roared past, sirens wailing.

'They took off hours ago,' Levine lied. Until he knew exactly what was going on, he wasn't about to drag his family back into this. 'If we don't get in touch with them within four hours, they take our story to the press.'

'And just what is your story?' Farsi asked.

Levine and Campbell looked at one another. 'Let's get Carl sorted out first,' Campbell said. Farsi nodded and told the driver to move out.

'It's a bit of a coincidence that you should show up just in time,' Levine said as they drove past the camp. He noticed that the fire had now spread to a third caravan and was thankful that the girl next door had let his daughter's indiscretion slip. There was no way any of them would have survived the blast or the resulting inferno if they'd been tucked up in bed.

'It was close,' Farsi said. 'We're guessing your daughter sent her boyfriend a text, but it didn't hit our desk until an hour and a half ago. The night shift didn't realise the importance; otherwise, we'd have been here hours ago.'

'Is that how the others found us?' Campbell asked.

'We believe so,' Farsi said, 'and we'd really like to know why they want you dead. Apart from the team that just tried to kill you, we know there's a contractor waiting for Simon Baines and Len Smart to land in South Africa tomorrow evening.'

'South Africa?' Campbell asked. 'What the hell are they doing there? I thought they were in the Philippines!'

'And what do you mean by contractor?' Levine asked. 'A hit man?'

'At least one,' Farsi told him. 'They're on a cargo ship that will be arriving in Durban, and we intercepted instructions that sound very much like a kill order. Unfortunately, we haven't been able to establish just who will be meeting them.'

The news confirmed what Campbell and Levine had thought all along: the government wanted rid of everyone who knew that Tom Gray was still alive.

So why couldn't Farsi put two and two together? Surely, it was obvious that the information they had could cause the entire government serious damage. The opposition, who had been ousted in the last election, were responsible for creating the subterfuge, and the current ruling party were complicit by not only maintaining the silence but also sending out kill squads.

There could only be one explanation—Farsi didn't know that Tom was still alive.

'So why are you helping us?' Levine asked. 'If the government are looking to kill us, surely MI5 would be involved in the plot.'

'You've been watching too many movies,' Farsi told him. 'Our mandate is to protect the citizens of the UK, not kill them. If someone has committed a crime, we seek justice through the courts.'

'Then how come you just shot that guy?' Campbell asked. 'You could have tried arresting him.'

'Because I knew he'd been sent to kill you, and it was his life or yours. Hopefully, that will convince you that we're on your side.'

A compelling argument, Levine thought. If they were just playing good cop/bad cop, burning one of their own to execute the charade was a bit extreme. Although Farsi's sentiment about following the proper judicial procedure was noble, Levine wondered how the man would react when he discovered the truth. Would he or his superiors allow Tom Gray to announce his return to the world once they realised how devastating it would be to the credibility of the government?

Levine decided that although he trusted Farsi—if only for the time being—he would keep that particular card close to his chest.

'When you get to the next village, you'll see a supermarket on the high street. Our families are in the car park at the rear.'

Campbell threw him a look, but Levine assured him it was okay. 'There's a loose end we need to tie up,' he told Farsi. 'The man you shot was due to report in once he'd finished his mission.'

'No problem,' Farsi said. 'We'll take care of it.'

Chapter Eleven

Monday, 7 May 2012

The chirping of his mobile woke Farrar from a fitful sleep. According to his watch, he'd been asleep for less than two hours.

'What?' he barked into the phone.

'It's Hill. The job's complete.'

'Where's Baker?' Farrar asked.

'He's … tidying up,' Hill told him.

'I'll give him a ring,' Farrar said, but Hill told him not to bother. 'During the takedown, Baker got into a skirmish, and his mobile was damaged.'

'Just get him to call me when he's got a new phone,' Farrar said and hit the 'End' button.

Durban was an hour ahead of the UK, which meant it was just after seven in the morning in Durban. Having woken Palmer just a few hours earlier, Farrar decided to wait until he got to the office, before contacting him again. He'd said he wouldn't have access to the website until the afternoon, so there was no point in depriving the man of any more sleep when he had an important hit to carry out.

Despite the abrupt wake-up call, Farrar found himself looking forward to the day ahead. He headed to the shower and began preparing his report for the home secretary, which he would deliver once Palmer confirmed his kills.

———⌣———

Even though it was barely six in the morning, Veronica Ellis found that she wasn't the first member of the team to make it into work. A light from the technical team office told her that Gerald Small had beaten her to it.

'Morning,' she said as she stuck her head through the doorway. 'What's got you in so early?'

'Just finishing up the website,' the technician told her. 'I managed to get the source code from Gordon's cloud storage account, and the ISP has graciously agreed to point the IP address to one of our machines.'

'So when Farrar uses the site, will he notice any difference?'

'None at all,' Small said, 'but we haven't been able to crack the encryption algorithm he used to generate the passwords. The best I could do was to pretend to authenticate, but in actual fact it will accept any password the user enters.'

'If you have the source code, why can't you figure it out?'

'It relies on a key in the web.config file,' Small explained. 'It reads the key and uses that as the hash for the encryption. Trouble is, this is his backup version, and the key is blank.'

'Surely, this would only be a problem if they intentionally entered the wrong password, wouldn't it?'

'That's right,' Small told her. 'The risk is tiny, but there nonetheless.'

Ellis wasn't about to second-guess him on anything technical, and if he said he couldn't do any more, that was the end of the matter. At least they had the site in place, and following the news she'd received an hour earlier, she only expected it to be in use for another twenty-four hours at the most. They already had logs that tied Farrar to the website, and one of his operatives was currently being more than cooperative in a safe house south of London. Although compelling reading, Andy Hill's testimony wouldn't be enough to get Farrar into court, let alone convict him. According to Hill, there'd been no written instructions beyond a workup file, which had been deleted once the plan had been drawn up and approved, so it would be Farrar's word against theirs. Farrar would no doubt paint his team as disgruntled, rogue employees and have some high-ranking figures offer testimony on his behalf, so the more proof she could gather, the better.

With that in mind, she thanked Small and went to her own office to let Andrew Harvey know about the latest developments.

With an hour remaining of the flight to London Heathrow Airport, Abdul Mansour carefully adjusted his *burqa*, unlocked the toilet door and returned to his seat. He hadn't spoken a single word to his male companion during the entire flight lest anyone discover the charade that had seen him pass easily through passport control at Lahore's Allama Iqbal International Airport. He hadn't really expected any problems leaving Pakistan, but he had to trust Al-Asiri when he said the arrival would be uneventful: that wasn't normally the case when walking into the lion's den.

Thirty minutes later, the plane began its descent. Mansour once again felt for the inhaler in his pocket, and he decided that if they were stopped on their way through the airport, he would set the device off and leave himself at the mercy of Allah.

When they eventually touched down, Mansour and his companion, Ali, joined the throng of other passengers heading towards the immigration desks. Mansour looked for a desk staffed by a likely ally, but Ali guided him to a queue manned by a burly male.

He kept his hands inside the *burqa* and removed the canister from his pocket, ready to activate it should there be any trouble.

It took ten agonising minutes for them to reach the head of the line, and Mansour prayed that they would be let through with just a cursory inspection of their documents.

It wasn't to be.

'Lift the veil, please,' the border guard said, flicking through the passports.

Mansour pretended not to understand the instructions, and they were repeated with hand gestures. Again he didn't move, but Ali lifted the thin material and Mansour found himself staring into the official's eyes.

He pressed down on the canister and began a silent count of ten, but he only got to two before the guard nodded, handed back the documents and waved them through. Mansour let out the breath he'd been holding and glanced back, but the man was already inspecting the paperwork for the next passenger.

They collected their single suitcase from the baggage hall and made their way to the exit, where they found a man holding a placard bearing Ali's surname. They followed him to his vehicle, which was located in the multi-storey car park. Once they'd cleared the airport, Mansour finally felt he could relax.

'I wish you'd warned me what to expect,' he told Ali.

'He has been working for us for quite some time now,' his companion told him. 'The man has a severe gambling problem, which we feed with a few thousand pounds every month.'

'Is money enough to ensure his obedience?' Mansour wondered aloud.

'It usually is. This one was about to lose his house because of his addiction, but we paid off the mortgage arrears, and he gets a gambling allowance in cash every month. He is happy with the current arrangement, but he also knows that if he tries to cross us, his precious home will go up in flames while he and his family sleep.'

'Sometimes the carrot works, sometimes the stick,' Mansour said, 'but a combination of both is better.'

Ali nodded. 'I have been here eleven times, and you are the eleventh wife he has allowed me to bring through immigration control. It has proven to be a valuable route into the country.'

Mansour agreed, though he did wonder why he hadn't been told of it on his last visit to England. Hadn't they trusted him? His masters had provided him with a forged passport and let him make his own way there, rather than disclose this more secure method of entry. Perhaps the operation had been so hurriedly put together that there simply hadn't been time to ensure their man would be working when he touched down.

That was a year ago, he reminded himself, and his exploits since had surely demonstrated his loyalty beyond any doubt.

His loyalty to the cause, at least.

In his pocket he had the flash card from the mobile he'd been carrying on his recent visit to Azhar Al-Asiri's home, and embedded on that drive were the GPS coordinates of the building. Once they reached the London safe house, he would send someone out to a local toy shop to buy the equipment he needed for the next part of his plan.

Andrew Harvey removed the magazine from the 9mm Beretta, checked the chamber was empty and stripped it down, as his firearms training dictated. The barrel looked clean, and the moving parts slid nicely into place. The well-oiled gun had obviously been properly maintained.

'Thanks, Dennis. Should I ask where you got this?'

'Best not to,' Owen smiled.

They were sitting in Harvey's hotel room, waiting for a phone call so that they could make a move. The plan was to check out the area around the port exit to see if they could spot anyone waiting for the Wenban haulage trucks to make an appearance. Unfortunately, they still had no idea just how many they were up against.

That information, according to Veronica Ellis, had died with Carl Gordon.

The good news was that they had managed to rebuild the website Farrar had been communicating through, though the latest message they'd intercepted an hour earlier hadn't made today's task easy.

Ellis had given Harvey a brief rundown on the events of the previous evening, and it seemed Farrar had believed the news he'd been fed by Andy Hill. On the understanding that Campbell and Levine were out of the way, Farrar had left a curt note on the website:

Information no longer required. Terminate their journey.

For Harvey, this changed the entire game. Up until a few hours ago he was looking for someone who wanted the people in the container alive, which meant being subtle and choosing the moment carefully. Now, however, the strike could occur at any time, and Harvey and Owen would be the only ones concerned about the passengers' safety.

He would have felt a lot better if he had a full team behind him, but when he suggested the idea to Ellis, she ruled it out. There simply wasn't time to get anyone else in place, and using the local cops was out of the question.

'What happens if you and the police catch some guy in the act,' Ellis had said, 'and the locals want to take him in? That's only natural, as it's their country. We might lose access to him and our case against Farrar falls apart.'

Her reasoning was sound, but it didn't make his job any easier. What did was the recent discovery made by Gerald Small. His eventual success at hacking the Port Authority servers meant they knew that the larger consignment was to be delivered to a small firm to the south of the city. The mom-and-pop company operated normal business hours, which meant that unless the truck could reach them before five in the afternoon, it would have to park up overnight, and the logical place to do so was the Wenban facility. Small had been searching for further details, such as the offloading time, when the server security systems recognised the intrusion and kicked him out. That information would have been handy, but at least they knew a lot more now than they did a few hours earlier.

Owen's mobile chirped and he hit the 'Accept' button. After the briefest of conversations, he nodded to Harvey, grabbed his jacket and headed towards the door.

Harvey tucked the pistol into his waistband and covered it with the Hawaiian print shirt. Owen was similarly dressed in order to create the impression that they were just tourists out enjoying a drive.

In the hotel reception, Owen was greeted by two young blondes from the Durban office whom he'd arranged to come along on the surveillance, adding to the pretence. After brief introductions, the girls led them to the car, an Audi A5 convertible. Harvey climbed in the back with Clara, and Elaine took the front passenger seat.

On the short drive to the port, Harvey gave Clara a phone and was glad to discover she was familiar with the model.

'It's set to record video,' he said. 'Just hold it up to your ear, and make sure you aren't covering the camera lens.'

As they drove, Clara pretended to make a short phone call, then handed the phone back to Harvey, who looked at the recording.

'All I'm getting is the wheels of the vehicles,' he told her. 'If you can hold it vertical, we should get some good images.'

Clara tried once more, this time with better results. Harvey wiped the test video and handed the phone back, then pulled his own from his pocket. After a dummy run, he declared them good to go.

Earlier in the day, Owen and Harvey had studied aerial shots of the port before spending a couple of hours monitoring movement from the main exit, Bayhead Road. They knew that the trucks would turn left onto South Coast Road and head south until they had a chance to join the M4 highway heading north towards their depot.

Following the likely route, both Harvey and Clara set their phones recording, placed them to their ears and pretended to be deep in conversation as they cruised along at a sedate pace. They passed shops and service stations built in the fifties and looking like they hadn't had a lick of paint since. Their job wasn't made easy by the sheer number of vehicles on the road, and though Harvey had a clear view of the occupants of the vehicles parked along his side of the street, Clara's phone was mostly capturing oncoming traffic.

It took almost fifteen minutes to travel the two miles to the M4 on-ramp, where Owen made a U-turn and retraced their route. Once they'd reached their starting point at the junction of Bayhead Road, Harvey uploaded the videos to a cloud storage site and emailed Hamad Farsi, asking him to scan through the images and see if any of the faces captured were known to the service. It was a long shot, but if they could identify their suspect before the truck arrived, it took the targets out of the equation.

'Let's go meet up with Kyle,' Owen said.

He drove down Bayhead Road and pulled up at the service station where he'd parked his BMW that morning. Kyle Ackerman was waiting by a Suzuki Jeep, and he came over as they parked up. Owen handled the introductions and thanked Kyle for helping out.

'No problem,' Kyle said. 'Two thousand rand for following a truck is the easiest money I've ever made.'

Harvey wasn't sure that having someone with no field experience on the operation was a good idea, but Kyle was the only person Owen could call on at short notice. When Owen had suggested the idea, Harvey had asked for someone who could handle himself in a tight situation, and Kyle had been Owen's only option. His four years spent in the Royal Marines would have to make up for his lack of fieldcraft, and hopefully his only task would be to tail a slow-moving vehicle for a few miles.

Owen thanked the girls for their help and promised to treat them when the mission was over, and Clara slipped Harvey a business card and a smile before climbing into the driver's seat and gunning the engine.

'You're a sly one,' Owen grinned as Harvey studied the phone number he'd been handed. 'She's not usually that forward.'

'Hey, I'm as surprised as you!'

'Trust me, that's one call you wanna make.'

Harvey was flattered by the invitation, but his first concern was ensuring Kyle knew what was expected of him.

'Dennis said I just had to stay behind the truck and wait for a phone call from you guys,' Ackerman smiled. 'Not really rocket science.'

Harvey found himself warming to Kyle, his easy-going approach making him a likeable sort, but concerns about his ability to pull off the mission pushed those thoughts aside.

'It might get a bit hairy,' he warned. 'If the first container looks big enough to hold a couple of dozen people, Dennis and I will follow it; otherwise, it's yours. We have no idea which one contains the people we're looking for, and we don't know where or when it's going to be hit. We don't even know how many people will be looking for it.'

'Lots of imponderables,' Ackerman said as the smile melted away, and his demeanour suddenly went into professional mode. 'Don't worry, I'm not stupid enough to take on an army all by myself. If I see anything suspicious, I'll let you guys know.'

Harvey nodded, his confidence in the man growing by the minute. He handed over the card Carla had given him.

'Take this,' he said. 'I prefer brunettes.'

Kyle screwed it up and tossed it into a nearby bin.

'Been there, done that,' he winked.

The ship was due to dock at any moment, but it could be hours before the containers they were interested in were ready to come ashore. Harvey knew they wouldn't be able to park at the service station for long without arousing suspicion, but for a while they would be a lot less conspicuous than if they were to park right on the junction, and the truck would have to pass them on its way to the highway.

They went into the service station and ordered coffee before finding seats near the window so that they could keep an eye out for the distinctive Wenban livery. Their thoughts turned to the mission ahead, and after all the preparation, all they could do now was wait. Owen had prepared passports for both Smart and Baines, and two more were waiting to be processed once they had new photos for the other two passengers. There was still no confirmation that the mysterious Sam Grant was one of them, and Harvey thought back to the file that was currently locked in his hotel room safe.

He'd studied the picture time and time again, and while it still seemed like a composite, the eyes had once again struck him as remarkably familiar.

Hopefully, the next few hours would provide some answers.

An hour and a half later, just as Hamad Farsi was informing Harvey that no matches had been found within the images—either within their own database or Interpol's—Sean Littlefield drove past the service station and continued down Bayhead Road until he reached the junction with Langeberg Road, the arterial route leading from the cargo terminal.

'It's going to be a long wait,' he observed as he parked the Mercedes Sprinter van.

Ben Palmer nodded, but his thoughts were on the operation that lay ahead.

Since getting the message from Farrar, he'd been thinking about the takedown, and they'd stopped off at a hardware store on the way to buy a few items. He got out of the passenger seat and climbed into the back of the van to prepare his improvised munitions.

With the need for subtlety gone, Palmer had wanted to get his hands on some proper grenades rather than the flash-bangs Littlefield had provided. He didn't know if his targets would be armed, but experience told him that it was always safer to assume they were. Unfortunately, it was too late in the day to acquire the real thing, so Palmer set to work adapting the flash-bangs so that they would be as lethal as fragmentation grenades.

His first task was to cut out a piece of cellophane the same height as the barrel of the M84 stun grenade and long enough to wrap around it, plus an extra three inches. The grenade had a thin aluminium core surrounded by a perforated steel body, which allowed the magnesium-based pyrotechnic to escape and temporarily blind the victims. Palmer's plan was to wrap layers of putty, heavily impregnated with small steel screws, around the barrel. It was based on the principle that if you set off a firecracker in the palm of your hand, you burn your hand; but if you wrap your fingers around it, you'll never play the piano again.

The M84 produces a subsonic deflagration rather than a supersonic detonation, but by encasing it in the putty, the effect of the blast would be magnified, and the screws would be as deadly as any bullet. He'd considered using ball bearings, just like those found in Claymore mines, but the irregular shape of the screws would produce more collateral damage, tumbling as they entered the bodies, tearing flesh and fragmenting bone. The idea wasn't to inflict pain, just to cause as much shock to the system as possible so that the body shut down.

Palmer used the first piece of cellophane as a template to produce another eight before cutting out slits in each one to accommodate the grenade's handle, then smeared the first three with a thin veneer of the putty. He sprinkled around fifty screws onto each sheet and used the putty tin to roll them flat. Once he'd trimmed off the excess, he wrapped a sheet around each of the M84s, using electrical tape to hold them in place. After waiting a few minutes to let each layer dry, Palmer repeated the process twice more until the grenades were completely encased.

The sun had set by the time the weapons were ready, and the container was still an hour away from being offloaded. Trucks filed past as he climbed back into the passenger seat, some destined for local trading estates, the majority heading inland.

'All set?' Littlefield asked, and Palmer nodded.

———⌣———

When Arnold Tang's car pulled up to the entrance of the Hong Wing restaurant, the owner was already standing near the entrance, ready to welcome him. The visitor was quickly shown to a table near the rear, where waiters were busy laying place settings.

'Are you dining alone?' the manager asked, and Tang informed him that a friend would be along shortly. His henchmen took their positions at a nearby table as Tang sat in a chair facing the door, and a bottle of Remy Martin Louis XIII was quickly placed in front of him.

A few minutes later, Koh Beng Lee arrived with his own entourage. Arnold greeted him and poured two glasses of cognac, and they exchanged small talk until the waiter arrived to take their order. Once he was gone, Lee steered the conversation towards business.

'I have another twenty people from Singapore ready to make the journey West,' he said. 'When is the next ship leaving?'

'On the twentieth,' Tang told him. 'How do you want them to travel once they reach Durban?'

Lee knew the options open to him. Tang had two tiers of travel, the first and cheapest being overland from Durban to Morocco. After a short ferry ride to Spain, it would be overland all the way to Calais for the short hop to Dover.

The second option cost an extra ten thousand US dollars and meant a plane ride to the north of the continent, shaving fifteen days off the journey and avoiding a lot of dicey border crossings.

As the people making the journey tended to be the poor looking for a better life, very few could afford option two.

'They will all be going overland,' Lee told him and gestured to one of his men, who brought over a briefcase. He opened it to reveal bundles of fifties, and Tang nodded. He wouldn't insult his friend by counting it, and Lee already knew the consequences of being so much as a dollar short.

Tang placed the case on the floor next to his feet and poured another two drinks.

'I trust you heard about Timmy Hughes,' Lee said as he savoured the spirit. 'He was a good customer of mine. I understand you had ... dealings with him, too.'

Tang's demeanour shifted instantly at the mention of the name. 'What about him?'

'You didn't hear?'

'Obviously not.'

'He was killed two weeks ago. Shot in the head, I was told.'

Tang rubbed the bridge of his nose as he digested the news, then suddenly banged a meaty fist on the table. One of his men ran over, hand inside his jacket and ready to draw down if his boss was in danger. Tang waved him away and pulled out his mobile phone.

'Where is the last shipment?' he barked. It took a moment for his new lieutenant to find the information, and that got Tang wondering.

Was Hughes's death somehow linked to the disappearance of two of his men a fortnight earlier? They were good men, and had handled the people-smuggling operation efficiently before they suddenly vanished. Was another player trying to move into his territory? Had they simply decided to work for someone else, or had they been taken out in an effort to cripple his business?

Anger boiled within him, his face taking on a crimson hue.

The first thing to deal with was Hughes's fare-dodging friends. When his lieutenant came back on the line, he was told that the ship had landed in South Africa an hour earlier.

Tang had already given instructions for the passengers to be killed once they'd arrived in England and he'd received his payment from Hughes, but as that money was never going to arrive, there was no point in paying for an unnecessary plane journey. He was going to be slightly out of pocket on the deal, and the passengers would pay for it.

'Call Leng in Durban. Get him to cancel the *gweilo*'s flight, then I want him to take them somewhere remote and dispose of them.' He thought for a moment, then added: 'Tell him to rape the woman and make the men watch, then kill them all.'

He hung up and poured himself a large measure of cognac. The possibility that someone might be making a move on his operation would gnaw at him for days, and the death of the *gweilos* would be small recompense.

Chapter Twelve

Monday, 7 May 2012

'Here we go.'

Andrew Harvey saw the blue truck with lightning flashes approach the service station, and he grabbed his coat, following Owen out of the door.

'Follow the next one, and be careful,' he warned Ackerman, who nodded solemnly.

They allowed several other vehicles to get between them and the target, both men making a mental note of the drivers and passengers. Owen eventually pulled into the traffic and saw the red container roughly a quarter of a mile down the road.

'Don't get too close unless it leaves the expected route,' Harvey said, angling the rear-view mirror so that he could see who was behind them.

The truck turned left onto the coast road, retracing their earlier steps, before obligingly hitting the M4 on-ramp which led to the Wenban compound. The road threaded its way through central Durban before heading to Durban Beach, hugging the coast as it meandered north. By now only three vehicles remained between them and the truck, and that soon fell to two. Traffic was disappointingly light at this time of night, and Owen held off the throttle to allow the gap to open up.

After twenty minutes, one of the cars ahead pulled off the M4 at an off-ramp, and Harvey checked the mirror for the hundredth time and saw that their tail was clear.

'That has to be our guy,' he said, indicating to the van up ahead.

Owen agreed. 'Sure you don't want me to just pull him over?'

'No,' Harvey said. 'Slowly overtake them both and then stay half a mile ahead of the truck.'

He pulled his phone out and prepared the video camera before holding it to his ear. The powerful BMW closed the gap easily, and they cruised past the van, Harvey recording the driver's face while simultaneously noting the licence number. By the time they'd eased ahead of both vehicles, Harvey had plenty of footage. He scanned through it quickly and saw the lone driver, a man in his fifties. Not recognising him, he sent the video to Farsi along with a note requesting details of the van's owner.

Owen opened up a lead on the target vehicles before slowing to match their speed.

'We should reach Wenban in about ten minutes,' he said.

Having scoped out the route a few days earlier, Harvey knew that there was just one more off-ramp before the highway took them past the compound, and it was just a few minutes up the road. If the truck continued past it, his gamble would have paid off. If it took the turning, it would be another fifteen minutes before they could get off the highway and try to find it again.

His heart beat faster as the BMW slid past the turnoff, and he willed the truck to follow. He watched the headlights in the mirror as they appeared to crawl along the tarmac, and he muttered to himself as the seconds ticked by.

'Come on, come on, a little more ...'

He let out an audible sigh of relief as the truck trundled past the off-ramp and continued to follow them.

'Okay, head for the warehouse opposite the Wenban compound. We'll park behind it and see what they do once they get there.'

Owen gunned the engine, and they pulled away from the miniature convoy. By the time they pulled off the highway and reached the warehouse, they were around four minutes ahead of the truck, and Owen parked up around the back of the derelict building. As Harvey got out, he noted that theirs were the only fresh tyre marks in the loose dirt, which meant it was unlikely their quarry would choose the same location—anyone worth their salt would have scoped the area out, and this place hadn't been visited in months.

He pushed his way through a hole in the fence and sprinted to the front of the warehouse, where he checked that the front gate he'd oiled on his previous visit moved without making a sound. Satisfied that he could get out of the compound without being heard, he tucked down behind a row of rusting oil drums. A moment later, Owen joined him, zipping up his black jacket as he sank to his knees.

'Where the hell did you get that?' Harvey asked, looking at the R4 assault rifle Owen was brandishing.

'Same place I got your pea-shooter,' Owen smiled. 'As we don't know the enemy strength, I thought it best to bring it along, just in case.'

'Couple that with your muscle car, and you must have the smallest dick in the world.'

Despite the banter, Harvey was grateful for the extra firepower.

It was another two minutes before headlights heralded the arrival of the truck. The driver swung the vehicle through the open gates and manoeuvred the flatbed to the back of the compound, where he reversed into a marked bay and climbed out of the cab. Harvey watched him head into the office, and a couple of minutes later he emerged and climbed into a car which sped away into the night.

There had been no sign of the van, and Harvey was beginning to wonder if they'd followed the wrong container when the Mercedes slowly cruised past his hiding place, the driver concentrating on the road ahead while the passenger's attention was focused on the haulage company's yard.

Just as he was wondering where the second person had appeared from, his phone vibrated. Farsi had sent him the file on Sean Littlefield, and he quickly scanned through it, sharing the information with Owen. There was nothing to link him to Farrar or any black ops teams, and none of his known associates matched the name the van was rented under.

Harvey was still no closer to discovering who his enemy was, and now he and Owen were facing at least two adversaries. There could even be more hidden away in the van, but he couldn't do anything about that at this late stage. He hadn't even had time to get a snap of the newcomer to send to Farsi, so all he could do now was exercise caution and hope to bring one of them in alive.

———

Ben Palmer had spent most of the journey in the back of the van, looking out of the small rear window to see if they were being followed. The BMW had caught his attention soon after they'd joined the highway, but once it had sped past and disappeared into the night, he began to relax.

Satisfied that they had no tail, he climbed over the central console and into the passenger seat.

'We're clean,' he said, and Littlefield looked in his wing mirror, seeing nothing but darkness.

They watched the truck pull off the highway, and Palmer ordered Littlefield to stop two hundred yards short of the compound. A few minutes later, a car drove out of the gates and roared past them, heading towards the city.

'Do a drive-by,' Palmer said. 'I want to see if anyone's still there.'

Littlefield rolled the van forwards, and as they crept past the gates, Palmer spotted a single car parked outside the office building. Lights shone through the windows, and he knew he'd have to wait a little longer to complete the mission.

'Sean, park up farther down the road, and I'll walk back. Once the last person's gone, I'll call you.'

His friend drove along until they rounded a corner, where he performed a U-turn and went off-road, parking the van behind a row of trees. Palmer hopped out and jogged parallel to the road until he was within a hundred yards of the perimeter fence, where he took a knee next to a bush, his eyes on the prize. He took a ski mask from his jacket pocket and pulled it over his head, a low-tech solution to the three CCTV cameras covering the target.

The nocturnal orchestra was in full swing, and insects buzzed around him as he waited impatiently for signs of movement. Eventually, he was rewarded as the lights went out and the office door opened. A male appeared, carrying a bowl, followed by the dog Palmer had encountered a few days earlier. It bounded to the fence to relieve itself and then ran back to its owner, barking for its food.

As the dog ate, the man climbed into his car and drove out of the gates, stopping at the roadside to lock them before heading into town, another shift over.

Palmer waited another few minutes, then called Littlefield on his mobile.

'Bring the van up to the gates. I'll meet you there.'

Sean joined him at the entrance thirty seconds later, and Palmer rattled the fence next to the gate. The dog came pounding towards him, teeth bared as it growled an ominous warning. When it was within ten feet, Palmer put a silenced bullet between the animal's eyes, and it dropped before it could even register the impact.

The final level of security to overcome was the chain securing the gates. Palmer slid open the side panel of the van and pulled out the bolt cutters, which made short work of the lock. He pushed the gates open, and Littlefield drove the van into the yard, spinning it around so that the nose was pointing towards the entrance, ready for a quick exit.

Harvey watched the masked man swing the gates open and the van drive in, and as soon as the driver jumped out of the cab and ran to the back, he was ready to move.

'I'm going in,' he said. 'Cover me.'

He squeezed through the warehouse gate and across the road, his rubber-soled sneakers minimising the sound. When he reached the van, he saw that the back doors were wide open, and he eased his way to the rear, his pistol extended in a two-handed grip.

Taking two steps to the side, he rounded the door and caught the two men unaware.

'Hands up, nice and slow, and move away from the van.'

Palmer froze, one hand on the 3-methylfentanyl aerosol, one of the improvised grenades in the other. Littlefield had the other two, and he looked over at his friend for guidance. When Palmer gave the slightest of nods, he put the munitions down and raised his hands.

Palmer depressed the nozzle on the canister and showed his hands. He turned to face Harvey, who gestured with the pistol for him to move away from the vehicle. He complied, Littlefield in tow.

'Masks off,' Harvey ordered. 'Slowly.'

Both men did as instructed, and then Harvey asked for their weapons.

'It's in the back of the van,' Palmer said, and Harvey backed up to the opening. He glanced in and saw the pistol, then reached in to grab it, his eyes back on his prisoners. Once it was tucked into his waistband, he ordered Littlefield to surrender his own gun.

Harvey told them both to unzip their jackets and lift their shirts, and satisfied that they were no longer armed, he ordered them to their knees.

Neither man moved.

'Down on the grou ...'

The words felt heavy in his throat, and the gun wavered as he tried to focus on the two men. He shook his head to clear it, but all he succeeded in doing was throw himself off balance. He slammed into one of the doors and collapsed to the ground. Palmer was on him in an instant, disarming him and giving him a kicking for good measure. He held his breath as he picked up the canister and threw it towards the fence, making a mental note to collect it on the way out.

'Drag him clear of the gas,' Palmer told Littlefield as he grabbed all three grenades. He scanned the area but saw no one else, and the questions came thick and fast. Who was this guy, and who had sent him? Only two people could possibly know about this mission, and between Carl Gordon and James Farrar, he knew who he trusted most.

It just didn't make sense for Farrar to double-cross him, but having dealt with the man on more than one occasion, he knew he could trust him about as far as he could throw him.

He needed to find some answers, and fortunately that was a field he excelled in.

'Why don't we just kill him?'

'Because he's not a local, Sean. This isn't some guy protecting his property, and I want to know what he's doing here.'

Littlefield shrugged and grabbed Harvey's ankles, dragging him towards the office building while Palmer headed for the truck. He got five yards before the shot rang out and he heard the scream of pain.

He swiveled to see Littlefield lying next to the prisoner, clutching his thigh as a crimson stain grew between his fingers, his hand outstretched in a plea for help.

Palmer ignored his cries and ducked behind a flatbed trailer as another round came in, missing his head by a whisker as it ricocheted off the vehicle's frame.

What the hell was happening?

It wasn't local police, he knew that much. They'd have swarmed the place by now. Everything pointed towards it being just one person with a rifle.

He got down on his knee and peered between the trailer's wheels, looking for the shooter.

There!

A flash gave away the gunman's position in the adjacent lot, and he knew his own weapons would be useless at this range. A glance around told him there wasn't enough cover for him to get closer, so he would have to draw the man in.

'Sean!' he shouted as loud as he could. 'Throw me the detonator!'

Littlefield was confused. What the hell was Palmer talking about? With his femoral artery shredded, he'd already lost a couple of pints of blood. Combined with the pain, he was unable to think clearly, and he patted his pockets looking for whatever it was Palmer was asking for.

Dennis Owen had heard the shout, and when he saw the injured man searching his pockets, he knew he had to stop him handing over whatever he was carrying. He took careful aim, looking to incapacitate him rather than end his life. The first shot flew an inch high, the second catching the man in the shoulder.

That was all the time Palmer needed. With the gunman concentrating on Littlefield, he dashed from cover and managed to get behind the cab of the target vehicle just as a volley followed inches behind him.

Owen cursed, knowing he'd fallen for a feint. Throwing the rifle strap over his shoulder, he drew his Beretta and broke cover, sprinting towards the gate. He stopped when he reached the van, scanning the area for signs of movement but seeing only the prostrate figure of Harvey lying next to Littlefield. He made his way over to them at a crouch, his pistol searching in vain for the other target.

He'd seen Harvey disappear behind the van and emerge a minute later, being dragged to his current position. At first glance he saw no wounds, and after removing the pistol from Littlefield's belt he turned Harvey over. Unconscious but breathing, there was a trickle of blood on the back of his head, although it didn't appear life-threatening.

Owen slapped him a couple of times on the face, but all he got in return was a grunt.

'What have you done to him?'

'Gas,' the injured man grimaced.

Littlefield was in bad shape. Owen pulled the man's belt free and applied a tourniquet to his thigh. If the other man was willing to use his friend as bait, he was unlikely to cheerfully hand over his weapons and come quietly, so keeping Littlefield alive was their best chance of getting the information Harvey wanted. In his present state he was unlikely to be a danger to Harvey, but just to be safe Owen yanked on Littlefield's index finger, dislocating it and rendering his good hand useless.

'You can still use it to apply pressure to the wound,' Owen said, 'just don't try anything funny with my friend. If I come back and he's dead, I'll introduce you to some real pain.'

Not waiting around for an answer, he dashed towards the truck. He'd just reached the cab when he heard the clang of the lock being breached and a squeal as the rusty door hinges protested at being opened.

Owen rolled under the truck and saw a pair of legs standing at the back of the vehicle. He took aim as he heard the doors slam shut and squeezed off a shot that grazed the man's trouser material as it flew a few millimetres wide of the mark. The legs suddenly disappeared behind an adjacent truck, and Owen was searching for his next shot when the whole world seemed to come crashing down around him.

The first grenade exploded inside the closed container, shaking the entire vehicle. Dirt and rust from the flatbed's ancient chassis assaulted his eyes, and the deafening noise threatened to burst his eardrums. One of the welds burst at its weakest point, buckling the side wall of the container, and blood quickly began dripping onto the dusty ground.

Screams of terror began emanating from the container when they were cut off by the second explosion, which caught Owen as he struggled for a breath. He coughed as he ingested a cloud of dirt, choking as the fine particles caked his throat. His lungs refused to cooperate, demanding an inward breath while all Owen wanted to do was clear the mess from his airways. It seemed an eternity before he was able to coax in just enough air to get the natural process going again, then heaved as the contents of his passages fought for a way out.

By the time he'd managed a few short breaths and regained a semblance of control, the cries from the container had died down to just a couple of barely perceptible moans.

Owen crawled out from under the truck and lay panting on the ground, staring at the container looming above him. Through the tear in the side he could see the lifeless limbs of a woman, her skin pockmarked with bloody entry wounds.

He staggered to his feet, anger at the senseless murder gripping him like a vice. He'd seen death in the Gulf War, but that was usually soldier on soldier, not premeditated murder. He tucked the Beretta into his waistband, pulled the R4 off his shoulder and turned to give chase.

And found himself staring down the barrel of a pistol.

'You know the drill,' Palmer said, and Owen dropped the rifle and slowly removed the pistol.

'Kick them under the truck.'

Owen swiped at them with his foot, and Palmer ordered him to assume the position, hands outstretched on the side of the truck. He expected a quick frisk but instead felt a prick at the base of his skull, and moments later his legs gave way beneath him. He scrambled for a handhold until his arms also refused to obey his commands, and within a minute he found himself lying on his back, staring up at the glacial face of his assailant.

'You and I are going to have a little chat,' Palmer said.

He picked Owen up and threw him over his shoulder in a fireman's lift and carried him to the van, throwing him in through the open doors. After grabbing a torch and checking that Littlefield was going to make it, he went back to the container to finish the job.

The gas he'd brought along would have been useless if he hadn't already wasted it, given the size of the hole the detonation had created in the side of the container, so he would have to go inside and make sure there were no survivors. He pulled the door open, and the fetid combination of coppery blood and cordite hit him square in the face, but he knew the kill had to be confirmed. He climbed in, his feet fighting for grip on the blood-soaked floor, and as he played the beam of light around, it was soon apparent that the majority were dead from a combination of shrapnel and blast concussion. He heard a faint moan and moved towards it, where he found a heavily pregnant woman cradling her bloodstained stomach.

Palmer stepped over her, ignoring her clutching fingers as he searched for his four targets. He moved the light from face to face until he reached the pile of bodies at the back of the metal box.

Kyle tapped the wheel of the Jeep to the beat of the eighties classics pumping out of the CD player. Over an hour after Owen and

Harvey had taken off, the second truck had left the port, and he'd followed it up the M4 until it switched to the N2, heading towards King Shaka International Airport. As instructed, he'd checked regularly for a tail, but the last set of headlights had disappeared from his mirror a few minutes earlier, and the only vehicle ahead was the Wenban Iveco.

With just fifteen minutes before they reached the junction leading to the cargo terminal, it was a bittersweet moment for Kyle. The prospect of easy money for an evening drive was nice, but a part of him had hoped for something a little more exciting than cruising along at sixty miles an hour listening to Billy Idol.

The track ended and he returned his attention to the road, spotting the headlights gaining ground fast. Kyle watched a blue Mitsubishi Evo with a yellow stripe on the bonnet power past him and draw level with the truck, and his heart skipped a beat as it matched the Iveco's pace for a brief moment. Just when he thought he might be called into action, the Evo driver hit the gas and the powerful car sped ahead, its taillights quickly disappearing in the distance.

Kyle realised his heart rate had jumped by twenty beats per minute, just as it did before combat, heightening the senses and focusing the mind. With the excitement over, he tried to calm himself, skipping a few tracks on the CD until he found a soothing ballad. The clock on the dashboard suggested they would hit the turnoff in just over twelve minutes, after which he would return to the city centre and have a beer in his hotel room before heading back to Johannesburg in the morning. Since he wasn't due back in the office until Wednesday morning, he could have a couple, perhaps in a local bar where he could look for some female company ...

The truck up ahead suddenly slowed as the brake lights came on, and all thoughts of a relaxing evening disappeared in an instant.

He couldn't see any reason for the driver to stop in the middle of nowhere, which told him something wasn't quite right. He flicked off his own headlights and pulled over to the side of the road a couple of hundred yards behind it, navigating his off-road vehicle between two clumps of trees.

Ahead, he saw the driver climb out and walk to the back of the vehicle, then kick the wheels in frustration before digging out a cell phone. Kyle thought about going to offer help, but realised it wouldn't be the same as changing the wheel on his own vehicle. All he could do was keep the Iveco in sight and wait for the tow truck to arrive.

He debated whether or not to call it in, but in truth there wasn't much to report, and he knew Owen and Harvey would probably have their hands full following the real target.

He decided to wait until either the Iveco was repaired and reached its destination or Owen called him to end the mission. One thing he couldn't wait for was the growing pressure in his bladder, so he climbed out of the Jeep to relieve himself in the bushes. He glanced up and down the road as the plants got a watering, and as the moon emerged from behind a cloud, he saw something glint in the road about fifty yards ahead of him.

Kyle zipped himself up and went to take a look, staying in the shadows as he advanced. In the road he saw a triangular tube around six feet long with metal spikes protruding from every side. He instantly recognised the stop-stick used by American law enforcement agencies to halt car chases. Each spike was a hollow metal tube which embedded itself in the tyre, allowing the air to escape slowly without causing a catastrophic blowout.

He was about to step into the carriageway to retrieve it when the sound of an engine drew his attention to the approaching headlights. He ducked back into the trees and watched as a dark-grey van slowed as it neared the truck. A Chinese youth, no more than seventeen, jumped from the passenger seat and picked up the stick, then jogged after the van as it pulled up behind the stricken truck.

Kyle's first thought was that this was preplanned rather than a good Samaritan coming to the truck driver's aid, and this was confirmed when the kid dropped the stop-stick and produced a blade from his waist. The truck driver immediately put his hands up, expecting to have his load stolen, but the boy continued to close on him. The driver backed away, sensing that he was involved in more than a simple hijacking, but as he backed into the rear of the truck, the boy plunged the knife into his stomach.

Kyle watched the man fall to the ground, but the assault wasn't over. He watched the youth strike again and again, hitting the man in the back and head. A shout from the driver of the grey van halted the attack, and the youth wiped his blade on the dead driver's shirt before dragging him into the undergrowth.

Another man had appeared from the van's cab and approached the driver at the rear of the truck. The youth joined them and got a rollicking in Cantonese from the elder of the trio. Kyle had no idea what was being said, but when the boy removed his T-shirt, it was obvious that the bloodstains hadn't been part of the plan. The chastised teenager was banished to the van while the other two began opening the container.

Kyle had his Glock 9mm in his right hand while he thumbed through the contact list on his phone. He selected Owen's number and held it close to his ear, but after five rings it went to voicemail.

'Shit!'

Until he knew for certain that this wasn't just a violent robbery, all he could do was watch.

Tom Gray screamed as the pain shot up his leg.

'What is it?' Vick asked, concerned.

'Cramp!' he said, gritting his teeth. He tried pointing his toes to get rid of it, but as soon as his foot went back to its normal position, the pain returned.

'Welcome to the annual meeting of the agoraphobic society,' Sonny deadpanned, but no one was in the mood for laughing.

'At least it smells a bit better in here,' Vick said, massaging Gray's calf as best she could.

It was an improvement, but not much. Two weeks of rudimentary bathing facilities and a shortage of shampoo meant her odour was worse now than it had been during her time in the jungle, and the others weren't exactly smelling of roses.

'I'd have happily put up with the stench for a few more hours if it meant I could lie down properly,' Gray moaned.

'If you ask me, those guys are going overland, which is why we got transferred into this shoebox.'

Gray knew Len was right. The cramped air-cargo container wasn't the ideal way to travel, but it beat another three weeks in the stinking box they'd called home for the past fortnight. According to the research he'd done before setting off from Port Kelang, he expected them to spend a couple of hours on the road, an hour or so in the airport and then a further ten to twelve in the air. After that, it would be around three days overland before they hit the ferry to Dover, and he hoped the final leg of the journey would be in more luxurious conditions.

Once they reached the UK, however, their problems wouldn't be over. He still had to deal with Farrar, and over the last week he'd been formulating a plan that relied on one man's help. Guaranteeing his cooperation wasn't a given, but the countless hours spent deliberating had thrown up no alternatives. With the man on board, it would be easier to sway the other players that would inevitably become embroiled, but if he didn't offer his support, Gray's plan would fall apart at the first hurdle.

'Anyone fancy a game of I Spy?' Baines asked, breaking Gray's train of thought and getting an elbow in the ribs from Vick for yet another poor attempt at humour.

'Can it, Sonny,' she said. 'Or stow it, or whatever it is you guys do.' Her lexicon had grown in the last month to include words such as 'tabbing' and 'jankers,' but she still couldn't keep up when the men were in full flow. One thing she had learned was the camaraderie that existed between them. They might be boastful when recounting their adventures together, and often disparaging towards each other, but their stories always hinted at an altruistic bond not found in other walks of life.

She went back to her daydream, picturing herself taking a long, hot shower in a luxury London hotel, followed by a head-to-toe massage accompanied by a few glasses of champagne. She was just about to slip beneath the satin sheets when the truck juddered and slowed to a halt, shattering her illusion and casting her back to the present.

'Are we at the airport already?'

'I don't think so,' Gray told her. 'I think we've got a flat.'

'Does that mean we'll miss our plane?'

Gray thought it unlikely that it would wait for four stowaways, but he remained hopeful that Arnold Tang would have contingencies in place. If his success rate was as high as he'd boasted, he would surely have people en route already.

'I'm sure we'll be fine,' he told her.

Minutes passed, and Gray was wondering what the implications would be if they had to wait for the next flight out of the country when he heard the door to the main container opening. Moments later the plastic sheet of the tiny AKE air cargo container was unfastened and the cardboard box shielding them from view was pulled aside.

A Chinese face appeared, giving the occupants a once-over, his eyes coming to rest on Vick. The beginnings of a smile crawled over his face, revealing yellow, nicotine-stained teeth.

In an instant it was gone.

'Come!' he ordered. 'You come now!'

Gray was the first to crawl out of the tight space, glad of the chance to get his circulation moving once more. The others followed and were shown to the van, the rear doors held open so that they could climb in.

'See? Told you we'd soon be on our way,' he grinned at Vick as he made himself comfortable on the bare floor. Vick snuggled up next to him, while Len pulled out his Kindle and Sonny sat with his back to the cab.

'Ooh, you're bleeding,' Vick said, pointing to Sonny's feet.

He looked at the soles of his shoes and saw fresh, red patches near the heels. He gave himself the once-over but found no sign of a wound.

'Must have stepped in something when we switched vehicles,' he shrugged. 'Probably road kill.'

The driver pulled away, and within seconds the passengers felt the van turn and bounce across the grassy median, heading towards the centre of the city.

'We're going the wrong way,' Sonny said, and despite the van having no side or rear windows, Gray knew he was right.

'Taking a shortcut?' he offered.

'Maybe they're taking us to another truck,' Vick suggested. 'We can hardly just walk onto a cargo plane.'

It's possible, Gray thought, but he wanted to hear it from the horse's mouth.

'Ask them what's going on,' he said to Sonny.

Baines turned and tapped the elder passenger on the shoulder. 'Where are we going?'

The man blew a cloud of cigarette smoke in Sonny's face and began gesturing out of the front window while rattling off a barrage of Cantonese.

'I don't understand a word you're saying,' Sonny said. The teenager joined in, a malicious grin on his face as he looked Sonny in the eye and added his two cents worth to the conversation. He was silenced by a dig in the ribs from his elder.

Baines shrugged noncommittally and went to sit down next to Smart.

'I think we've got a problem,' he whispered. 'From what little I understood, the kid is looking forward to having his way with Vick before he kills us.'

A look of horror crept over Vick's face, and Gray quickly pulled her head into his chest, just in case her reaction drew any unwanted attention. He kissed her hair and whispered for her to stay calm.

'I'm not going to let anything happen to you,' he promised and threw Baines a stern look.

'I thought you only knew a few Chinese phrases,' Len said quietly.

'I do,' Sonny said. 'I know when someone mentions sex, and I also know when they want to kill me. That kid ticks all the boxes.'

'Even I know that in most languages words have several meanings,' Len said.

Sonny knew the point was valid, but he had an uneasy feeling. 'The old guy was carrying a crowbar,' he pointed out, 'and there was no sign of the truck driver. Surely, they would have got him to open the container instead of breaking the lock off.'

'You think they killed him?' Gray asked.

'It would explain this,' Sonny said, waggling his feet and drawing their attention back to the bloodstains.

Gray considered the options and came up with just two: take the Chinese men on, here, on the road, or wait until they reach their destination and see what happened. If they chose the latter, there was no way of knowing how many people they'd have to face if Sonny had correctly understood the kid's intentions. On the other hand, if Sonny had got his wires crossed, they could end up blowing their only chance of getting home.

With every passing second they were motoring towards option one, and Gray knew they'd have to make a decision. He asked his friends for their thoughts, and not for the first time, they were in agreement.

'It's your call, Sonny,' Gray said.

'I know what I heard,' Baines said flatly, and the others nodded. Each of them looked around for a weapon, but the van was sterile. They were going to have to use their bare hands, but there wasn't enough room behind the seats for them to effectively tackle the Chinese one-on-one.

'I'll take the kid and the one on the right,' Len said. 'Tom, you take the driver.'

'Aren't we forgetting someone?' Gray asked, gesturing towards Vick. 'It'll be dicey while we're moving. Let's see if we can get them to stop first.'

The others agreed, and Gray asked Vick to pretend she needed a rest stop. As it wasn't the hardest acting job in the world, she squeezed her knees together and put on a pained expression.

Gray tapped the kid on the shoulder and nodded towards her. 'The lady needs to go to the toilet. Can we pull over?'

The teenager spoke quickly to the older man and got a bark in reply. He looked at Gray. 'You wait. Go soon.'

'She can't wait. She's gonna piss all over your nice clean floor.'

The youth ignored him, turning his attention back to the front window. Gray sat back down next to Vick and explained that things might get a little bumpy. The van had a series of webbing restraint straps down each side, and Gray told her to grab one and hold on with all her might. He saw the look of apprehension but assured her it was going to be okay.

Still uncertain, Vick clutched the nearest strap as tight as she could and nodded. Gray gave her a smile and kissed the top of her head, then knelt behind the driver. Smart got down on one knee, two feet to his right.

The youth felt their presence and was turning around to decline what he thought was another toilet break request when Smart cupped his hands around the elder's forehead and pulled down and back sharply. The crack was clearly audible over the roar of the diesel engine and the man fell forward, his body held in place by the seatbelt, head hanging at an unnatural angle.

Smart turned his attention to the kid, anticipating another easy kill, but the youth recovered quickly from the shock of the initial assault. As he wasn't wearing a seatbelt, he was able to swivel and face Smart, eluding his grasp and pulling his knife from the sheath on his belt.

Gray had his man in a headlock and was shouting for him to pull over, but the driver ignored the order and yanked the wheel to the right, trying to unbalance Gray. All he succeeded in doing was to throw the teenager off balance, and instead of the blade driving through Smart's throat, it glanced the side of his neck, drawing blood but doing no serious damage. Smart pulled back, wary of the knife, and the kid turned his attention to helping the driver.

Switching the knife to an overhand grip, he brought it down hard, aiming for Gray's head. Tom saw it coming and jerked away from the blade but not far enough to prevent it slicing through his upper arm. Blood gushed from the wound, but he didn't even have time to register pain before the knife came flashing down again. Gray jerked the driver backwards and the van jerked violently to the right once more, throwing the youngster off balance. He fell into the driver, the strike missing everyone and deflecting off the side window. He was righting himself when the van bounced onto the median and he was thrown up against the roof of the van before collapsing in the foot well.

Smart came to Gray's help, delivering a powerful punch that took the last of the fight out of the driver. He went limp and Gray let him go, reaching over him to grab the wheel. He had one hand on it when they hit a huge rut and the wheel tore from his hand. He was thrown upwards, slamming into the roof before collapsing in a heap next to Vick. The van rolled, throwing the occupants about like socks in a tumble dryer as it spun across the grass before ending up on its side.

They untangled themselves and took stock. Vick had a cut on her cheek and a sprained ankle where someone had landed on her. Smart and Baines had minor scratches and a few bruises, but Gray was worst hit. Blood poured from the wound on his arm and he was lying motionless near the back doors, which had torn open during the crash.

Smart went to tend to him, checking for and finding a faint pulse, and he tore Tom's T-shirt and used it to create a tourniquet.

Vick cradled Tom's head. Tears were streaming down her face, partly due to Tom's condition, but ultimately brought on by the ferocity of the brief, chaotic exchange. Her body shook as she fought for control, her breath ragged and laboured. Sonny saw the signs and went to comfort her, trying to calm her down before she went into shock.

Behind them, in the cab, the youth wiped the blood from his face. A three-inch gash in his forehead leaked crimson into his eyes, but his focus was on the four *gweilo*. There was no thought of running, taking flight so that he could live to fight another day, despite being outnumbered. Instead, he weighed up the opposition and decided that the larger man was the more dangerous. He would die first, followed by the little fair-haired one and then the female. He wouldn't get his few moments of fun with the woman, but he'd complete the task the team had been assigned and his stock would rise as a result.

He got quietly to his feet, knife in hand, and took two silent steps towards Smart. Vick caught the movement from the corner of her eye but the warning shout stuck in her throat as she froze in terror. The knife hand came up as Baines saw the look on her face, and he snapped his head round as the teenager took a final step to get within range of Smart's back. Sonny thrust a leg out at the side of the boy's kneecap and the snap of bone and cruciate ligament resounded through the vehicle. The teenager collapsed, dropping the knife as he fell. Sonny grabbed it and knelt on the adolescent's arm and stomach, clamping his hand over the kid's mouth.

Taking prisoners was out of the question, and there was no way they could simply let the Chinese kid go. Sonny looked behind him and saw that Vick and Len were watching him.

'Look away, Vick,' he said, and Smart shielded her while Sonny administered the *coup de grâce*, plunging the knife into the boy's heart and twisting. When the life finally drained from the young killer's eyes, Sonny withdrew the knife and wiped it clean before putting it in his inside pocket.

'We're getting lazy,' he said to Smart. 'We should have made sure they were all dead before we did anything.'

Smart agreed, and it struck Vick just how little she knew these men. She'd listened to their tales over the last couple of weeks, how they'd fought their way out of seemingly countless situations—and taken a Thai brothel apart with their bare hands in one of their less sober moments—but the stories didn't convey the ease with which they could take another human life. Those stories had seemed so ... detached from reality, as if she'd been watching a movie or reading a book. Sonny, who she'd thought of as a loveable rogue, had just turned dispassionate killer in front of her eyes and ...

Her thoughts were interrupted by the sight of the armed figure standing near the twisted back doors. Smart followed her gaze, and when he saw the Chinese features, his shoulders sagged.

Kyle Ackerman had watched the four people climb down from the truck and pile into the van, and was surprised to see a woman amongst their number. Regardless, he knew these had to be the people Owen and Harvey were looking for, and he reached for his phone, stabbing the preset number. The van took off across the median, heading back the way it had come, and by the time he got to the Jeep, he saw the distinctive Evo pass by in pursuit.

It must have been a team effort, with the Mitsubishi setting the trap and the van picking up the pieces.

He climbed into his own vehicle and backed out onto the tarmac, then crossed over into the southbound lane. He was about to turn the headlights on, then thought better of it. He could see the taillights of the vehicles ahead and there was no point announcing his presence, especially with so little traffic on the road.

He followed for three or four miles, constantly hitting the 'Redial' button on his mobile but getting no further than the electronic voice asking him to leave a message. He'd done so once, and that was enough.

Without warning, the van veered into the right-hand lane before correcting itself, and Ackerman knew something was amiss. He toyed with the idea of pulling them over, but he had no idea if they were armed beyond the teenager's knife, and he was outnumbered at least five to one if he included the two in the Mitsubishi.

He was trying the mobile for the umpteenth time when the van skewed to the side once more and bounced onto the grass. He watched it nosedive before bouncing onto its side and rolling half a dozen times.

Ackerman pulled up against the side of the road as the van settled on its side. His first instinct was to get out and go to their aid, but then he remembered the Evo. It had stopped in the inside lane, and he saw one of the occupants get out, drawing a weapon and approaching the wreckage.

He pulled out the Glock but knew it would be useless at this distance, and going on foot was not an option as there was no cover to hide behind if it turned into a gunfight. He was wondering how close he could get in the Jeep before they heard him, when an idea struck. It was a downhill run to the van, so he put his vehicle in first and gently popped the clutch. It rolled forwards, and once he'd built up enough momentum he selected neutral and turned the engine off, coasting towards the Evo. At the last moment he tugged the wheel to the right until he was on a collision course with the van.

The driver of the Mitsubishi saw him and leaned out of the window, shouting a warning to his accomplice. The gunman heard the shout but didn't understand the message, and he shouted back over his shoulder for the driver to repeat it while keeping his eyes on the *gweilo*.

It was the right thing to do if he didn't want to get jumped from the front, but it still cost him his life.

At the last moment he caught sight of the Jeep barrelling towards him, but there was little time to react. Instinctively, he turned and aimed the gun at the windshield, getting off a single, wayward round that flew harmlessly high. Ackerman ploughed into him at just short of thirty miles an hour and the man disappeared beneath the front of the wheels, his body mangled as the combination of ground and undercarriage chewed him up and spat him out the back.

Kyle applied the handbrake and jumped out. He fired off three quick shots at the Mitsubishi and the driver got the message, hitting the gas and speeding off into the night.

With the immediate area clear, he checked inside the van, gun up and ready for any surprises.

There were none, apart from the amount of carnage. Three bodies were quite clearly dead, and one wasn't looking too clever. The three walking wounded regarded him dolefully, as if at the end of their tether.

'You guys okay?' Kyle said, focusing on the lady.

Smart was relieved to hear an English voice, but the questions began piling up in his head. What was he doing here? How did he know they would be in the van? Who was he working for?

'Depends who's asking,' he said.

'I work for the government,' Kyle told him. He lowered the gun and looked at Gray. 'How's he doing?'

'He's out cold and his arm needs attention.'

Kyle disappeared and returned moments later, carrying a first aid kit. He began to open it, but Sonny stopped him.

'We need to get out of here,' he said. 'Let's load him into your car and get as far away from here as possible.'

Smart liked the plan, and they carefully carried Gray to the Jeep before Ackerman could have his say. Sonny climbed in the back seat and pulled Tom in, then Smart joined him and they rested their friend on their laps.

Vick got in the front passenger seat and fastened her seat belt.

'I'm Kyle,' Ackerman said, and the others introduced themselves.

'Who's your friend?'

'That's Tom,' Vick said.

'It's Sam,' Sonny corrected her.

Ackerman looked in the mirror quizzically.

'It's complicated,' Smart told him as he extracted a bandage from the first aid box and began tending to the wound on Gray's arm.

Ackerman shrugged. Their names didn't concern him, but the lack of contact with Owen and Harvey did. If he'd found the people they were looking for, and the bad guys were dead, what in God's name had happened to them?

Gray gave a moan and opened his eyes tentatively.

'How're you feeling?' Sonny asked.

'Like I was run over by a train,' Gray said, trying to focus. 'Where are we?'

'We're heading towards…hey, Kyle, where exactly are we going?'

'I'm going to drop you off at the hospital; then I have to go and help my friends. They went after the other truck, and I think they're in trouble. They're not answering the phone.'

'Who is this guy?' Gray asked, his head still groggy.

Sonny filled him in on what had happened while he was out cold, and asked Kyle to give them the bigger picture.

'Dennis Owen asked me to provide backup for his operation. He and Andrew had intelligence that you four would be on the cargo ship and that someone had been sent to intercept and kill you. They didn't know which container you were in, so they followed the largest one, and I was asked to follow the truck you were in.'

'Who's Dennis Owen?'

Ackerman explained that Owen was his boss at the Trade and Investment Department, and what their real role entailed.

'What's Andrew's story?' Sonny asked.

'He's based in England,' Kyle said. 'Five would be my guess.'

Gray was still trying to clear his head, but the mention of MI5 suddenly brought clarity. He sat bolt upright.

'Are you talking about Andrew Harvey?' he asked.

'That's right,' Ackerman told him. 'You know him?'

Gray didn't answer. He was too busy trying to digest the news. Andrew Harvey, in Durban? Someone sent to kill them? A Chinese kill team?

He needed answers, and only one man could provide them. 'Forget the hospital—we need to find Andrew.'

'Are you sure?' Ackerman asked. 'That wound looks pretty nasty.'

'I'll live,' Gray said. 'Where is Andrew now?'

'They were following the other container to the depot. I expect they'll be there or thereabouts.'

'Then that's where we go.'

After double-checking every corpse, Ben Palmer knew he'd followed the wrong container. He whipped out his camera and thumbed through the images he'd taken on his last visit until he found the itinerary for the other truck. It had been due to leave the port an hour after the first, which meant it would be en route right about now.

Catching it up shouldn't be a problem, but having been surprised by the two men who'd jumped him, he was beginning to have doubts about the whole mission.

Another glance at the itinerary told him the other container was going to the airport, and if it boarded a plane, he could lose it forever. Carl Gordon might be able to get into the airport servers and follow the trail, but he would only pursue that once he'd finished with his interrogations.

Palmer moved to the container doors, stepping over the pregnant woman who once again cried for his help. He ignored her pleas, climbing down and closing the container door. His first stop was the office, where he kicked in the door and found the CCTV equipment. He extracted the VHS tape from the machine and took it back to the van, where he found Owen unconscious.

He realised the gas hadn't fully dispersed, which meant using the van was out of the question. He knew his attackers must have come in their own vehicle, but with both out cold, he could hardly ask them where it was.

Palmer went over to where Littlefield was lying next to the unconscious man. Sean was fading fast, the blood still seeping from his wounds despite the tourniquet. There wasn't a lot Palmer could do for him, but he didn't say as much.

'I'm going to find their car and get you to a hospital,' he lied. He would take Littlefield from the scene, but only so the connection between the two men couldn't be established. If Sean's body were found, one of the first things they would do was a forensic sweep of his farm, a building riddled with Palmer's fingerprints. Although he religiously wore surgical gloves on every mission, he hadn't used them during his recent visit.

He moved over to the motionless figure and slapped him on the face.

Nothing.

He tried harder and this time got a reaction, a moan and shake of the head. Palmer glanced around, looking for some water to splash on the man's face, then remembered the coffee pot in the office. He got up to fetch it just as the headlights appeared on the road a few hundred yards away.

It wasn't a well-travelled road, just a spur off the highway that led to the industrial units and beyond that a small village a mile or so further on. Palmer had to make a decision, and he erred on the side of caution, sprinting back to the truck, where he found the R4 rifle. A quick check revealed an almost full clip, and he carried it back to the front of the rig, staying in the shadows, with a clear view of the main gate.

The vehicle cruised past at barely fifteen miles an hour. That in itself meant nothing, Palmer knew. It could be locals being cautious after a few too many beers, or one of the many gangs casing the area for something to steal.

As the vehicle neared, Palmer could make out the driver and a female passenger, though he couldn't tell if there was anyone in the rear, as the windows were tinted. The driver didn't seem to be paying the compound any attention, his focus on the blonde sitting next to him.

The Jeep continued down the road until the lights disappeared around the corner, and the sound of the engine eventually faded.

Palmer waited a few moments. Once he was satisfied that it had been a false alarm, he ran back to the office and grabbed the coffee pot, which he emptied out and filled with water from the cooler. He took it back into the yard and poured half of it over the supine figure's face, shaking the man from his deep slumber.

Harvey shook his head, which felt heavy, turgid. He opened his eyes, but they refused to focus, the world a blur of dark shapes and flitting movement. A dark shadow moved over him and morphed into the shape of a human head.

'Where's your car?'

Harvey fought for clarity, but it was a long time coming.

'Where is it?' the voice repeated.

'I ... er ...'

Palmer gave him another slap, gentler, just enough to get the man to focus. He squatted next to him, the rifle on the floor replaced by his silenced pistol, which dug into Harvey's ribs.

'I haven't got all night,' Palmer said calmly. 'Tell me where your vehicle is, or lose a kneecap.'

He moved the gun to Harvey's knee and began the countdown, while Harvey frantically tried to get his bearings. Palmer reached four when Harvey raised his hand and pointed towards the gate.

'It's behind that building,' he said, his voice sounding alien in his own ears.

Palmer grabbed Harvey's collar and dragged him to his feet, pushing him towards the main road. Bending down to retrieve the rifle, he spotted movement from the corner of his eye, in the direction the Jeep had disappeared. He walked nonchalantly behind the van, then got down to see if he could see anything out of the ordinary.

He saw nothing apart from a few bushes swaying in the breeze, but to be on the safe side he let off a couple of three-round bursts.

There was no return fire and no screams, and Palmer chastised himself for jumping at shadows. He got back to his feet and walked around the van in time to see Harvey stumbling towards the main gate, his legs barely obeying his commands.

Palmer realised this one could be trouble once he fully recovered from the effects of the gas, and decided he could get the information he needed from the one who was still in the van. He raised the rifle and fired a round an inch above Harvey's head, causing him to stop in his tracks.

'Just give me the keys,' he said, and Harvey patted his pockets in a vain attempt to find them. It took a few seconds for him to realise he didn't have them. He explained this to Palmer, who responded by raising the rifle.

'Drop it!'

The voice came from Palmer's right, and he moved his head to see the slight figure advancing towards him, a Glock held in a double-handed grip.

'Looks like we've got ourselves a standoff,' he smiled, keeping the R4 pointing at Harvey's lower back. 'Aren't you a bit young to be out so late?'

'One last chance,' the newcomer said, continuing to close on his target.

'That's far enough, sonny. Stand down—'

The first bullet tore through Palmer's skull, the second, redundant round hitting an inch lower. He collapsed in a heap, and

Baines held the gun on the corpse until he was close enough to confirm the kill.

'Only my friends call me Sonny,' he said and then turned to check that Harvey was okay. He seemed a little confused, almost as if he were drunk, and Baines told him to take a seat on the ground.

'How many more?' he asked, but Harvey was still catching up on events, his brain having difficulty maintaining a normal pace. Baines gave up and signaled Smart to join him, indicating that he should use the rifle to help clear the area.

A minute later, two others helped Harvey to his feet. One he didn't recognise, but the other was strikingly familiar.

'Sam?' he asked quizzically. 'Sam Grant?'

'Hello, Andrew,' Gray smiled.

'You know me?'

Explanations were put on hold as Baines and Smart returned with news of the carnage at the rear of the compound.

'We also found someone in the van,' Sonny told them. 'He's out for the moment, but no sign of injuries.'

Harvey started towards the Mercedes, and Gray offered him a shoulder. They got to the rear doors and saw Owen lying on his back.

'We'd better get out of here,' Sonny said, and Gray agreed. He asked Harvey where their car was, and it took a few moments for him to clear his head and pass on the information. Smart grabbed the keys from Owen's pocket and trotted off, while Kyle and Sonny pulled Owen from the van and laid him on the floor.

'We need to know who this guy is,' Harvey said, pointing to Palmer's corpse.

Kyle checked the man's pockets and came out with a wallet, then pulled out his phone and took snaps from several angles.

'Do you need fingerprints?' he asked, but Harvey decided that what they had was enough.

When Smart returned with the BMW, they loaded Owen and Harvey inside, then drove down the road to where Vick was waiting in the Jeep, while the others made their way back on foot.

'Where do we go from here?' Sonny asked once they'd all assembled.

'We've got passports for you and Len in Pretoria,' Harvey said, beginning to get his head together. 'We also have one ready and waiting for Sam, though we need a new photo. We didn't know who the fourth person would be, but it won't take long to knock one up.'

Gray introduced Vick, and it took Harvey a few moments to realise that Vick was the Victoria Phillips he'd been asking questions about a week earlier.

'How on earth did you end up with these three?' Harvey asked, and Vick told him that it was a long story.

'That's fine,' Harvey said. 'It's also a long drive back to Pretoria.'

They split themselves between the vehicles, with Len driving the BMW carrying Vick, Tom and Andrew, and the rest taking the lead in the Jeep.

Harvey turned to Gray once they'd set off. 'And the mysterious Sam Grant, the complete stranger who seems to know me. What's your story?'

Even as he asked the question, his attention was drawn to Gray's eyes, and when the penny dropped, he couldn't believe what he'd stumbled upon.

'Tom? But you're ...'

'He gets that a lot,' Len said before Vick could get the words out.

'I was actually coming to look for you,' Gray told him, 'but as you're here, how about I tell you our story, and you decide if you're willing to help us?'

'Just leave it!'

Uddin grabbed the bag containing the family ornaments and hurled it onto the bed. 'We can only take the bare essentials,' he told his wife, Fatima. Their luggage already exceeded the baggage allowance for the flight, and there simply wasn't room for sentimentality at the moment.

'But why do we have to leave?' she asked yet again.

Fatima had been preparing the evening meal when her husband had arrived home agitated and broke the news that they would be taking a flight later that night. When asked how long they would be away, he'd told her that it would be a one-way trip. Her subsequent protestations had been met with anger, and she went about the task of packing with a sense of dread. She knew her husband's work was shrouded in secrecy, and his behaviour told her this had something to do with the laboratory.

'I was given instructions and I ... disobeyed them,' he told her.

Fatima knew Munawar was an honourable man, so whatever order he had refused must have been in stark contrast with his principles.

'Surely, the pharmaceutical company will understand,' she said, but the look she received told her this was something more than a squabble with a supervisor.

The steps he'd taken had, he'd told himself, been for the greater good of mankind, but he knew that the driving force behind his decision had been the welfare of his family. Having driven them into hiding, the least he could do was explain why.

'The laboratory I work for doesn't make cold remedies,' he said, sitting her down on the bed. He explained who his ultimate boss was and the kind of product he was tasked with manufacturing.

'The virus they asked me to make was almost ready when a newcomer changed everything. He told me Al-Asiri had changed his mind about the agent to be delivered, but on reflection it didn't seem probable. It was the leader's pet project, and when we met he seemed more than happy with my projections, yet this Mansour was determined to use another, more virulent strain.

'The only one we had was too unstable, with no cure. If it were released before we had a means to control it, ninety per cent of the world's population would be annihilated within months. Only the most remote regions of the planet would escape.'

'So you refused to give it to him?' his wife asked.

'Whether I gave it to him or my replacement does, it makes no difference,' Uddin told her. 'What is important is that he not be allowed to use it.'

The look Uddin gave her suggested there was more to come, and when he eventually told her the rest of the story, Fatima knew there was no way they could ever return to their homeland.

Chapter Thirteen

Tuesday, 8 May 2012

Tom sat across the desk from Veronica Ellis and laid out the plan, just as he'd explained it to Harvey during their journey from Durban back to the UK.

They'd made a brief stop at the Durban office, where a doctor took a look at Gray's arm and declared him fit to fly. He'd also given the others a once-over and found no lasting damage. After Tom and Vick had their passport photos taken and emailed to the Johannesburg office, they had driven north to collect their diplomatic passports and airline tickets. During the journey, Tom had given Harvey a full rundown of the last four weeks, starting with Farrar's unannounced visit to his Manila home and culminating in their two-week no-frills cruise.

Harvey had reciprocated, giving his account of their successful effort to locate Campbell and Levine before Farrar could dispose of them. Gray had been concerned about his friends' conditions, but Harvey assured him that both men were responding well at a private clinic, and the women were bearing up.

The conversation had turned to Farrar, and Tom had shared the plan he'd been working on for the last fortnight. After Harvey explained that all the evidence they had was circumstantial backed up with hearsay, they'd agreed that Tom's idea was the only way to make Farrar accountable for his actions.

Ellis had been as shocked as anyone when she'd learned that Tom Gray was still alive, and what had started out as a bid to bring Farrar to task had escalated to the point where it could bring down an entire government. There was no way she could have foreseen this a fortnight earlier, and the decision to help Gray hadn't been an easy one to make.

It had been a battle of conscience over pragmatism. When this broke, any trust the people had in parliament would be destroyed. The home secretary would certainly be the first to fall, and it might even reach as high as the prime minister himself.

If the current government fell, the opposition wouldn't fare much better. It was they who had made the decision to lie to the world, spiriting Gray away and ordering his subsequent death. That left the fringe parties, none of whom were—in her opinion—capable of running the country.

That said, it was either leave the country in political turmoil or allow them to continue their dark practices and execute citizens at will, and that simplification had made the decision a lot easier.

Ellis smiled when Tom wrapped up. She liked the way he thought, and given the planning that had gone into his last escapade, she had every confidence in him pulling this one off.

Farsi handed Tom a piece of paper. 'Here's the number you asked for,' he said as he left the room.

Gray nodded towards Ellis's desk phone. 'May I?'

'Be my guest,' she smiled.

Gray dialled the number and asked for Paul Gross. When asked who was calling, he said, 'Just tell him it's Icarus.'

It took a minute before he was put through, and the voice that came on the line sounded curious. 'Hello?'

'Hi, Paul. Remember me? It's Tom Gray.'

'I'm sorry, I haven't got time for pranks,' Gross said.

'Would it help if I said I once sent an email to your personal email account, and that I threatened to take the story to a rival channel when you pestered me to go on the air?'

There was silence for a while as Gross recalled the incidents. 'Suppose I believe you. What do you want from me?'

Gray gave him a condensed version of the events of the last year and explained what he wanted from the producer of the BBC news channel.

'That's a great story, Tom, but what you're asking is far too risky. Besides, I have a DA order which prevents me featuring any story about you still being alive.'

'Doesn't it feel a little strange that the government doesn't want you to let people know I survived the explosion last year? What possible motive could they have?'

Gross was silent again as he considered the question. Ellis looked at Gray and offered to take over the conversation, but he shook his head, confident he could wear the man down.

'You make a compelling case, Tom, but the DA-Notice—'

'Is an advisory notice, or so I've been informed. If you ignore one, you cannot be prosecuted.'

'Perhaps not,' Gross agreed, 'but it could be career defining.'

Gray wasn't convinced. 'Only if your superiors came out and said they disagreed with your actions. The director general would have to go on record as saying the BBC fully supports the government's practice of killing innocent civilians.'

Both men knew it would never happen, but Gross still needed more.

'What if I do as you ask, but there's no confession?'

Gray once more explained the plan, and while not as confident as Ellis had been, Gross did think it workable.

'When is this going to happen?' he asked.

'Tomorrow,' Gray told him. 'There are a few technical aspects to work out, so you'll be getting a call from someone called Gerald Small in a few minutes.'

He thanked the producer and hung up. 'Can I tag along with Gerald?' he asked Ellis. 'I'd like to try out the equipment once it's in place.'

'Sure,' she said. 'Andrew can take you—'

Hamad Farsi knocked on the door and walked in without waiting for an invitation. 'Something you should take a look at,' he said, handing a file to his boss. She read quickly, her expression giving nothing away, before she put the papers down and turned to Gray.

'Sorry, Tom, but you'll have to excuse us,' she said, holding up the file. 'Business as usual.' She showed Gray to Small's office, then led Harvey and Farsi to the conference room and asked when the news had come in.

'Just a couple of minutes ago,' Hamad said.

Ellis read it through again, this time aloud for Harvey's benefit.

'Abdul Mansour will be travelling to England via Heathrow Airport in the next few days with the intention of releasing a malevolent variant of the Ebola virus. His target has biological defences against an external attack, and he is hoping to use this to contain the virus within the building itself. There is currently no known cure for this particular variant.'

'Short and sweet,' Harvey noted. 'Origin?'

'The British High Commission in Islamabad. A kid delivered it along with those images.'

Ellis looked through them but couldn't make head nor tail of the information. It appeared that someone had taken pictures of documents explaining the genetic make-up of the virus, through the hieroglyphs meant nothing to her.

'Is anyone verifying this?' she asked Hamad, who told her that copies were on their way to the Health Protection Agency.

Small knocked and entered the room, explaining that he'd spoken to the BBC technical controller, and there would be no problems setting up for the next morning.

'Thanks, Gerald,' she said. To Hamad: 'The facial recognition at Heathrow should pick him up when he tries to get through immigration. Check through the logs to see if there are any near hits.'

'Yeah, right,' Small murmured, catching Ellis's attention.

'Something wrong with my instructions, Gerald?' she asked, wearing her most indignant face.

'No, it's just ...'

Ellis urged him to continue, knowing how little he thought of the technology.

'If I was to go through immigration wearing the most basic theatrical prosthetic, such as a fake nose, it would throw the system off by at least forty per cent.'

'Possibly,' Hamad agreed, 'but make-up would easily be spotted by the border guard. Besides, you said yourself that it was the eyes that gave the biggest indicator.'

'Exactly, and eyes can be covered up with glasses, eye patches, veils, anything that you would see if you walk down any high street. These things don't raise suspicion and can easily be overlooked.

'Check the logs by all means, but I'm just saying, don't be too reliant on them.'

Ellis thanked him for his input, and Gerald left them to discuss the latest events.

'Bear that in mind,' Ellis told Hamad. 'I want people watching all of his old haunts, plus a team at Heathrow in case he hasn't arrived yet. Also, get onto every informer we have and see what they've heard.'

She turned to Harvey. 'Dig around and see which buildings have the bio-defence mentioned in the note. There can't be that many, but start with high-profile targets.'

'The US Embassy has one,' Harvey told her. 'Perhaps we should give them the heads-up.'

Ellis nodded. 'I'll let them know,' she said, standing and tacitly ending the meeting. 'Hopefully, they'll share any chatter they've had in the last forty-eight hours.'

They split up to take care of their respective tasks, with Harvey doing a search for bio-defence installations over the last fifty years. The list that came back was not substantial, but it did include some high-profile targets. He was prioritising them when Ellis came over to their desks, her face like thunder.

'Cancel the Heathrow team,' she told Hamad. 'He's already here.'

'We've got him?' Harvey asked, but her look told him otherwise.

'It seems our American friends have a new policy: you scratch our backs, we'll piss on your chips and call it vinegar.'

Both men were confused but let her continue in her own time. 'It seems they received a card handwritten by Mansour himself, delivered to their embassy this morning. Fingerprints confirm it was handled by him, and ink analysis shows it was written only a few hours earlier.'

'Did they tell you what the message said?'

'They told me they couldn't share that information until they'd followed up on it, but we'd hear about it soon enough.'

Farsi was suitably unimpressed. 'They know that the world's most wanted man is in the UK, but they don't feel the need to share that with us? That's bullshit.'

Ellis agreed. 'Andrew, you know someone over there who can speak off the record. Any chance they'd know anything about this?'

'I can try,' Harvey said. 'What did they make of the news you gave them?'

'I didn't tell them,' she said. 'I got as far as saying Mansour was on his way when they dropped their bomb. If that's the game they want to play, they'll find it works both ways.'

It made sense to Harvey, at least from a bargaining point of view. He pulled out his mobile and moved to a quiet corner of the office. Doug Wallis answered on the second ring.

'Andrew, how's things?'

'I'm good, Doug. Can you make lunch today?'

Wallis sensed the urgency in his voice and agreed to meet up within the hour. Harvey thanked him and hung up, then told Ellis about the upcoming meeting.

'I don't know how helpful he'll be,' Harvey admitted. 'Our arrangement does have its limits.'

Ellis was glad to hear it. She wanted to press him on the information they'd previously shared, but decided to save that conversation for later.

Harvey printed off the list of possible targets and gave it to Ellis before helping Farsi with his workload. While Hamad went through the list of informers and undercover operatives, he started on the facial recognition logs.

After uploading the most recent image of Mansour and setting it as the search parameter, he waited for the system to go through all entries for the last seventy-two hours. With over ninety-five thousand passengers arriving each day, the system would have to compare the image with well over a quarter of a million faces. Harvey decided to filter the list to disregard planes arriving from the West, which cut the number in half but still left a huge amount to go through. After setting the match threshold to 60 per cent, he hit the 'Search' button and left it running while he went to meet up with Wallis.

He arrived at the sandwich shop five minutes early and ordered an egg and cress baguette to take away. When Doug arrived, he waited until his CIA counterpart chose a bacon, stilton and cranberry on wholemeal before they headed towards the river.

'My boss is a bit pissed with you guys.' Harvey opened the conversation when they found an empty bench. 'She doesn't like the fact that you kept Abdul Mansour's arrival to yourselves.'

'Thought it might have something to do with him,' Wallis said before taking a bite of his sandwich and taking his time chewing it. Harvey realised he was asking a lot from his friend, perhaps even stretching the relationship, but he had to at least try.

'Not really much I can give you, I'm afraid,' Wallis eventually said, to Harvey's obvious disappointment.

'Can you at least pinpoint his arrival time?' Harvey pressed. 'We know how he got in, why he's here, and his probable target. If we knew when he got here we'd have a better chance of tracing him.'

Wallis was taken aback. 'You're kidding, right?'

'Deadly serious, Doug. We even have the genetic make-up of the virus and a good idea of which bio-defence he plans to circumvent, but, as you say, maybe this stuff is above our pay grade.'

He had Wallis's attention. The American looked at his watch and did a quick calculation.

'I suppose it will be on the news soon enough,' he said. 'Mansour gave us the coordinates to Azhar Al-Asiri's current home. We have a drone en route to take him out.'

It was Harvey's turn to be shocked. 'You get a note claiming to be from a known terrorist and you send in the bombers, no questions asked?'

'Don't be facetious, Andy; it doesn't suit you.'

'I'm not trying to be, Doug, but if you'd shared this with us you could have got the whole picture. Doesn't it seem strange that Mansour is handing you Al-Asiri on a plate, and shortly afterwards we're given a tipoff that could help take Mansour out?'

Wallis had to agree that it was too much of a coincidence. 'Can I share that with my people?' he asked, and Harvey said it would be better if it came through official channels. 'Tell your people to contact Ellis and give her everything you have, and she'll share the details we received.'

He could have told Wallis that he'd effectively given him every morsel they had, but in order to get the agencies talking to each other he knew he would have to keep that to himself. It meant jeopardising their friendship as well as their professional relationship, but Harvey knew the time would come when he would have a chance to rebuild that bridge.

They parted company, Wallis dumping his half-eaten sandwich in a bin before walking away with his phone to his ear.

The BBC news channel opened with an announcement that the Bank of England planned to inject another forty billion into the economy in an attempt to kick-start the recovery, but still no reports of an air strike in Quetta.

Mansour wasn't particularly concerned as he knew it would take some time for the US government to sanction the hit on Al-Asiri's home. In his note, he'd said that Al-Qaeda's leader would only be at the location for a short period, hoping that the idea of a forty-eight hour window of opportunity would force their hand.

Apparently not.

The sound of laughter floated upstairs, heralding the return of the men from their morning's testing. He went to join them and found the four of them in the living room, surrounded by their new toys. After a quick greeting he asked how their morning had gone.

'It was fun,' the younger one said, but his levity wasn't well received by Mansour.

'I didn't send you out to have fun,' he said, wiping the smile off the teenager's face. 'Are you able to control them using the phone app?'

'It was tricky at first, but we have the hang of it now,' another said as Mansour picked up one of the remote-controlled helicopters.

The machine was twenty-four inches long and sturdily built, with a purported range of over five hundred yards, but they told him it was only really effective at four hundred.

'After that, it becomes erratic.'

Mansour wasn't concerned. That was more than enough for their purposes.

'How long will it take to fit the attachment?'

They told him it would take less than two hours. 'I want you to go out and test them again with the smoke canisters attached. Let me know if it affects performance.'

The plan was a simple one. The four men would launch the helicopters close to the Palace of Westminster and guide them over the building, where the canisters would release their contents. The yellow smoke would be interpreted as a chemical attack, causing the triggering of the building's defences. Those inside would consider themselves safe from harm, but in fact they would be the only people exposed to his virus.

At the same time as the building was being locked down, he would have his note delivered to the security services, letting them know the fate of those inside.

And what a fine collection they would be. The Queen would be delivering her speech at the State Opening of Parliament, where the prime minister and his entire government would be in attendance.

This single strike would be the greatest victory in Al-Qaeda's history, bigger and bolder than anything the organisation had ever attempted, cementing his reputation for all time. Once Al-Asiri was gone, Mansour would assume control of the organisation, and few would dispute his right to lead the struggle towards ultimate victory.

The only part of the plan remaining was to hand the inhalers to the BBC cameraman who would be filming the event, and Mansour would do that personally the following day.

Chapter Fourteen

Wednesday, 9 May 2012

The sun had barely shown its face when Andrew Harvey reached Thames House and took the stairs up to the office. He expected to be one of the first in, but the place was already a hive of activity as the search for Abdul Mansour continued apace.

He took a seat at his desk and turned on the monitor, then entered his username and password combination to unlock the screen. He saw that the search he'd left running overnight had finished, but the number of matches was low.

Hamad Farsi arrived a few minutes later, armed with coffee and a sandwich.

'Any word from the street?' Harvey asked, but Hamad shook his head.

'No one's heard a thing. I'm beginning to wonder if the note was disinformation, just to get us chasing our own tails.'

'Or to see who we go to for answers,' Harvey offered. 'Maybe they just wanted to see which cages we rattled so that they could spot those who'd infiltrated their operation.'

Hamad agreed that it was possible. 'I thought with the CIA confirming his presence on UK soil it was a certainty, but he could have written that note anywhere in the world and had it flown in by a courier.'

Despite their own misgivings, and until told otherwise, they had to assume the threat was real.

'I've had no luck with the facial recognition. Closest we got was someone four inches shorter than Mansour, and that's not easy to fake.'

Farsi walked round to Andrew's desk and took the mouse off him. He clicked the filter option, selected 0 per cent for an eye match and ran the query against the current set of results. 'Let's see if Gerald's idea pans out. If Mansour really did come through Heathrow, it's likely he used countermeasures to fool the software.'

While the search ran, they pored over the chatter coming through the normal channels, but there was no mention of Mansour or a biological threat. Harvey was about to go and grab a coffee when a notification blinked in his taskbar, and he opened it to see that the search had finished, producing just thirty-one results.

Farsi joined him as he flicked through them, seeing a blind male but discounting him because of his tender age. Another male was wearing sunglasses, but again, he was too short. Harvey came across a woman in a *burqa* and quickly moved on to the next image. One by one he went through the selection until he came to the end.

'Nothing.'

'Go back to the start,' Hamad said, and Harvey went to the first image.

'Okay, flick through them until I say stop.'

Harvey hit the 'Next' button, then again.

'Stop.'

'Hamad, I know you don't get out much, but that's what we in the real world call a "woman".'

Farsi ignored the jibe. 'Got beautiful lips, hasn't she?'

'How can you tell when she's wearing … that … veil.'

Farsi clapped Harvey on the shoulder. 'The boy cottons on fast,' he smiled. 'Send me the arrival time, and I'll follow her through the airport.'

He returned to his desk and brought up the airport security system. He set the date and time to three minutes before the flight arrived and then started to fast forward until the passengers emerged from the gangway. While he watched the target make her way through the terminal, Harvey collated the details of the other veiled women in the search results and sent them to Hamad's screen.

'I'll start at the bottom of the list, you take the top.'

They studied the recordings for two hours before Farsi called Harvey over.

'Check this one out.'

Farsi rewound the footage and they watched the woman walk from the arrival gate through to the immigration area.

'Play it again,' Harvey said, and Farsi obliged.

'Definitely something not right in her gait,' Harvey noted. 'If she gets to immigration and they don't ask her to lift her veil, I'd say we had a hit.'

Farsi fast-forwarded to that point, and both were disappointed to see the woman's companion lift the veil and the border guard study the face, comparing it against the passport.

'Damn!' Farsi said, throwing the mouse across the desk. 'I thought we had him.'

'Me, too.' Harvey stood and checked his watch. 'I have to go and check on our guests. Let me know if you get anything from the other possibilities.'

The resident security officer at the safe house looked at the monitor and recognised Harvey standing at the front door. She hit the door release and went to meet him in the hallway.

'Morning, Andrew.'

He approached the lady and gave her a peck on the cheek. 'Morning, Linda. You're looking gorgeous, as ever.'

The fifty-year-old gave him a coy smile. 'Charmer.'

'How's everyone doing?'

'Fine,' Linda told him. 'Just finished breakfast and they're washing up.'

Harvey thanked her and went through to the kitchen, where he found Vick with her hands in the sink and Gray doing his fair share with the towel.

'Ready for your big performance, Tom?'

'Hi, Andrew,' Gray said, almost dropping the plate he was drying. 'To be honest, I'm crapping myself.'

Harvey laughed, unable to envisage Gray caving in under the pressure. 'I'm sure you'll be fine.'

'I'm surprised it's still on,' Gray said. 'You said yesterday that something big was on the cards. I expected that to take priority.'

'I checked with Ellis on the way over, and she's happy for this to go ahead. We're at a bit of an impasse at the moment.'

Harvey poured himself a coffee. *Impasse is an understatement,* he thought. The CIA had decided it might be prudent to know what information MI5 had received and had suddenly been keen to share all they had on Mansour.

Their discussions had led to the drone being recalled while they figured out what was happening within Al-Qaeda. Until they could get a handle on what was causing the in-fighting, they thought it best to maintain the status quo.

'Any thoughts as to what you'll do once this is over?' Harvey asked Gray.

'First thing is to get my money back,' Gray told him. 'I checked the balance of my PNB account this morning, and it was cleaned out a couple of weeks ago. There was over half a million dollars in there, and Farrar is the only other person with access to it.'

'I'm sure that once the government's involvement in this is established, a suitable compensation package will be arranged.'

Gray shook his head. 'I'm not going to take millions in tax-payer's money. All I want is what's mine, and Farrar to get what's coming to him.'

'I think that last one's a given.' Harvey said, finishing off his drink. 'I'll give you half an hour to get in position. Call me when you're set to go and I'll give Veronica the nod.'

Gray shook his hand. 'Thanks, Andrew, for everything. I know you didn't agree with what we did last year, but ...'

'Yeah, I know,' Harvey said. 'Look, I gotta go. Call me when you're set.'

Farrar was just about to tuck into a chicken Caesar sandwich when his mobile chirped, and he wiped his fingers on a handkerchief before answering it.

'Farrar.'

'Hi, James.'

Farrar immediately lost his appetite, though he tried his best to be pleasant.

'What can I do for you, Veronica?'

'I know the operation is over, James, but we've come across some information that suggests there may have been more to the Levine and Campbell case than first meets the eye.'

'Really?' he asked, trying to remain calm despite the feeling of dread that accompanied every conversation with Ellis. 'What would that be?'

'Something about an agreement they made with the government,' Ellis said, and Farrar almost dropped the phone.

How could she possibly have known about that? Had one of Gray's cronies left instructions with a solicitor to leak the details if they died, or had one or more of them shared their little secret with a third party?

Whatever it was, he would have to nip it in the bud.

'Sounds interesting,' he said. 'What kind of agreement?'

'I can't tell you over the phone,' Ellis replied. 'How about we meet up. Are you free in thirty minutes?'

For this, he would miss his own funeral. 'Sure. We can take a walk along the embankment, just like the old days.'

Ellis agreed and hung up, and Farrar's mind began racing as he considered his next move. Denying any knowledge was a starting point, but Ellis was tenacious, like a terrier with a tennis ball. The first thing he needed to do was find out how much she really knew and how much was speculation. Whatever she brought to the table, he would dismiss it as conspiracy theorists seeking their fifteen minutes of fame and get her to drop it. With Gray and his buddies gone, there would be no one to corroborate any stories, and the DA-Notices he'd sent to the media would ensure the public never got to hear about it.

Coming up with an explanation for the notice was easy: they had intelligence that a group was planning to claim Tom Gray was still alive in the hope of reigniting the debate on judicial process. This group had been threatening vigilante activity, and the government felt it wasn't in the country's best interest to give them the publicity they craved.

He left his office feeling a little apprehensive, but with the i's dotted, he just had to cross this final t to put the matter to rest. When he reached the street, he opened his umbrella and sidestepped a few of the deeper puddles, then made his way to the Albert Embankment. Footfall was sparse, save for the few joggers who braved the elements day in, day out. That suited Farrar perfectly. The fewer people around to eavesdrop on their conversation, the better.

His watch told him he was seven minutes early, and he hoped Ellis would be punctual so that he could get out of the rain and back to his meager lunch. He walked slowly towards Lambeth Bridge, the murky, grey waters of the Thames on his left, the snarling traffic crawling past on his right. Coupled with the awful weather, he found the entire scene depressing and promised to treat himself later in the evening. Perhaps an evening in with a bottle of wine and the intern he'd been seeing on and off for the last two years.

Yes, an evening with Michael would cheer him up.

'Hello, James.'

Farrar spun, but a hand gripped his elbow and urged him onwards.

'Keep walking,' Tom Gray said. 'There's a van ten yards ahead. I want you to get in.'

Farrar planted his feet, his jaw hanging open as he struggled to understand how a dead man could be standing next to him. Palmer had confirmed the kill himself, which meant the assassin had either been compromised, or he'd chosen to switch sides. Had Gray offered him more money not to complete the job?

'How ... ?'

Gray turned to face him. 'Come with me and I'll explain everything.'

Farrar tried to pull away but couldn't escape Gray's grip. 'Don't be stupid, James. You've read our files, so you know what Jeff Campbell can do with a sniper rifle at a thousand yards. Do as you're told, or he'll put a round through the base of your spine, and as you lie screaming on the floor, he'll take out each kneecap and elbow. If you survive, you'll be paying someone to wipe your arse for the rest of your life.'

Campbell was alive, too? The news just got worse and worse, and Farrar was overwhelmed by so many revelations in such a short time. One minute he thought the operation had been wrapped up, and now he discovered that his targets were alive and well, not to mention armed.

Gray could see Farrar was finding it difficult to make a decision, so he pushed him up against the embankment wall and pulled his collar mic up to his mouth. 'Warning shot, please.'

A second later he heard the *thwang* as the 7.62mm round hit the top of the wall an inch away from Farrar's back before ricocheting off into the river.

Farrar got the message and began walking, his mind still straining to come to terms with the situation.

In the car the surprises kept coming. Carl Levine twisted in the driver's seat and smiled with a distinct lack of benevolence.

'Hi, Jimmy. Bet you didn't expect to see me again.'

Farrar ignored him and turned to Gray. 'So what happens now, Tom?' He tried to sound confident, defiant, but his voice dripped fear as the car set off.

'You're going to record your confession and admit everything you've done over the last thirteen months.'

After a moment's thought, Farrar began to relax. With the initial prospect of pain and death banished, his mind began to focus once more. He looked out of the window as the city flashed past, and a smile appeared on his face when he realised that once again he had the upper hand. He would play Gray's game and walk away, if not totally unscathed, then at least with his life intact. It would require some clean-up work and a lot of political spin, but those mechanisms were already available and he would make best use of them.

'What's so funny?' Gray asked.

Farrar looked him in the eye. 'The irony,' he said. 'Here we are, a year on, and you're about to parade yet another hostage in front of the cameras. Not a tactic that's worked well for you in the past.'

Gray ignored him and gave him a quick frisk search, being none too gentle in his approach. Farrar was unarmed, but Gray took his phone, cranked open the window and dropped it into the street.

They drove for another twenty minutes in silence, both men deep in thought.

Levine eventually pulled up at an old industrial estate in the east end, the businesses long since gone, each falling victim to the global recession. They pulled up next to the door of the last unit, and Gray urged Farrar out of the car. He unlocked the chain securing the entrance and pushed Farrar forward, along a corridor, and into what had once been the warehouse of a greetings card manufacturer. The fixtures and fittings had gone, but boxes and rubbish littered the floor.

Levine followed them in, but Gray stopped him near the door. 'I've got this, Carl.'

'Tom, the guy's a snake. I don't trust him.'

'Nor do I,' Gray agreed, 'but I can handle him on my own.'

Levine looked disconsolate. 'I'll be waiting outside,' he said.

'No need, Carl,' Gray said, pulling the Browning from his jacket. 'I'm armed, he's not. Take the car back to the hotel, and I'll join you when I'm done.' Levine was about to protest again, but Gray put a hand on his shoulder. 'Go. I'll walk back.' As an afterthought, he called Carl back. 'If I'm not there by two, you know what to do.'

Levine threw one last malevolent look at Farrar and left.

Gray waited until he heard the car start and pull away before waving to a chair, which was facing a video camera mounted on a tripod.

'Sit.'

Farrar obligingly took a seat, unbuttoning his coat and making himself comfortable.

'You know, there's really not a lot of point in going through with this charade, Tom. No one's going to let this air to the public, and I mean no one.'

'You seem pretty sure of yourself,' Gray said as he stood behind the camera, working on the focus. 'What if I told you I had a British news channel ready and waiting for me to deliver this recording, eh?'

Farrar seemed less cocksure. 'I don't believe you.'

'Why not? Because of the DA-Notice you slapped on them?'

Gray watched his expression and smiled. 'They were more than happy to help once they found out that the person who'd issued the notice would be the one confessing.'

Farrar went from uncomfortable to angry in an instant. 'You're wasting your time,' he snarled, getting to his feet. 'You really think anyone will take notice of a confession extracted under duress?'

'They'll listen,' Gray said. 'They have to listen.'

Farrar took a couple of steps towards him. 'You really are as stupid as you look, aren't you? You're a little kid playing a big boys' game, and you don't even realise how—'

Gray fired at the floor a few inches from Farrar's feet, the sound of the shot echoing around the room.

'That was your last chance.' Gray pointed the gun at Farrar's face and his demeanor turned sour. 'You either sit down and answer my questions, or I find another way.'

Farrar was about to suggest he do just that when Gray forced him into the chair with the barrel of the pistol.

'And if I have to find another way, there'll be no need to keep you alive.'

Farrar held his tongue. The last thing he wanted to do was push Gray too far and overplay his hand.

'Get on with it,' he said, straightening his already immaculate tie.

Gray went to the camera and hit the 'Record' button and then moved next to Farrar, careful to keep the gun out of view.

'My name is Tom Gray.' He paused, more to compose himself than for dramatic effect. 'Some of you may not believe me, but I'm sure subsequent audio comparisons with my recordings last year will convince you.'

Farrar winced. He hadn't considered forensic confirmation, so any attempt to dismiss Gray as a delusional imposter was not going to fly.

'I have a remarkable tale to tell,' Gray continued, 'and this man, James Farrar from Her Majesty's Government, is going to confirm everything I say.'

Gray moved back behind the camera and zoomed in on his subject. Once he was happy with the way Farrar was framed, he placed the pistol on the camera case and pulled a set of prompt cards from his inside pocket.

'On the thirtieth of April last year, it was announced to the world that I had died from the injuries I'd suffered ten days earlier. In actual fact, I was secreted out of Britain on a military transport plane and taken to Subic Bay in the Philippines. The order to do this came from the home secretary.'

Gray looked at Farrar. 'Is that what happened?'

'That is correct.'

Gray moved on to the next card, but before he could read it, Farrar jumped in. 'I also want to say that I am agreeing to everything because this man is armed and I fear for my life.'

'Duly noted,' Gray said. 'Last month, I was taken hostage by members of Abu Sayyaf, and you sent Len Smart and Simon Baines to rescue me. You gave them unserviceable ammunition in order to increase the chances of them being captured and killed. Is that correct?'

Farrar again acknowledged the statement as being true.

'When we managed to escape from the Philippines, you found out which route we were taking and hired a hit man to intercept and kill us in Durban.'

He looked at Farrar, who nodded. 'Correct.'

'The same hit man who killed British national Timmy Hughes in Singapore two weeks ago.'

'Yes.'

'You also sent a hit team to kill Carl Levine; his wife, Sandra; and their daughter, Alana; as well as Jeff Campbell and his wife, Anne. They were staying in a caravan in Dorset, which was recently destroyed in an explosion.'

'That's right.'

Farrar noticed that Gray was becoming complacent, strolling around the room as he made his accusations, and he'd taken his eye off the pistol near the camera. Farrar didn't yet have an opportunity to grab the weapon as Gray was still too close, but with a handful of cards still to be read, there was still time. He calculated it to be three steps, so even a two-second start should be enough.

He kept his focus on Gray, deliberately keeping his gaze off the gun, just in case he telegraphed his intentions.

The next question, when it came, caught him off guard.

'Why did you do it?'

'I don't know what you're talking about,' he said. 'You're the one who invented this nonsense. I can hardly be expected to explain what goes on inside your mind.'

'Then how about I give you the theory presented to me by Jeff Campbell?'

'By all means, go ahead.'

Gray read from the card, explaining how the government had made a deal with the six surviving men in return for their silence, and how Farrar had been instrumental in trying to eliminate everyone involved.

'Does that sound right?'

Farrar waved a dismissive hand. 'Whatever.'

Gray strode purposefully towards him, his face ending up inches from Farrar's, the venom in his eyes palpable.

'Don't give me "whatever"!' he shouted. *'Is that what happened?'*

'Yes! Yes! Exactly like that!'

Gray straightened up. He turned his back and walked away, studying the next card in the pile. Farrar watched him take two, three, four steps, still concentrating on the next question, and he saw his chance.

Gray heard the sound of the chair leg scraping against the floor as Farrar made a bolt for it, and by the time he looked at where his captive had been, he'd already reached the gun. Gray started to charge towards him, but the pistol came up, pointing at his face. He stopped dead.

'The safety's still on,' he said, hoping to get Farrar to take his eye off the target.

'Nice try,' Farrar said. 'I know my way around a Browning and that's the first thing I checked. I also know there's a round in the chamber.'

Farrar ejected the magazine, the gun never wavering. The clip was full and he rammed it back into the grip. 'Turn the camera off.'

Gray moved slowly over to the recorder and hit the 'Stop' button.

'Give me the recording.'

Gray ejected the USB flash drive and threw it on the floor near Farrar's feet. 'Now what?' he asked. 'Are you going to shoot an unarmed man, a delusional imposter?'

'Enough games, Tom.'

'Oh, so now you acknowledge that I'm Tom Gray. Too much of a coward to admit it to the world?'

'I said *enough!*' Farrar shouted. He tried to gather himself, concentrating on turning this in his favour. 'Tell me where the others are.'

'That's not going to happen and you know it,' Tom spat. 'If I don't meet up with them in thirty minutes, they'll disappear.'

'Tom, I'll give you one last chance. Tell me where they are and I'll make it a quick death; otherwise…'

Gray laughed. 'You know, when you try to sound intimidating it just comes off as desperate.' He sat down on the chair. 'And just what would you do if you found them? Apologise for the inconvenience you've caused over the last year or so? You've sent teams to kill them and they failed. What makes you think you can get it right this time?'

'I'll do it myself if I have to,' Farrar said.

Gray snorted. 'You haven't got it in you. You're happy to sit behind a desk and let others do the dirty work, but you're nowhere near man enough to pull the trigger yourself.'

Farrar took two steps towards him, the gun aiming at the centre of Gray's face. 'I'll give you one last chance, Tom. *Where are they?*'

Gray ignored the question. 'What are you going to do when this gets out, James? You can't bury the truth forever—you know that.'

'Very apt choice of phrase,' Farrar said, 'because that's exactly what I intend to do, starting with you.'

Gray just smiled back. 'It's over, James.' He got to his feet and started walking towards Farrar. He had three paces to cover, but only managed one before the trigger sent the firing pin smashing down on the percussion cap of the next round in the chamber.

Click!

Farrar looked stunned. He ejected the round, thinking he had a blockage. He tried the next round, and the next, both with the same result.

Gray grabbed the gun from him and pushed him to the floor. He removed the clip, then extracted the top bullet and pulled a penknife from his pocket. He eased the bullet from the cartridge and tipped the contents onto Farrar's chest.

'Sand,' he said, dropping the empty brass casing into Farrar's hand. 'Seems to be happening quite a lot these days.'

Farrar scrambled to his feet, his fists clenched, but Gray ignored him and walked over to a pile of boxes covered by an old tarpaulin. He dragged it aside to reveal a television set, which he switched on.

Farrar looked at a picture of himself, streaming live to the nation via the BBC news channel. He raised a hand, and a moment later the figure on the screen did the same.

Gray waved to the four corners of the room. 'Fibre-optic cameras and state-of-the-art microphones, courtesy, ironically, of Her Majesty's Government.'

He clicked his throat mic. 'All yours, Andrew.'

———— ————

Harvey entered the room, accompanied by two armed police officers. 'Don't forget to read him his rights,' Harvey told them as they forced Farrar to the floor and cuffed him.

Farrar was dragged to his feet and marched out of the building. Harvey and Gray followed, and Tom watched his nemesis take a seat in the back of the unmarked car.

'We got some great footage,' Gerald Small said, handing Gray a tablet PC. 'You ought to be on the stage.'

'Can I get a copy?' Gray asked, handing over the comms kit.

'Already done,' Small smiled. 'I'll get Andrew to drop it off at the safe house later today.'

Gray thanked him for his help and joined Harvey in the Skoda saloon. They drove away from the city, heading for the quiet residential area which housed the four-storey building Gray and the others would call home for the next few days.

There was no telling what immediate effect his transmission would have, though Gray knew the prime minister's spin doctor would no doubt be working overtime to play it down. The next step was to get a live interview on the BBC and give his side of the story before the political machine had a chance to bury the story as a hoax. Paul Gross hadn't been convinced that he'd be allowed to broadcast a live interview, but Gray would simply take it to the other news outlets if the BBC hierarchy refused to play ball, and he'd already created a home video that would hit the top dozen social media sites if no broadcaster was willing to run the story.

Harvey's phone chirped and he put it on speakerphone. 'Hi, Hamad.'

'Andrew, we may have found Mansour.'

'Abdul Mansour?' Gray asked, perking up on hearing the name, and Harvey suddenly remembered he wasn't alone in the car. He went to take the phone from its dashboard mounting, but Gray stopped him. After all he'd been through at Mansour's hand, he thought he was entitled to hear this.

Harvey saw the look of determination and decided not to make a fight of it. 'What did you find, Hamad?'

'Remember the lady we followed through the airport this morning? The one we thought was walking strange?'

'Yeah, but we discounted her. She showed her face to the border guard.'

'I know, but there were no other hits, so I went back to her. If the guard hadn't seen her face, I would have been certain we had our man, so I checked him out. Turns out he had over thirty grand of gambling debts until three years ago, when they were suddenly paid off. He's been debt-free since.'

'That's not unusual,' Harvey said. 'Maybe he just stopped gambling.'

'That was my thought, but I checked with the casino he used to frequent. He still goes there six days a week, and spends an average of two hundred pounds a night.'

'Doesn't sound like something you could do on a border guard's salary.'

'I know,' Hamad said. 'Someone's been giving him a shitload of cash each month, and you'd expect him to be giving something in return.'

'Such as turning a blind eye now and again,' Harvey agreed. 'So assuming it is Mansour, where did he go once he left the airport?'

'We tracked his car through the Highway Agency's network of cameras to a place in Stratford.'

Harvey pulled over and asked for the address, which he typed into the satnav. 'I can be there in twenty minutes,' he said and pulled out into the traffic.

'SO15 won't be there for another thirty,' Farsi said. 'They're in the middle of an operation at the moment.'

'Okay, I'll hang back when I get there.'

Harvey steered the car through side streets, trying to avoid the main arteries of the city that would be clogged at this time of day.

'Abdul Mansour is here, in the UK?' Gray asked, incredulous, and Harvey nodded. He explained that they'd received intelligence and were working it up, though he didn't go as far as telling Gray about the specific threat. 'We think he came in dressed as a Muslim woman and was helped through customs by an officer on the take.'

They arrived at the target street seventeen minutes later. Harvey parked close to the junction and told Gray to wait in the car.

'I'm going to do a walk-past,' he said, taking the phone from its holder. 'I want you to stay here, Tom.'

Gray nodded. It wasn't his operation, and the last thing he wanted to do was antagonise Harvey after all he'd done for him.

<hr />

'Abdul, we may have a problem!'

Mansour had just finished taking a shower, and he went to the living room to see what Mohammad, the house owner, was concerned about. He found the man looking through a small gap in the net curtains.

'What is it?'

'A stranger in the street,' Mohammad said, and Mansour watched the man walking slowly past the house. He was on the other side of the street and didn't seem to have any particular destination, simply ambling from one end of the street to the other.

'He could be a salesman, or an estate agent. How can you be sure he's a threat?'

'Because he parked his car down there,' Mohammad said, pointing to a Skoda, 'and there's someone in the passenger seat.'

Mansour could see the occupant of the car but couldn't make out the facial features. He asked Mohammad for a camera and used it to zoom in on the car.

His heart almost stopped. He instantly recognised the man from his time in the southern Philippines, and a strange, alien feeling washed over him.

It took him some time to realise that it was fear.

Mansour was torn between confronting the man and running, and prudence dictated he choose the latter. He took a photo of the man and handed the camera to Mohammad.

'You are right,' he said. 'I must leave, but I want you to find out who this man is.'

'What of the operation?'

The cameraman was due to arrive in twenty minutes to collect the virus, but Mansour knew it was too late. Somehow they had found him, which meant it was time to disappear again.

'It is postponed.' He ran up the stairs and threw on the *burqa*, then collected the inhaler and spare canister and put them in his pocket. He left the passport, as it had probably been compromised, but he grabbed the cash on the dressing table.

When he descended the stairs, Mohammad was waiting in the hallway.

'I haven't seen anyone else arrive,' he said and gave Mansour a slip of paper. 'You can stay here for a few days until the heat dies down.'

Mansour committed the address to memory and handed it back. 'Can you distract them while I go out the back?'

'Of course. Go, and may Allah watch over you.'

Gray watched the man appear from the front of the house and cross the road on a collision course with Harvey.

'Hey! I know you! You stole my bike!'

Harvey turned to see an angry-looking man bearing down on him. The last thing he needed was a scene, so he tried to walk away, but the stranger grabbed his collar and swung a punch. Harvey easily avoided it, but the man kept coming, so he tried talking his way out of it.

Gray was watching the drama unfold when a flash of movement caught his eye. In a gap between two semi-detached houses, he saw a figure in black hurdle a fence and disappear into the next garden, and he knew instantly that Harvey's attacker was a distraction.

He jumped into the driver's seat, but the ignition was empty: Harvey must have taken the keys with him. He debated helping, but he knew that with every passing second, Mansour's chance of escape increased exponentially.

Harvey seemed to be holding his own, and with the armed police due in the next few minutes, he decided to take up the chase.

By the time he climbed out of the car and reached the end of the road, Mansour had cleared the garden and was running towards an alleyway, his *burqa* flapping around his legs. Gray followed a hundred yards behind and hit the alley just as his target exited the other end, turning to the right. He'd closed by ten yards, but Mansour still had a healthy lead.

When Gray got to the end of the alley, he saw the black clothes disappear around another corner and sprinted to catch up, the exertion already beginning to tell after weeks with no proper exercise. When he reached the main road, he saw a sea of pedestrians parting as Mansour barged his way through. An elderly lady was knocked to the ground, but Mansour didn't give her a second thought as he dashed across the road, narrowly avoiding a van which just managed to slam its brakes on. The driver of the car behind wasn't as quick to react, and she ploughed into the back of the van, but Gray didn't break stride as he ran past the two damaged vehicles.

He was beginning to close on his target, and Mansour could sense it. He turned and saw the pursuer less than fifty yards behind him, and his first thought was to find a weapon. He saw a hardware store and dived inside, scattering customers as he searched for the aisle containing knives. Mansour grabbed two from the shelf and turned to the front of the store, only to find his way blocked by an employee. He ripped off his headpiece and gave the teenager a look which offered two options: get out of the way, or die.

The young man got the message. He stood aside and Mansour ran out of the shop.

Where he found the mystery man waiting for him.

They stared at each other for what seemed a lifetime, oblivious to the crowd gathering around them—albeit at a respectful distance.

'Drop the knives,' Gray said, his voice tinged with anger.

Mansour ignored the command, instead trying desperately to think where he'd seen the man before.

'Who the hell are you?'

Mansour may not have recognised him, but a few of the shoppers had seen the BBC news transmission and knew exactly who they were looking at. Whispers of 'Tom Gray' began to grow, and when they reached the terrorist's ears, he wondered if it could possibly be true.

He looked Gray in the eyes, and at that moment, he knew.

He'd tried to kill this man twice, but this time he wouldn't delegate responsibility to someone else. He gripped the handles of the knives until his knuckles turned white and took a step towards his opponent, expecting him to move backwards.

Gray held his ground.

The attack, when it came, was lightning fast. Mansour raised his right arm and brought it down hard, aiming at Gray's head. That blow was easily blocked, but the simultaneous jab with the left punctured a one-inch hole in Gray's side.

Mansour danced back, bobbing on the balls of his feet, while Gray put a hand to the wound. It came away covered in crimson.

'You'll have to do better than that,' he said, adjusting his position to move closer to a street light.

Mansour came again, this time thrusting at Gray's face, but Gray was ready and caught the knifeman's forearm in a vice-like grip before slamming Mansour's knuckles against the steel lamppost. The blade clattered to the floor, but Mansour brought up the other one, aiming for Gray's kidney. The move was telegraphed, and Gray easily avoided further injury by backing into his enemy and switching his attention to the knife hand.

Mansour tried to bring the blade up to Gray's neck, but his strength was no match for the ex-soldier, who held his wrist tightly while slowly pivoting so that they were once again face to face, the knife poised delicately between them.

Both men heard the sirens approaching, and Mansour knew his time had run out.

But there was still time for one last, defiant action.

He brought his knee up sharply into Gray's groin and pushed him away, sending him sprawling to the ground. Instead of stepping in to deliver the killer strike, though, Mansour put his hands into his pockets and brought out the inhalers.

'The difference between you and me,' he said to Gray as he pressed both canisters into their housings and held them in position, 'is that I am willing to die.'

The crowd, thinking he was holding a detonator, scattered in all directions, screaming incoherently and trampling each other in their bid to clear the area.

... two, three, four ...

The first of the armed response vehicles pulled up, and two officers decamped, shouting for Mansour to get to the floor as they aimed their single-shot MP5 rifles at his chest.

...*five, six, seven...*

'Allahu Akbar...'

'Drop it, now!'

...*eight, nine, ten.*

Mansour closed his eyes just as the rifles spat, and the inhalers fell from his dying grasp. One of them rolled towards Tom Gray, and he felt a breeze on his face as the canister dispensed its entire contents.

Epilogue

Monday, 17 June 2013

'Push!'

Vick Phillips screamed and dug her nails into Tom's hand, hoping to cause him as much pain as she was experiencing.

'You're doing well, darling,' Tom said through gritted teeth. In truth, she'd been in labour for over thirty hours, and neither was at their peak.

Vick did her breathing exercises as best she could, but all she could focus on was the seven pounds of human trying to navigate a four-centimetre passage.

'Do you know the sex of the child?' the nurse asked, trying to take Vick's mind off the pain.

'No,' Tom told her. 'We wanted it to be a surprise.'

'What about names?'

'Vick wanted to do the celebrity thing and name it after the place it was conceived, but there's no way I'm calling a kid Machu Picchu.'

The joke was lost on the nurse, but Vick showed her appreciation by squeezing his hand with enough force to draw blood, and Tom wondered if she'd had her nails sharpened just for the occasion.

'Just kidding,' Gray winced. 'We chose the names weeks ago.'

The obstetrician, sitting at the foot of the bed, saw the crown of the baby's head appear.

'One more big push,' he said, and Vick obliged, her face contorted as beads of sweat coursed down her crimson forehead. She produced a scream befitting a horror movie, and then it was over.

A nurse cut the umbilical and took the baby away to be weighed and checked over. A minute later it was wrapped up and placed on its mother's chest. Vick looked down at the screaming, purple bundle and thought it the most beautiful thing she'd ever seen.

'Congratulations, you've got a beautiful little girl,' the nurse told her, and Vick cooed over her daughter.

'Hello, Melissa.' Vick shed a tear, but finally one of joy rather than pain.

Tom Gray gently traced a finger down her tiny wrinkled face, and his thoughts turned to little Daniel, stolen from him at such a tender age. His son might be gone, but he would never be forgotten, and Gray made a silent promise to give his daughter enough love for two.

The one thing he was truly grateful for was that she could at least lead a normal life.

The political fallout hadn't been as bad as some commentators had predicted, with just the home secretary and a couple of his minions giving way, awaiting a decision as to whether or not they would face criminal charges. Farrar, for his part, had already been charged with multiple counts of murder and attempted murder and was awaiting trial, along with the remnants of his team.

Although those bad guys had been taken off the streets, Gray was pleased to know that there were still many more out there. Viking Security Services had nosedived since he'd sold it to the venture capitalists, who had increased their prices and lowered salaries to the point where those staff who hadn't fled to sign up with Timmy Hughes had been demoralised. The effect on the company's reputation had been quick and harsh, with contracts drying up. They'd been at their lowest point when Gray walked into the office and made them a generous offer, which had been readily accepted.

With Gray back at the helm and Hughes gone, his staff had come back in droves, as had the customers, and he knew he would be able to give his daughter—not to mention his new wife—a more than comfortable life.

Melissa wouldn't be spoiled by any means. At least, that's what Gray told himself, though he knew it was going to be hard to say no, just as it had been with Daniel. All he wanted was for his daughter to grow up with the same morals as her father, and he'd consider that the perfect foundation on which to build her life.

The obstetrician checked mother and child over, and happy that they were doing well, he left to complete the paperwork.

He also decided to check with the Department of Health to see if any other maternity hospital had gone a whole calendar month without delivering a single male child ...

THE END

About the Author

Alan McDermott is a husband, father to beautiful twin girls and a software developer from the south of England.

Born in West Germany of Scottish parents, Alan spent his early years moving from town to town as his father was posted to different Army units around the United Kingdom. Alan had a number of jobs after leaving school, including working on a cruise ship in Hong Kong and Singapore, where he met his wife. Since 2005 he has been working as a software developer and currently creates clinical applications for the National Health Service.

Alan's writing career began in 2011 and the action thriller *Gray Justice* was his first full-length novel.

21704938R00139

Printed in Great Britain
by Amazon